PRAISE FOR SALLY GUNNING AND HER DELIGHTFUL MYSTERY SERIES FEATURING PETER BARTHOLOMEW

"Fascinating people, a setting that leaps to life. . . . Marvelous."

—*The Armchair Detective*

"Gunning does a wonderful job with her locale and many characters [and] delivers a dandy mystery puzzle at the same time."

—*Wilson Library Bulletin*

"A kind of Cape Cod *Death on the Nile*—don't miss it."
—*Bookbeat*

"Gunning proves her ideas are still fresh, her touch still golden. . . . Fun and intelligent."

—*Cape Cod Times*

"Loaded with red herrings. . . . A most entertaining mystery."

—*Murder Under Cover*

"Gunning brings a deep understanding of small-town life . . . and an unforgettable cast of characters. . . ."
—*Mystery News*

Books by Sally Gunning

Hot Water
Under Water
Ice Water
Troubled Water
Rough Water
Still Water
Deep Water

Published by POCKET BOOKS

For orders other than by individual consumers, Pocket Books grants a discount on the purchase of **10 or more** copies of single titles for special markets or premium use. For further details, please write to the Vice-President of Special Markets, Pocket Books, 1633 Broadway, New York, NY 10019-6785, 8th Floor.

For information on how individual consumers can place orders, please write to Mail Order Department, Simon & Schuster Inc., 200 Old Tappan Road, Old Tappan, NJ 07675.

DEEP WATER

A PETER BARTHOLOMEW MYSTERY

SALLY GUNNING

POCKET BOOKS

New York   London   Toronto   Sydney   Tokyo   Singapore

This book is a work of fiction. Names, characters, places and incidents are products of the author's imagination or are used fictitiously. Any resemblance to actual events or locales or persons, living or dead, is entirely coincidental.

An *Original* Publication of POCKET BOOKS

POCKET BOOKS, a division of Simon & Schuster Inc.
1230 Avenue of the Americas, New York, NY 10020

Copyright © 1996 by Sally Gunning

ISBN: 0-671-56313-0

First Pocket Books printing December 1996

10 9 8 7 6 5 4 3 2 1

POCKET and colophon are registered trademarks of Simon & Schuster Inc.

Cover art by Tristan Elwell

Printed in the U.S.A.

For my nephew Alex,
Weir man, music man, good man.
With love and thanks.

Author's Note

The quotations that introduce each chapter of this book were excerpted from Robert Louis Stevenson's *Treasure Island*.

My tale of the shipwreck of the *General Newcomb*, including the heroics of the townspeople and (some of) the ship's crew, is based on the real-life saga of the *General Arnold*, which ran aground in Plymouth Harbor on December 25, 1778.

The plaques in the Mariner's Chapel document the actual histories of the nineteenth-century sea captains of the First Parish Church in Brewster, although the names have been changed.

The tale of the Paul Revere spike is historically accurate, but again, the name of the ship has been changed.

My thanks to Christopher J. Dolan for guiding me through the gap between police fact and Nashtoba fiction, to Bill Appleton for suggesting the perfect car for Polly, to Jill Prager for sorting out my shellfish prices, to Frank Travers for allowing me to absorb some of the local color aboard the *Great Heart*, to Al Franz of Lee Stamp & Coin Co. for sharing the delightful atmosphere of his shop, and, as always, to Tom, with love, for the usual long list.

DEEP WATER

Chapter

1

"This is a handy cove," says he, at length; "and
a pleasant sittyated grog-shop."

Peter Bartholomew settled his shoulders against the hard
wood planks of the booth, lifted his Ballantine Ale in the
direction of his ex-wife, and heaved a sigh that had been
three years in the making. "To us."

Connie clinked his glass with such gusto, he checked for
cracks before he drank. "To us," she repeated. "I can't
believe it. Are we really doing this?"

"We're doing it," said Pete. "We're on vacation. It's just
us. For two whole weeks."

Connie started to grin, but the grin faltered halfway
through. "And Factotum is really closed, right, Pete? I mean
really closed?"

"It's really closed." Not that he could blame her for
checking. He had started the odd-job company, Factotum,
twenty years ago when he was a high school sophomore and
had stumbled over the word on a vocabulary quiz.
Factotum—person employed to do all kinds of work. It had
begun in his parents' garage, had moved with him into his
cottage on the marsh, had survived his hiring, marrying,
divorcing, and rehiring Connie, and in all that time Pete
couldn't remember ever closing Factotum. At least not for

1

two whole weeks. There were only eight hundred or so year-round residents on the island of Nashtoba, but the islanders had come to depend on Factotum. Factotum patched their boats, stacked their firewood, and hung their storm windows. It also did their Christmas shopping, fetched their relatives, and chased their lost pigs. Occasionally, sometimes accidentally and sometimes on purpose, it solved murders. And it did all this twenty-four hours a day, seven days a week, fifty-two weeks a year. No wonder their marriage had gone bust.

But not this time, thought Pete. This time they'd decided that if they were going to cohabit again, they'd cohabit right. After a winter's delay caused partly by cold weather and partly, Pete had to admit, by his own cold feet, they'd finally completed two dormers on top of Pete's tiny cottage. They now had some breathing room above the paint cans and chicken wire and birdhouses and broken beach umbrellas that had become part of Factotum's inventory. The last bed slat on Pete's ancient bed had been tapped into place at four o'clock that afternoon, and they'd been lugging mattresses and sheets and pillows and lamps and alarm clocks up the stairs ever since. Half an hour ago Pete's partner, Rita, had switched the office phone to the answering machine, hung a Closed sign on the door, and left.

Factotum was closed. Pete and Connie were on vacation. Nashtoba could go hang. The world could go hang.

Pete leaned toward Connie, grinning like a fool, about to give in to a dangerous impulse to say something sappy, but a huge cheer at the bar drowned him out.

Connie peered around Pete. "It's Cobie," she reported. "Cobie Small. Everyone's clapping him on the back."

"I don't care," said Pete. "So what do you want to do first?"

Connie reached across the red-checked tablecloth and ran her hands under the sleeves of his T-shirt. Pete felt the shiver all the way to his feet. "I want to go home, lock the door . . . but I forgot. Your door doesn't have a lock."

"I'll nail it shut. Then what?"

Connie stretched luxuriously. She had the kind of body that did unnerving things when stretched. Pete was sorry when she bolted to attention, peering at the bar again. "Oh, *no,*" she said. "Cobie's drinking."

"Cobie?" Against his will, Pete turned around.

The bar at Lupo's Restaurant was not necessarily its main feature, but neither did it serve solely as a stopover for the diners on the way to the cozy booths and tables. On any given night a handful of regulars leaned on their elbows in front of an altar of gleaming bottles and well-worn brass taps, comparing weather reports, chewing over the latest world events. Tonight Pete saw half a dozen familiar faces— a couple of fishermen, a shopkeeper, a reporter, a bank teller, the fellow who had helped him roof his house. And plunked down beaming from ear to ear in the middle of all of them, beer glass in hand, was Cobie Small.

Pete had seen Cobie, a shellfisherman-beachcomber who lived on an abandoned wreck in the harbor, stand in that very spot not three weeks ago and announce he'd taken the last drink of his life. But tonight the glass in his hand wasn't full of his recent soda water. Neither was it full of beer. It was full of something darker, something without the head. Cobie handled the tall glass like a shot, tossing its contents into his mouth in one. Pete could almost feel the liquor burn into his own gut in despair.

No, thought Pete, wrenching around to face Connie. It wasn't his pain. It wasn't his problem. He was on vacation, dammit. "So after I've nailed the door shut," he said. "Then what?"

Connie grinned. *"Then . . ."*

"Hey, Pete. Where the hell have you been? I've been looking all over for you."

The minute Joe Putnam slid into the booth next to Connie, her grin froze, but somehow Pete didn't think it had anything to do with the faint smell of fish that wafted from Joe's jacket. After all, it wasn't the smell of *rotten* fish.

There was another roar at the bar. "I don't believe it," said Connie. "Cobie's buying drinks. For the whole bar."

Cobie buying drinks? Cobie, whose usual style was to bum drinks rather than buy them? But this time Pete refused to turn around.

Joe Putnam leaned out of the booth to check out the action at the bar, but when he settled back, he dropped his boot heels on the floor with a thump that suggested an extended stay. "I'm glad I found you, Pete. Eight thousand pounds of fish sitting out in those weirs, and guess what that idiot Elmont did? Fell downstairs and broke three ribs. He's out for the season. I need somebody to help me sling fish."

"Sorry, Joe," said Pete. "Can't help you. We're on vacation."

"Vacation? Shit. Where are you going?"

"We're not going anywhere. We're just not working. That's what vacation means. No work."

"What is this, a joke?"

"No joke. Factotum's closed. For two weeks."

Suddenly Cobie Small's voice rose out of the babble at the bar. "Drop ina bucket. Jus' a drop ina bucket, see?"

"My God," said Connie, "he's got a fistful of *twenties*. And what's he babbling about now? Something about pearls."

"Pearls in oysters," said Joe.

"Or pearls for Esther," said Pete.

Joe snorted. "Cobie buying his wife pearls? Not likely."

"Why?" asked Connie. "What happened to her?"

"Who knows. Cobie sure never said. Just gone one day. So stop fooling around, okay, Pete? You can't close up on me, not when I'm desperate. What am I supposed to do with eight thousand pounds of mackerel, let it rot?"

Pete had to admit eight thousand pounds of mackerel was a lot of rotten fish. But before he could assemble his arguments, another bellow reached him from the bar, this time from the lobsterman, Pit Patterson. "Cobie you old goat, where'd you get all this cash? Been stealing from my traps again?"

"Piss on your lobsters," said Cobie. "Drinks are on the general."

At a booth across the way Pete saw one of his fellow diners, the president of the historical society, tighten his lips. Clearly, this was not his crowd.

Pete turned back to Joe. "There must be somebody else."

"Yeah? Name him. Any fisherman worth his salt is out there on the water already. If you don't help, the season's a bust. You've known me a long time, Pete. I wouldn't be bugging you if I weren't in a jam."

Pete and Connie exchanged a look. Pete noticed Joe didn't miss it, either, and like all good fishermen, he seemed to have a nose for the prevailing wind. He stood up. "You talk about it, and while you're talking, as long as Cobie's buying, I'll grab us a round at the bar."

"Okay," said Connie once he'd gone. "It's your call."

"No, it isn't. It's our vacation."

"Right. And if I say don't do it, you sit around looking like *that* for two weeks."

"Like what?"

"Like Benedict Arnold as he drafted a short note to Washington to tell him he was terribly sorry, but he'd be fighting on the other side for a while."

Pete rubbed his face. "Okay. So I do this one thing, just the weirs, nothing else. Joe's in every day by midday. There'll still be time to—"

"To what? Catch up on the soaps?"

Pete grinned. "To nail the door shut. Which reminds me. You were saying something about what comes after that?"

This time it was the voice of the bartender, Dave Snow, that cut between them. "Yeah, Cobie, my restaurant opens Memorial Day. And that's how long you've got to stop whizzing off your boat in front of my patrons."

Cobie cackled wildly. "Water view! You wanna water view."

And that did it for the sole remaining diner, the librarian, Eva Chase. Pete watched her stuff her napkin under her plate and march stiff-heeled for the door.

"Uh-oh," said Connie, eyes still trained on the bar. "Kiss your beer goodbye. Pit's got hold of Joe. He's jabbing his finger in his chest. What's he saying? Joe looks pretty steamed."

Pete turned.

Pit's voice got louder. "Hey, Putnam. I said I saw Kay row in from Cobie's wreck pretty early this morning."

Pete groaned. He knew what had to come next. Joe Putnam would take a swing at Pit to protect the honor of his woman, and all hell would break loose.

But no. It was Cobie Small, not Joe Putnam, who plowed his fist into Pit.

It wasn't much of a punch. Pit shoved Cobie away with a hand on his face that sent him sprawling.

The men at the bar laughed.

Pete didn't.

He slid out of the booth, and by the time he got Cobie to his feet, Connie was beside him. Between them they propelled him toward the door.

"Jail?" asked Cobie. "Goin' to jail?"

"No," said Pete. "We're taking you home."

Chapter

2

"The name of rum for you is death."

Connie gave a shove that accidentally, or maybe not so accidentally, sent Cobie Small knocking into Pete, and climbed into the truck after him. She stayed as close to the door handle as she could. On the whole, she preferred the smell of Joe Putnam's fish to Cobie Small's unwashed body.

"Thankeeoo," said Cobie. "Thankeeoo, Pete. Coulda walk home, y'know."

"Sure you could."

"Coulda calla cab, too. Money, y'know."

"I saw. What'd you do, rob a bank?"

"No bank. The general. Gotta thank the general."

But Connie, for one, didn't feel much like thanking him. Cobie's greasy head was sinking dangerously close to her shoulder. She pushed him vertical, and a blue eye, made bluer by the redness around it, swung her way.

"Who're you? Not my wife. Where's my wife? Where's Esther?"

"This is *my* wife," said Pete. "Or ex-wife, rather. You know Connie."

"Connie? Connie left you. Who's this you say?"

"Connie," said Connie. "I came back, remember?"

Cobie peered at her harder. "Esther came back, too. Jus' like that. Minute I called her."

Okay, so it had taken Connie a little longer. Still, she might have made her way back sooner if Pete hadn't divorced her so fast. "Clearly," she told him now, "you'd have done better with Esther."

She saw Pete's teeth gleam in the dashboard light. At least they could joke about it now. The fact seemed significant, and Connie pondered on it in silence until the old truck rattled over a frost heave and Cobie burped. It occurred to her she should have given him the window seat, but it was too late now. Still, they were almost there. She could hear the sound under the wheels where the tar of Shore Road had succumbed to the sand blown in from the beach.

They bumped to a stop on the soft shoulder. Connie peered into the night. She knew Cobie's floating wreck was moored no more than a hundred and fifty yards off Close Harbor's shore, but the only visible evidence was a light that winked as the boat tossed back and forth. She could *hear* the boat, though—the suck and slap as it rose and fell in the waves. It could be worse, she supposed—it could be raining, or blowing a gale, or . . .

"Not feeling so good," said Cobie.

Connie was out of the truck in a flash, pulling Cobie by the collar until his head, at least, was over the edge of the seat. She danced sideways as he spewed into the sand, barely missing her sneakers. Yeah, this vacation was starting off just great.

Pete rounded the back of the truck and, for the second time that night, helped her wrestle Cobie to his feet. "Hang on to him, I'll get the dinghy." He yanked off his work boots and socks, rolled up his jeans, and disappeared into the dark.

Connie hung on to Cobie, following Pete's progress with her ears. She heard the chunk of the metal on wood as he tossed the anchor into the bow of the boat, followed by the

8

sandpapery sound of the hull sliding over the beach, then a groan as Pete made contact with the icy May water, followed by the smack of a wave against the bottom of the boat, then another and another.

"Okay, let's go."

The voice came alien and distant in the dark. Connie steered Cobie toward it, her eyes slowly adjusting, so that when she reached the dinghy she could see Pete standing soaked to the thighs at its bow.

She dumped Cobie in the stern seat and hopped in beside him. Somehow Pete clambered in without swamping them. He grabbed the oars and reached and pulled. The little boat leaped through the chop.

"Oooh, muscles."

"No, tide. Outgoing. And an offshore wind. We'll end up in Spain if we don't watch out."

Swell. Connie kept her eye on the light ahead, bobbing rapidly closer, and suddenly the wreck loomed in front of them. Pete slew the dinghy around. The beam of light swung over the bow and away again. A wave came at them sideways and a sheet of spray smacked Connie in the face. Pete grabbed the mooring line and made the dinghy fast. He gave Connie a boost, and she landed sprawled on deck, then she pulled and Pete pushed until Cobie lay stretched beside her. The first thing Connie saw of Pete was a salt-stiffened cowlick as he chinned himself up, then a bare foot over the gunwale, and, finally, the long length of the rest of him hurtling over the side. Together they hustled Cobie across the deck to the gangway, stuffed him down, and followed him in.

The compactness of the cabin took Connie by surprise. Short, narrow bunks lined each side of the bow, one bare, one with a mattress and unmade-up bedding. There were cupboards built underneath each bunk and under the gimballed table that jutted from one wall. A miniature stove and refrigerator were tucked against the other. The light Connie had seen from shore came from a lantern suspended over the table.

"He has electricity?"

"Generator," said Pete. "It charges the boat's battery. It's just about all that runs on this thing."

He deposited Cobie on the bunk and began to wrestle him out of his clothes. Suddenly a ripped, brown envelope flew out from somewhere and landed at Connie's feet, spilling its contents wide.

"Wallet!" Cobie hollered. "Gimme my wallet!"

Connie bent to collect the things from the floor. Six twenties, a ten, two ones. An old picture. A new library card. She stuffed it back into the envelope and held it out to Cobie.

"Turn 'round," he ordered. "Both of you. Turn 'round."

Pete turned, rolling his eyes. Connie turned, too, but not as fast—she caught Cobie fumble the envelope under his mattress.

Connie looked around as the undressing resumed. Cobie's walls were decorated with the few beach treasures he probably couldn't trade for a bottle of booze—a jawbone of a blue shark, a vertebra from a pilot whale, and a bleached piece of driftwood curved like a leaping fish, with a knot where the eye should be and a split to form a tail. One of his finds seemed to have been put to use as a closet— in the bow between the bunks an old anchor shaped like Popeye's tattoo swung on a hook, a worn shirt hanging from one of its flukes.

Behind Connie, Cobie groaned. "Thirsty. Godawful thirsty."

Connie went to the refrigerator and peered in. The contents were typical of an alcoholic shellfisherman, she supposed—lots of beer, but the only food in sight, a couple of dozen unopened quahogs. She found a bottle of water and brought it to Cobie. By now Pete had him down to his union suit.

"Thankeeoo," said Cobie. He drank, lay down, pulled an old army blanket over him, and snored.

The row to shore was slower going now that Pete had to buck wind and tide, but despite his denials, there were muscles in there somewhere—he ran the boat onto the beach with such a firm, final thrust that Connie was able to hop out onto dry sand.

Pete splashed out after her. They each slid a hand under the seat of the dinghy and pulled it up the beach. "Here," said Pete, stopping where they'd found it, but then he looked behind him. "Spring tide. Maybe we'd better pull it into the grass."

They hauled the dinghy twenty feet farther, sank the anchor in the sand, and ran for the truck.

Pete started the engine. Connie jacked up the heat and moved close. A sleeve of heavy, soggy yarn came around her. The backs of his fingers brushed her cheek. She turned to him, and there he was, all of him, solid against her. She still wasn't used to it, this turning and finding him there, finding him looking for *her*.

No, she decided, this vacation wasn't sunk yet.

Chapter
3

"It was not very long after this that there occurred the first of the mysterious events that rid us at last of the captain, though not, as you will see, of his affairs."

Pete's shoulders burned. His back was so abused, it had locked up an hour ago. His right ear, the one heading straight into the northeast wind, throbbed like an exposed nerve in a tooth, and judging by the numbness under two pairs of wool socks and thick rubber boots, he was pretty sure his feet had gone home.

Pete wanted to go with them. Oh, boy, did he want to go with them. But here he was out on a pitching boat at six-thirty on a typical forty-two-degree Nashtoba May morning, tossing fifty-pound netfuls of stinking, squirming mackerel over his shoulder and into the fish totes. And to think, when he'd first got here he'd felt sorry for the *fish*.

The weirs were a trap for fish, built out of sapling poles strung with net, or twine, that worked on the principle of a maze. A straight line of netted poles, the "leader," led into a heart-shaped core. Joe Putnam had set his leader across the prevailing current just outside Nashtoba's Close Harbor. The fish rode the tide out, hit the leader, and, following some fight-or-flight instinct that had been with them since the world began, turned left toward deep water. It was an instinct that had never failed to save them in the past, but this time the deeper water only led them farther into the heart of the maze, where they circled, unable to find their way out.

So eight thousand pounds of mackerel at fifty pounds a netful made what? One hundred and sixty backbreaking dips into the sea and out. And now, 'round about forty dips in, all Pete wanted to do was to shove the long handle of his net up Joe Putnam's ass, open up the throttle for shore, and climb back into bed with Connie. But instead, he tossed another mess of mackerel into the nearest bin and shot a look at the back of Joe's head that should have forced steam from his ears.

"Whew!" said Joe. "Take a break, huh?" He tossed his empty net into the back of the skiff and pulled a Coke out of a cooler. "Coke?"

Coke. At six-thirty in the morning. Pete shook his head. The trouble was, his ear and his feet were freezing, but the rest of him was sweating, and he knew the minute he stopped moving, all that dripping sweat would turn into ice. While Joe settled himself on the top of the cooler, Pete kept going.

"Some laugh about Cobie last night," said Joe.

Pete didn't answer him. For one thing, he hadn't found the episode amusing. For another, he needed to conserve wind.

"Drunk. Jeez, I've never seen him so drunk. Taking a swing at Pit Patterson."

Pete heaved another load of fish behind him and stopped to wipe his face. "What was all that about Cobie and Kay, anyway?"

Joe snorted. "Didn't bug me any. Who'd believe it?"

Pete had to admit it was unlikely. He knew Kay Dodd, an old friend of his sister Polly's, a photographer for *The Islander* newspaper. She had to be twenty-five years younger than Cobie, and a whole lot classier. She and Joe had been a standard island item for years.

"Pit's steamed at Cobie," said Joe. "That's why he said it.

Can't blame him, not the way Cobie's been rifling his traps."

"Cobie's really been stealing his lobsters?"

"Stealing him blind. No call to pick on Kay, though. Everybody knows the only reason she went out to that wreck last month was to take those pictures for the paper. She's moving in with me, did I tell you?"

"No," said Pete. He realized he'd stopped swinging his net some minutes ago—he could tell because his joints had locked. He shook out his limbs and got moving again. He was right, though, it didn't pay to rest. He jabbed his net into the roiling fish, gritted his teeth, and yanked, but the net went nowhere. Two minutes' rest and now he couldn't get fifty pounds of fish to break the surface of the water.

Pete peered over the side. He was caught on a piece of driftwood. He could see the bleached wood through the green-black fish. He leaned over and pulled. The net came free, the log rolled, and a crab-eaten eye socket popped out at him.

But the crabs hadn't touched the long underwear. That's what Pete recognized first—the long underwear.

"I need a hand here."

His voice must have sounded normal. Joe tossed down the last of his Coke, got up off the cooler, and joined Pete at the rail. "Yeah? What you got?"

"Cobie," said Pete. "What's left of him."

Chapter
4

"But he was dead enough, for all that . . . and was
food for fish . . ."

They hauled the body into the skiff and steamed for shore.
Pete called the police chief from the harbormaster's office
while Joe Putnam unloaded the catch into the truck. Minus
Cobie, it didn't amount to much.

They milled around the dock, as far from the skiff and
Cobie's body as they could get, waiting for the chief. When
he arrived he had Hardiman Rogers, the island's sole doctor
in tow. Neither man greeted Pete. They went straight to the
boat and bent over Cobie's body in unison, the older man,
well over sixty but thin to the point of being skeletal, easing
himself down a lot faster than the forty-year-old chief. Pete
could hear the chief's holster creak. Or was it his seams? He
wasn't exactly fat, but he packed a lot of what Pete would
have to call gristle.

"What happened?" asked the chief.

"Nothing. He was caught in the weirs. I hooked him with
my net."

"Naturally," said Hardy.

"I took him back to the wreck last night. Drunk."

"You or Cobie?"

"Cobie," said Pete testily. "I shoved him in bed and left."

15

"Time?"

Pete thought. "I'd say it was around nine-thirty."

Hardy pumped Cobie's chest, and a fine froth erupted from his mouth and nostrils. He ran the pad of his thumb over the wrinkles on his hands and feet, then grasped Cobie's shoulder and rolled him. He bent closer, feeling his scalp, his neck. "He's bumped along the bottom some."

"There was a good stiff ebb last night," chimed in Joe. "High tide was around eight-thirty. It ran strong till one or two o'clock."

Hardy straightened. The wind hadn't let up any, and his hair, as wild and white as Mark Twain's, whipped around his shirt collar. The chief's hair hardly budged, but his ran more along the lines of Jack Webb's.

"If you want me to hazard a guess," said Hardy, "this is what I'd say happened. Cobie got up not long after you left him, Pete. Probably to relieve himself. He toppled overboard and went out with the current, into the weirs."

"Not long after I left him," Pete repeated.

"Considering the tide and the condition of the body, I'd say so," said Hardy. "Look what the crabs have managed to accomplish. Nifty little scavengers, aren't they?"

Joe Putnam gazed at Cobie morosely. "Crabs, lobsters, they'll pick you clean in two or three days. The soft parts, anyway."

Pete winced.

There followed the usual bushel of red and yellow tape. The trip to the police station to officially record the facts. The wait while the chief arranged for the autopsy required in a case of unattended death. The attempt, only mildly successful, to dodge the usual grilling by Jean Martell, the dispatcher. It seemed to Pete she was worse than usual, but then he remembered that Ted Ball, the island's only other police officer, was on vacation in Hawaii, and Pete, and Jean, knew that if you wanted to get something out of the chief that he didn't want gotten out, your only hope was to catch him when he was under the gas at the dentist.

On the other hand, the chief seemed to have learned that if he wanted to get something out of Pete, all he had to do was look overworked and underpaid and ask. He sat behind his desk, rubbed a large hand over a long, corrugated forehead, and said, "Goddamn Ted. Who in his right mind would want to go to Hawaii? So who's next of kin?"

The question didn't surprise Pete. It was the kind of question the chief usually asked him, since Pete was born and raised on Nashtoba and the chief was from Somewhere Else, a fact which most of the islanders figured meant he couldn't know much of anything about anything.

"I don't know," said Pete. "Cobie had a wife once. Esther. I never heard of anybody else. I don't know where Esther is, though."

"See what you can find out, will you?"

"Sure. No problem. See what I can find out about somebody who hasn't been seen in fifteen years. Who may even be dead. And in the meantime you'll be doing what?"

"Securing that boat, taking inventory, looking for witnesses."

The chief mopped his careworn brow a second time.

Next year, thought Pete, *I'm taking my vacation in Hawaii.*

What made Pete take the long way home he couldn't say. Neither could he say, when he got to the spot where Cobie's wreck was moored, what made him pull over. He looked out over the beach. The old wooden fishing boat still wallowed on its tether. The dinghy still sat in the sand, waiting for its owner.

It would be a long wait.

Pete pulled out and drove home to break the news to Connie.

"I don't believe it," said Connie for the third time, eyes blinking like a signal light. Connie hated to cry. "We were just out there last night. We put him to bed. He was *snoring.*"

17

Yes, thought Pete. Snoring. Breathing. Alive. Cobie Small. Not a friend. Pete wouldn't have called Cobie a friend. But he was a part of life here, a part of Nashtoba island. And on those rare moments when Pete had caught him sober, he'd liked Cobie.

The teakettle whistled. Pete got up, tossed instant coffee into two mugs, poured the boiling water over it, and carried the mugs to the kitchen table. He sat down and hunkered over the steam, using it as a portable heater. Connie left her cup untouched in front of her.

"So he drowned," she said finally. "After we left him. He went out on deck and fell over."

"According to Hardy. They have to do an autopsy to be sure."

Connie shuddered. But somehow the act of dissecting Cobie, verbally if not physically, seemed to calm her. She stopped blinking and gazed past Pete, out the window, toward the water. "It's weird, isn't it? Here Cobie totters around that boat for years. He was overdue for this, really. But the one night we decide to see him safely home, he—" Connie stopped. "Oh God."

"What's the matter?"

"The dinghy, Pete! We forgot about the dinghy. We rowed Cobie out. Then we rowed ourselves back. We left the boat on the beach. Cobie was stuck on the wreck without the dinghy. That's why he drowned. He tried to swim in this morning!"

"No, he didn't. He was still in his underwear when we found him. And besides—"

"Of course he was still in his underwear. You think he'd swim to shore in his coat and boots? We should tell Willy."

"Wait."

But Connie didn't wait. Connie never waited. She was halfway to the door before his words caught and held. "Connie. He went over the side right after we left him. Hardy said so, and Joe Putnam agreed with him, because of the tide, and because of where Cobie was found and what

18

the crabs had done to him. Cobie never saw daylight. He never missed his dinghy. Now will you sit down?"

Pete was mildly surprised when she returned to the table, pulled out her chair, and landed in it hard. Still, true to form, she didn't knuckle under completely. "I still can't believe we forgot the dinghy."

The dinghy. Yes, there was something niggling at Pete, too, about that dinghy, but it wasn't the same thing that niggled at Connie. "So what should we have done? Row Cobie out and swim in?"

"We should have gone back this morning to get him."

"He wasn't there this morning. He was in Joe Putnam's fish weirs. Dead. Now can we stop talking about this dinghy?"

"No," said Connie. "I can't help it. It's not just the dinghy. I feel responsible somehow, as if we should have *done* something."

Yes, that was the other thing that bothered Pete. "I know," he said quietly. "Or done something different. Stayed with him longer. Brought him back here. Made him some coffee."

But Connie shook her head. "Coffee's no help, don't you know that? Besides, he was asleep. Snoring. And if you'd brought him back here last night, I'd have left you for a second time."

Pete forced a smile. He didn't enjoy this new, joking phase of hers and hoped she'd pass through it in a hurry. Still, it served to remind him of something. "The chief asked me to see what I could find out about Esther."

"Of course he did. And of course you said yes. What's the matter with Ted Ball, the guy who gets paid to do all this?"

"He's on vacation."

"Ah, of course. So that explains it. And you're not on vacation. For a minute I was confused, but now it makes perfect—"

Pete rose. "Ted's in Hawaii, all right? And I said I'd do it, so I'm doing it."

"So go," said Connie.

But he didn't.

Connie's eyes, usually the pale green of Nashtoba Sound at low tide, were growing darker, the way the sound did in foul weather. "He smelled, you know."

"I know." Pete started around the table toward her.

"He almost *barfed* on me." She pushed back her chair and stood up.

Pete dodged her chair and reached for her just as it began, that sound that always reminded him of a honking goose, the sound of Connie crying.

It was almost noon when Pete arrived at Beston's Store. It was the logical first stop in his quest for Esther Small—somehow Beston's Store had become the center of all commerce on the island of Nashtoba, and the three perennial residents of the bench in the front of the store had become the repositories of all its news. You got three different versions of the news, of course, but once you knew what to expect, you could adjust the three reports accordingly—censor Bert Barker's, expand Evan Spender's, edit Ed Healey's.

"Well, well, well," said Bert as Pete climbed the steps. "Here comes just the fellow who can tell you, Ed. Okay, Pete, when did Cobie become fish food? Last night or this morning?"

Pete eyed Bert's pinched face with distaste. "As far as they know, Cobie Small went overboard last night shortly after nine-thirty." Pete turned to Evan. Evan was a telephone repairman. The salt spray and northeast winds were not kind to the telephone lines on Nashtoba, and Evan was in and out of every home on the island almost as often as the mailman. He never said much, but he listened plenty, and if anyone knew what had happened to Cobie's wife, Pete bet it would be Evan. "Any idea where I'd find Esther Small?" Pete asked him.

Evan's skin was as battered by the wind and spray as the

phone lines—it creased and divided as he thought. That was his mistake, thinking; it gave Ed Healey the chance to start talking. Still, Pete couldn't blame Ed—since he was too fat to move much, talk was the one recreation left him.

"Ah, Esther," said Ed. "Esther Simms, she was. 'Course, that was before she married Cobie. Her brother was the one who went down in the *Mary Lee,* you know. Funny business, that business with the *Mary Lee.* Not a cloud in sight. Nobody—"

"They used to live in that nice little saltbox on Paine Road," said Evan. "Can't seem to recollect what happened after that."

"Why yes, Paine Road," said Ed. "Now it's Dick and Nancy Murchison's place. Dick just got out of the hospital, you know. Got bitten by a brown recluse spider. They had to put twenty-two—"

"Brown recluse spider bite's worse than a tick bite," said Bert.

"Don't try to tell that to George Beston," said Ed. "He got bit by a tick and had intravenous—"

"About Esther," said Pete.

"Oh, give it up," said Bert. "Who gives a hoot about old Cobie? Not Esther, I bet you. When Cobie was *alive* he was dead. Or comatose, anyway."

"Seemed sober when he was in here the other day buying glue," said Evan quietly.

"Well he wasn't sober last night," said Bert. "Heard he was sauced as a Christmas goose. Picked a fight with Pit Patterson, too."

"And over Kay Dodd," said Ed Healey. "Imagine *that,* if you will. That lovely Kay, and sorry old Cobie. Joe Putnam had enough sense to laugh it off, but not old Cobie."

So Nashtoba's rumor mill was as thorough as it was fast, about everything except where to find Esther, apparently. "No one knows where she is now?" asked Pete.

"For the life of me," said Ed, "I can't seem to recall what happened after Paine Road. Seemed all of a sudden Esther

21

was gone, and Cobie was out on that wreck. That's Joss Finch's old dragger, you know. Once the engine seized, he gave up on it. He said it would have cost him—"

Pete turned to Evan. "Evan? No clues?"

Evan shook his head.

"Didn't Cobie say something that day he was in here after the glue?" asked Ed. "He said something about Esther. Almost sounded as if he expected her, didn't it, Evan?"

Evan only shrugged.

Still, it seemed to Pete that Ed might have been right about Cobie expecting Esther. What had Cobie said last night? Something that had made Pete think of Lassie. *Came when I called her,* that was it.

Well, she came, maybe, but she didn't stay; and as of last night, Cobie, too, had seemed at a loss where to find her.

Chapter
5

_____

"What good wind brings you here?"

Pete gave up and headed home. It was still gray and damp and cold, and when he walked inside, the house felt warm and cozy by default. He could hear Connie walking around upstairs in the extra room whose character remained as yet undetermined. Right now it was the room where they'd dumped everything they didn't know what to do with. They called it simply the other room, with emphasis on the _other_.

As Pete listened he could hear a multilayered thump overhead, as if a heavy carton had been upended. They had lined one wall with bookshelves—Connie was probably filling them with all the old books they'd been storing in cartons. Good. The empty space was getting on Pete's nerves. He'd help her fill up the shelves, and then they could curl up on the couch with a bowl of popcorn. It was just what the first day of vacation required, although he was sure the old Puritans would have considered it illegal—to sit around in the middle of the day doing nothing. The only trouble was, first they'd have to dig the couch out from under all the junk. But didn't Pete see in the paper that _The African Queen_ was on television that afternoon? They could

23

forget the couch and climb under the quilt in the bedroom and watch *The African Queen*. With the popcorn. Maybe it would start to rain. Thunder, even. Pete's spirits rose. Either way, this was going to be a great vacation. Despite the weirs. Despite Cobie. Maybe even because of him. It seemed to Pete you respected life more when death hung there next to it.

But while Pete was busy conjuring up his dream vacation, he forgot one small detail—unplugging the phone. When Pete walked in, Connie was on it.

"Oh, good," she said when she saw him. "Hold on. Here's Pete now."

She stretched the phone in his direction and mouthed the word *Polly*. Pete raised his eyebrows inquiringly. Connie shook her head. Not good.

Pete's spirits took a dive. Not that he was surprised. It had been a while since things had been good with his sister. First there was a string of questionable romances. Then a sudden, and, to Pete at least, highly objectionable engagement, but when Polly's fiance had been murdered, even Pete had to admit things hadn't picked up any. From there Polly had spiraled upward and downward, more or less with the weather, usually calling her brother from ninety sea miles away when things were at their worst.

Pete girded his loins, wound his way through the cartons, and took the phone from Connie. "Hi, Pol. How's everything?"

"Okay. Good. I guess."

"Yeah?" said Pete lamely. He never seemed to know what to say to Polly lately.

"Connie told me about Cobie. Poor guy. So you're weir fishing?"

"Yeah," said Pete.

"Oh," said Polly.

"So," said Pete, "how's the job going?"

"Oh, I don't know. I quit. No big deal. I'll look for another one, one of these days. I guess."

There seemed be some sort of effort on the other end of the phone to rally. "So how's Factotum doing?"

"It isn't. Not for a while. We're on vacation."

"Vacation," repeated Polly, as if vacation were her worst enemy.

"Although I am working the weirs for Joe Putnam. And trying to find Esther Small for the chief, so far, unsuccessfully. I got her as far as the saltbox on Paine Road and lost every trace."

Polly sighed wistfully. "Do you know, I always loved that house on Paine Road."

"You did?"

"Don't you remember? I went in there with Mom once when she was collecting for the Heart Fund. Esther showed us all over. She called it her dream house. And speaking of Mom, I got a *horrible* letter yesterday. The usual party line. 'Today is the first day of the rest of your life.' Honestly, it almost made me slit my throat."

"You know," said Pete, fast. "You haven't been up here since Thanksgiving. You should come up sometime."

"Yeah?"

"Yeah. In a month the weather will be—"

"You know, I should," said Polly, and suddenly the rally seemed genuine. "You know, Pete, that sounds good. I mean, really good. I'm not working now or anything. And I don't care about the weather. But you're on vacation. Are you going someplace or something?"

"No, we're not going someplace. But—"

"Wow. Okay, great. So maybe I will come up. I could be there by noon. Eleven, even."

"Eleven . . . tomorrow?"

"Yeah, tomorrow. I mean, why not?"

"I'll be out on the weirs. And I don't know if Connie—"

"Oh, that's okay," said Polly. "I know my way around, don't I? If nobody's home, I'll drop my luggage and go for a ride." A pause. "I mean, it's okay if I come? It's not a problem or anything?"

"No," said Pete. "Of course not. No problem."

"Oh, man. Okay, great. So I'll see you tomorrow, then."

"Okay. See you tomorrow." Pete hung up and turned around.

Connie's back was to him. She was jamming Pete's 1939 world atlas into the shelf. Pete supposed he should get a new one, but what for? Nashtoba, at least, hadn't changed any.

"She sounded awful," said Pete.

"I know," said Connie.

"She started in about slitting throats. So I happened to mention why doesn't she come up sometime."

"I heard," said Connie.

"And she said great, she'll be here at eleven."

"Tomorrow."

"Yeah," said Pete.

Connie squeezed an unfamiliar *Fodor's Guide to New Zealand* onto the shelf next to his old atlas. The Fodor's was this year's, he noticed. Was she planning on going someplace? The other side of the world, maybe?

"How long is she staying?" asked Connie.

"Who knows. She said something about luggage. So if she arrives with a steamer trunk—" Pete waited, watching Connie's back. She was tall and big-boned, leaner, it seemed, of late. Her rib cage expanded and contracted with a mammoth sigh, and she turned. She looked at the clock.

"So we have twenty-one hours," she said. "What do you want to do first?"

The popcorn, quilt, and *The African Queen* came in second. They had just reached the leeches in the Ulanga River and the hard kernels in the bottom of the bowl when the phone rang again. *Damn.* He knew he should have unplugged it. And for once, Connie was thinking like he was. As he picked it up she said "Don't answer that."

"Nice," said Willy McOwat. "You tell her I owe her one. I have one question and then you can get back to whatever you were doing. What *were* you doing, anyway?"

"Get a life. And if that was your question—"

"It wasn't. It's about Cobie's cabin. What did it look like when you were out there last night?"

"What did it look like? The furnishings, you mean?"

"The condition of the furnishings."

"The bed wasn't made, if that's what you mean. But there wasn't much else to see. Some stuff on the walls."

"What about the things in the cupboards?"

"I didn't look in the cupboards. It wasn't a search party."

"But whatever was in the cupboards—"

"Whatever was in the cupboards was in the cupboards. And you're up to three questions. So if you're through—"

"I'm through," said Willy. "Thanks. Say hi to Connie."

Perversely, the minute the chief hung up, Pete wished he'd hadn't. What did he care about the state of Cobie's cabin, anyway?

Pete lay back down. Connie put the popcorn bowl on the floor, nestled her ear into the hollow of his shoulder, and slid a hot hand under his shirt. "Mm," she said, and almost at once her breathing fell into the slow rhythm of sleep.

But if anyone was ready for an afternoon nap it should have been Pete. He'd been up before dawn, he'd worked like a galley slave all morning, he'd found Cobie's dead body. So why was he lying there wide awake, watching Connie? He could just see the dark fan of her lashes, the clean line of her cheek, and, even as she slept, the signs of constant struggle in her brow. He hugged her to him fiercely. *This is all I need,* he thought. *Leave me this, and I'll take anything else they throw at me.*

But soon the events of the day and the warm body and the low murmur of Hepburn and Bogey caught up with him. He fell asleep and dreamed he was eaten alive by mosquitoes in the Belgian Congo.

It was the phone, of course, that woke them. *Three strikes and you're out,* thought Pete, not opening his eyes, but this time it was Connie who grabbed it.

"Hello?" she said sleepily, and almost at once Pete felt her jerk upright beside him.

He opened his eyes. Connie waved at him frantically to turn off the set. "Tell me that again. *What* happened? *Where* is she?"

"Who is it?" asked Pete.

"Dad. Are they sure? Is she all right?"

"Is who all right?" asked Pete.

"My mother. She's in the hospital. Okay, Dad. What time is it? Okay. Sure I can. Yes. Tonight. Don't worry. All right. Good-bye. *Yes,* Dad. Tonight."

She hung up and threw back the quilt. "Something's wrong with her heart. It's not beating right. I don't think it's anything serious, but Dad's having a fit. I have to go down there."

"To New Jersey? Now?"

Connie looked at him mournfully. "Now."

"I'll come."

"No, Polly's coming, remember? You stay here and resurrect her. I'll call you later."

It had been Pete's experience that when things started to unravel, they unraveled fast. Putting them back together took months, years, even, but the coming undone could be neatly effected in a matter of hours. Two hours and sixteen minutes, to be exact.

Connie was gone, in a flurry of desperate kisses and one agonized hug, by 5:32 that evening.

As was the usual way with the telephone, if you spent all day willing it to shut up, the minute you wanted it to ring, it thumbed its nose at you. Pete listened, and paced, and put books in the shelves, and took them out again, and paced some more, and finally dozed off on the couch at two in the morning.

Connie called at 2:20.

"It's something called atrial fibrillation. They've got it controlled with medication, but she has to stay overnight."

"But she's okay?"

"That's what two doctors and three nurses have told us. I believe them. Dad doesn't."

"And you're okay?"

"No," said Connie. "Dad's driving me crazy, this place smells like a refinery, and I miss you already."

"I'll come down," said Pete again, but Connie laughed over the wires.

"You do and you'll pass me on the turnpike. Go to bed. I'll see you tomorrow."

Pete went to bed, but it didn't help things any. He lay awake running through his usual middle-of-the-night worst-case-scenarios list, remembering, as he rolled over onto another popcorn kernel, why he'd made it a rule never to eat in bed, wondering if Connie's mother was really all right, and, finally, what the chief had found that made him curious about the state of Cobie's cabin.

Chapter
6

_____

"He had been well brought up . . . before he came to
sea and fell among bad companions."

Pete was tired and sore the next morning, and he had
enough on his mind, what with Connie going and Polly
coming, to distract him from the task at hand. He didn't
need the fog on top of it. Not that Pete cared if he could see
past the end of his dip net—some of what he'd seen so far
hadn't thrilled him. But the fog did cause him to slow down,
and he found himself floating from weir to fish tote and
back again as if he were in slow motion.

But when the voice boomed through the gray wall he
dropped his dip net quick enough.

"Police!"

Pete clutched at his net as the mackerel dribbled back
into the sea. Behind him, Joe stood motionless, peering
blindly into the fog.

The voice echoed again. "Clear the premises, do you read
me? Exit the impound area immediately."

A bow broke through the fog. It was the harbormaster's
launch with the harbormaster, Freeman Studley, at the
wheel, and Willy McOwat beside him. The man with the
bullhorn was a stranger. Maybe that explained why he

seemed so bent on making his occupation known. "Police!" he bellowed again.

Freeman Studley cut the engine and pulled up outside the weirs. The unknown police officer raised the bullhorn again, but Willy moved beside him, and pushed it down with two fingers. "I think they heard you."

Still, the stranger barked again. "These weirs are off limits as of now!"

That did it. "Oh yeah?" said Joe. "And who the hell says?"

Willy raised his own voice a warning notch. "This gentleman is Lieutenant Collins of the State Crime Prevention and Control Unit."

"Oh, yeah?" said Joe. "So what? These are my weirs, and he's got no—"

"They may be your weirs, but they're sitting in state waters," said Willy calmly, but he said it fast, as if he wanted to get it in before the lieutenant's jaw unclenched. "The investigation into Cobie's death falls under the jurisdiction of the state police. Lieutenant Collins is here to look the place over. Let's call it a day, boys."

Joe Putnam looked like he might have a stroke. Even in the gray mist Pete could see the blood rush to his face. "Right! A day off. And most of yesterday, too. And what do I get for it?"

"Nothing," said Willy quietly. "Unless you don't get moving. Then you get arrested."

"What's happened?" asked Pete. "I thought Cobie drowned."

"He did," said Willy. "For the most part. But in addition—"

The lieutenant cut him off. "An officer is waiting on the dock. He'll escort you to the station to collect your statements."

"*What* statements?" Joe shouted. "We already made our goddamned statements yesterday when we brought him in. You think I can take a month off every time a body washes up in my trap? I'm trying to make a living here. I've got four, six weeks tops—"

Pete laid a hand on Joe's shoulder. "Come on, Joe. Give it up. Let's head her in."

Joe's face was the color of a raw steak, fresh off the cow. He kicked a half-full fish tote, and the mackerel in it trembled. But he fired up the engine, yanked the wheel hard over, and roared out of the heart of the weir. Still, it took a few more boots aimed at the fish and a steady stream of the usual adjectives aimed at the lieutenant before they reached shore.

The Nashtoba Police Station looked like the rest of the white-trimmed, weathered-shingle cottages on Nashtoba, only it was smaller, and the ramrod-straight trooper who had led them there from the dock locked his knees uncertainly at the door.

"It's okay," said Pete. "They have a radio and everything."

The trooper turned his gleamingly shaved cheeks in Pete's direction, but nothing else in his face moved. He led Pete and Joe past the dispatcher's desk and pointed them down the hall. Pete figured it was a good measure of what the state police could do to the atmosphere when even Jean Martell said nothing as they passed.

The trooper waved Joe into the empty room Willy used as a lost and found, and with only one door left, was forced to usher Pete into the chief's office. Pete didn't know what happened to Joe. All he knew was that the trooper took his statement and left him there to stew.

Pete stewed, all right. And he'd managed to whip himself into a pretty good froth by the time Willy and the lieutenant came through the door.

"Jesus Christ, Willy. I have a mother-in-law in the hospital, and my sister's arriving any minute. What's the big holdup here?"

Willy raised an eyebrow, the one nearest the lieutenant. But all he said was, "Ex-mother-in-law, isn't it?"

"One or two questions," said Lieutenant Collins. "Then you may go." He walked around Willy's desk and sat down in Willy's chair. Willy moved to the window. The lieutenant held Pete's statement in his hand, but he didn't look at it. "You say Cobie Small was 'drunk.' Did you witness him drinking?"

"I saw him drink eight ounces of whiskey in about twenty seconds. I'd say that's witnessing—"

"His drinking problem is well known?"

"Yes," snapped Pete, but then he took a deep breath. This wasn't going to get anybody anywhere. "Yes and no," he amended. "He drank for years, but he supposedly stopped a couple of weeks ago."

"Yet he was intoxicated Friday evening."

"Yes," said Pete glumly. "He was intoxicated Friday evening."

"And what was the state of his cabin when you left it at nine-thirty?"

Pete looked at Willy curiously. "The chief already asked me that. I didn't see anything too odd. Why?"

"No unusual disarray? No clothes or kitchen items strewn around, no bedding disrupted?"

"His bed wasn't made," said Pete. "And Cobie himself was plenty disarrayed. But other than that, everything looked pretty normal."

The lieutenant placed a plastic envelope containing a photograph of a man and woman on the table in front of Pete. "Do you recognize these people?"

The picture must have been thirty years old. Pete didn't recognize the man, but he knew who the woman was. She was fleshier and blonder than Pete ever remembered her, but there was no mistaking the distinctive, heart-shaped face. "That's Esther Small." She was smiling and leaning against the man, a strapping young fellow in a dark suit. Pete looked again at the man. There was something familiar . . . Pete looked closer and noticed a crooked eye-tooth. "Jesus," he said. "It's Cobie."

"Thank you," said the lieutenant. "You may go."

But now, perversely, Pete wanted to stay. "What's going on? Did Cobie fall overboard or didn't he?"

The lieutenant jerked his head first at Willy, then at the door. Willy clapped a huge hand on Pete's shoulder and encouraged him toward the exit.

Once out of earshot, the chief said, "What's wrong with Connie's mother?"

"Something called atrial fibrillation. They fixed it, but they want to watch her overnight. Now will you tell me something? What's going on around here?"

"I'll stop by," said Willy. He hesitated outside the office door. "So Polly's coming."

Pete looked at his watch. "She should be here already."

"I'll stop by soon," said Willy.

But Polly wasn't there. And nobody answered the phone at Connie's parents' house. Pete called the hospital and got disconnected twice. He gave up. Connie was probably on her way home, anyway. He stripped out of his fishing garb, took a shower, and stumbled around looking for his clothes. Nothing was in the same place anymore. He had just gotten as far as clean Jockey shorts and jeans when someone pounded on his door. The downstairs office door. Pete grabbed a shirt out of the closet and heard the outer door open. Someone hallooed, and feet hit the stairs. What was the point in adding on a whole second floor to hide in if everyone was going to walk right up anyway?

Pete reached the hall bare-chested, shirt in hand, just as Willy's head crested the top of the stairs. "Hi," said Pete. "Come on up, why don't you?"

"Don't mind if I do. I figured it was safe since Connie wasn't here. Any word from New Jersey?"

Pete shook his head.

"I didn't see Polly's car out there."

"Neither did I." Pete went back into the bedroom, pulling on his shirt as he went. He collected a clean pair of socks from a bureau that was on the wrong side of the room and sat down on the foot of a bed whose head seemed to face the wrong way. "So when are you going to tell me what's going on with Cobie?"

"He drowned," said Willy. He walked over to the bureau and picked up a vase full of long brown stems and small yellow blooms. "What's this?"

"Forsythia. Connie picked them. So if Cobie fell off the deck and drowned, what's the lieutenant so worked up about?"

"I have this stuff behind my house," said Willy, still examining the flowers. "At least I think I do. The lieutenant's worked up because there's some question whether Cobie fell off the deck of his own accord. I thought you said Polly would be here."

"Well, she isn't," said Pete, but as he spoke, they heard a car. It sputtered to a halt outside in a way its driver couldn't possibly have intended. Polly? She had about as much luck with cars as she did with men. The chief went to the window, looked out, sucked in his gut.

Yes, Polly.

Pete went downstairs, the chief behind him. Polly, too, had walked right in and was standing in the hallway next to her bags, two full ones, Pete noticed. She hugged Pete, saw the chief, and raised a hand awkwardly. Her acquaintance with the chief was short—a six-hour car ride from Maine, where he'd extricated them from the red tape surrounding her fiance's murder, and a shared Thanksgiving dinner at Pete's house. As a matter of fact, Thanksgiving was the last time *Pete* had seen Polly.

She'd looked better at Thanksgiving. Now the skin in her face seemed too tight, turning her eye sockets into black wells, and the eyes themselves lacked their usual glimmer.

They stood awkwardly in the hall. "What's the matter with the Renault?" said Pete.

"Who knows," said Polly. "It never stops or starts when I want it to. Will you look at it later?"

"Sure."

Silence.

"I have to go," said Willy.

"No, you don't," said Pete, suddenly panicked at the thought of being left alone with this stranger, his sister, but he needn't have worried. The chief hadn't moved. "Come into the kitchen," said Pete. "I'll make coffee."

They went into the kitchen. Pete felt more comfortable in the kitchen. The kitchen, at least, hadn't changed any.

It didn't take long to exchange the immediate news—Polly's delay due to detour, Connie's absence due to her mother.

More silence.

Pete filled the kettle. Polly and Willy sat at the table. Polly said something about the house, but Pete was too busy worrying to hear it.

Finally Polly turned to the chief. "So what are you here for, business or pleasure?"

"Business," said Pete, just as Willy said, "Pleasure."

"So you're arresting my brother?"

Pete winced. Willy hated cop jokes. Then Pete looked at Willy. His grin was wide, Pete could see all his molars.

"We got called off the weirs by the state cops this morning," said Pete. "Willy was just about to tell me why. What happened, did something turn up on Cobie's autopsy?"

"As a matter of fact, yes," said Willy. "But I'm sure Polly doesn't want to—"

"Are you kidding?" said Polly.

Willy looked from brother to sister as if trying to pinpoint the defective gene.

Polly leaned forward on her elbows. Pete wasn't sure, but she seemed to look a little perkier. "Come on. Did Cobie drown or didn't he?"

"The official cause of death was indeed asphyxiation due to drowning," said Willy formally. "Sometime between nine-thirty and eleven-thirty. And he had plenty of alcohol in him. But before he died, he sustained a wound to the back of the head."

Polly blinked, eyes brighter, surely. "A wound? You mean like somebody clobbered him?"

"No, not necessarily. But the wound was an interesting shape. Three-sided. Triangular." Willy pulled a pad and pen out of his pocket and drew. Pete moved closer and saw a circle that was presumably Cobie's skull, and something irregularly triangular on the upper right-hand corner. A sensation similar to the dread he used to feel on the first day of school assailed him.

No. Not again. Not Cobie.

But Polly snatched up the pad and examined it eagerly.

"So that's what brought the lieutenant out here," continued Willy. "That and what you told me about the cabin."

"I don't get all this fuss about the cabin."

Willy's eyes grew gloomy. "You implied that other than an unmade bed, everything was shipshape. But when I was out there the next afternoon, it had been pretty thoroughly turned upside down. And inside out."

"Oh, wow," said Polly.

Pete stared at her. Yes, she was definitely perkier. But Pete wasn't going to get suckered in to this one. Not this time. "So maybe Cobie woke up and went through his stuff looking for something. Then he climbed out on deck, fell down, cracked his head, and went over."

Polly snorted.

The kettle whistled. Pete spooned out the granules, added the water, and delivered two mugs to the table.

"*Instant* coffee?" asked Polly.

"I've been trying to tell him," said Willy.

Pete added the sugar canister and the milk carton and rummaged in the drawer for spoons. Over the clatter he could just hear the chief ask Polly, "How long do you plan to stay?"

Pete stopped rummaging and listened carefully.

"I don't know. I didn't know about Connie's mother. Maybe I'll be in the way."

The phone rang. Pete lunged for it. Just before he got it to his ear, he heard Willy drop his voice and say, "Frankly, Polly, I think Pete could use some company."

Thank God the call was for Willy. Pete hustled him to the phone before he'd booked Polly for the season.

It was Jean Martell, the dispatcher at the station. Pete could hear snatches of her voice from where he stood, leaning against the kitchen counter, and the gist was clear. *Get your ass back here.*

Willy hung up.

"What I don't get is where exactly this wound *is*," said Polly, eyes still fixed on the drawing.

Willy sauntered back to the table and placed a hand on the upper rear corner of Polly's dark curls. "Here."

Jesus, thought Pete.

"So it came from behind," said Polly. "And above. Say from someone taller, sneaking up on him."

"Or from in front and below, from something that snuck up on him as he fell on it," said Pete.

Polly glared at him.

"If indeed there were an assailant, he was taller and he came from behind," said Willy.

"Don't you have to go?" asked Pete.

"Eventually," said Willy.

Chapter
7

I could scarce persuade myself that murder had actually been done and a human life cruelly cut short a moment since . . .

The second time the phone rang it *was* Connie. Pete was so glad to hear her voice, it scared him. "Hi," he said. "Where are you?"

"New Jersey." She sounded cranky. "They're keeping her one more night. Why, I don't know. She's already had every possible test there is, and the medication has straightened out her heartbeat nicely."

"How is she?"

"*She's* fine. Dad's the one who's losing it. He kept me up till four A.M. delivering her eulogy." Connie yawned. "Is Polly there?"

Pete turned to the window where Polly had been standing ever since the chief left them.

"Just arrived."

"Everything okay?"

"I don't know. I guess so."

"Did you find Esther?"

"No," said Pete. "I've been a little busy." He filled Connie in on the events of the morning.

"A triangular wound, and the cabin was trashed. With Cobie, that could mean something or nothing."

39

"Exactly," said Pete. "On the whole, I favor nothing. So what do you think? How long will you be there?"

"Who knows. Till they let her out, I guess. Hey, it wouldn't be from the anchor, would it?"

"What anchor?"

"The one hanging in the bow of Cobie's boat. Between the bunks. He hung clothes on it. Maybe the wound is from the anchor. Its flukes were sort of triangular."

"You mean he could have pitched into the anchor, hurt his head, wandered out on deck feeling woozy, and flopped over the side?"

"Something like that. And what about the money?"

"What money?"

"The one hundred and thirty-two dollars Cobie had in an envelope stashed under the mattress. Along with an old picture and a library card."

Pete thought. "I think I saw the picture. Nobody said anything about any money."

"Oh. Hey, I'd better go. Say hi to Polly."

"Okay," said Pete. He might have said something else, but Polly was in the room. Then again, Connie didn't say anything else, either.

They hung up.

Polly turned around. "Everything okay?"

"I guess so. But she's staying another night."

"What was all that about the anchor?"

"She says there's an anchor hanging next to Cobie's bunk. Its flukes could have made a triangular-shaped wound."

Polly's eyes grew brighter.

The part Pete hated most about having company was having to think up things to feed them. When he and Connie were alone their menu varied little, and they relied heavily on takeout or what they called catch-as-catch-can, which meant they each made individual raids on the refrigerator whenever they felt hungry. Now Pete foraged around and came up with something he felt was presentable for Polly—a thick ham and cheese sandwich, which she devoured, along with the last quarter of a bag of potato chips, an apple, and two more cups of coffee. She was still sitting at the kitchen table, probably expecting dessert, when Willy McOwat reappeared in front of them.

The chief was still in his departmental khaki pants, but Pete was interested to note he'd changed into a clean blue shirt and sneakers so new they were blinding.

"That's it," said Willy. "The lieutenant's packed up and gone. Accidental death. They figure he hit his head on something as he fell overboard."

"Ah," said Pete, relieved. He wanted it to be over. He had enough on his mind without having to worry about Cobie. Connie's mother was in the hospital. Connie was in New Jersey. Polly was in his kitchen. And there were a whole lot of dirty dishes in his sink.

Pete stopped up the drain, turned on the water full force, squished out some soap, and plunged in up to the elbows.

"Well, I'd like to know what they think he hit his head *on,*" said Polly. "Did you tell him about the anchor, Pete? Connie called—"

Willy swiveled to face Pete. "How's her mother?"

"Okay, but they're keeping her another night." He wondered if he sounded as pathetically bereft to the others as he did to himself.

Apparently not.

"Connie told Pete about this anchor," said Polly. "It's hanging in Cobie's cabin. It has those triangular pointy things—"

"So Cobie might have hit his head on it," Pete cut in. "No big deal."

To Pete's dismay, the chief frowned. "I didn't see any anchor."

"It's hanging in the bow between the bunks. Cobie hung his clothes on it. I remember it. Vaguely."

There was a noise like a summer wind. Polly, sucking in her breath. "Somebody took it! Somebody stole the anchor."

41

"Who'd steal an old anchor? It's probably right there. It probably fell down, or—"

"I didn't see it," said the chief stubbornly. "I was out there twice, once alone, once with the lieutenant. I'd remember something like that."

"We'd better go look," said Polly. "It might be a clue."

Pete emptied the sink and swiped crossly at the suds clinging to the hair on his forearms. "A clue to *what?*"

But it was Willy who answered him. "It can't hurt to look."

Pete glared at the chief, but the chief didn't see him. He was too busy getting beamed at by Polly. Pete gave up. "So go ahead. Go out there."

Now Willy looked at him. "Oh, you're coming. You're the one who remembers what it looked like. *Vaguely.*"

"And me?" asked Polly.

Willy smiled at her. It wasn't the same smile he used on Pete, on those rare occasions when he'd ever smiled at Pete. "Of course you're coming, Polly."

Pete still thought it was a dumb idea and he said so, all the way to the harbor. He had better things to do. Exactly what those things were he couldn't have said, but it had to be better than rowing out to Cobie's wreck for the second time in forty-eight hours. But when they reached the beach, Pete fell silent.

It was one of those thickly gray, deadly still days where nothing moved—not the clouds, not the beach grass, not the water. The sand stretched out in a pale, undisturbed curve. Cobie's boat sat at its mooring as stationary as a hen on a nest.

But *something* was different. And it was something to do with that damned dinghy. Only when Willy grasped the boat to drag it to the water did it come to him.

"Wait. You said you went out to the wreck yesterday?"

Willy nodded.

"In this dinghy?"

"I don't see any others around here, do you?"

"But that would have been after I drove by. I left you at the dock with the body. I drove straight here, and the dinghy was just where it is now. I remember distinctly. It was in the sand right here."

"So what?" asked Polly.

"Connie and I left it up there in the grass. I was worried about the tide. We pulled it into the grass Friday night. The next morning Cobie's dead, and the dinghy's twenty feet closer to the water. Somebody else went out to the wreck either later Friday night or early Saturday morning."

But what was he saying? He wanted no part of this. He refused to believe that anyone would intentionally harm a helpless drunk like Cobie. It was just Polly, trying to make something out of nothing because her own life wasn't measuring up at the moment. Well, Pete's life was measuring up just fine. Or almost fine. Or it would be fine once Connie came home and they could get going on this vacation. "It was probably some kids out joyriding," he amended hopefully.

"Right," said Polly. "In Cobie's dinghy. The very night he happened to be murdered."

"Nobody says Cobie was *murdered.*" Pete looked to the chief for backup.

"An odd coincidence, you must admit," said Willy.

But Pete would admit nothing until they reached the wreck. Then he was forced to admit it wasn't the cabin he'd seen Friday night. The bedding was stripped off the bunk and heaped on the floor, the mattress ripped open, the drawers pulled out and spilling their few clothes, and the cupboard in the galley was bare, contents emptied into the sink or rolling around underfoot.

"Jesus," said Pete.

A can of Dinty Moore beef stew rolled toward him and he kicked it aside. Willy picked up a box of Kraft macaroni and cheese and handed it to Pete. It wasn't the deluxe, but Pete had always thought the regular was better.

"Would Cobie have done this?" asked Willy. "And if so, what was he looking for?"

"Who knows? Aspirin, maybe."

"In the clothes drawer?" asked Polly.

"He was drunk," said Pete. "He wasn't making sense. He kept thanking the General and looking for Esther. Maybe that's it. Maybe Cobie ransacked this place looking for Esther."

"That's not funny," said Polly. "The poor old thing got bludgeoned to death and you—"

"Nobody says he got *bludgeoned*." But Pete could tell his voice carried less conviction this time. He was thinking again about the dinghy. Sure, Cobie could have turned the cabin over this way, especially if he were in a drunken snit about something, but *somebody* rowed out here after Pete and Connie left, either that same night or early the next morning.

And Cobie was dead the next morning.

Pete turned his attention to the anchor. Only after Connie mentioned it had he remembered it—swinging back and forth between the bunks with a shirt or a coat hanging from one of the flukes. Pete moved into the bow. All he found was an empty hook screwed into the ceiling. "No anchor. But it was hanging from this hook when I was here. I remember it now. It had a ring at the top, and a crossbar, and these flukes shaped like spades."

"How big?" asked Willy.

Pete sketched the dimensions of the anchor in the air.

"And the flukes?"

Pete held up his forefingers, three inches apart. "Somewhere in there."

Willy nodded. "That would account for the wound, all right. So if somebody else did this, what were they looking for?"

"Cobie's money." Pete moved across the littered floor and picked up the corner of the torn mattress, not that he was really expecting to find anything. He didn't. He turned to the chief. "That picture the lieutenant showed me. The picture of Esther and Cobie. Where did that come from?"

"From a dog-eared old envelope lying in the middle of the floor."

"What else was in it?"

"A library card."

"No money?"

"No money."

"So a hundred and thirty-two dollars is missing."

"*Aha!*" said Polly. "Somebody was looking for his money."

But Willy shook his head at her. "I don't think so. At least not completely. If whoever did this found what he was looking for, he'd have stopped looking, right? And under the mattress is probably one of the first places anyone would look. This guy kept going."

"All the more reason to think it was Cobie," said Pete.

Polly snorted.

"Come on," said Willy finally. "Let's get moving. We're looking for the anchor and whatever else whoever else was looking for before they did whatever it was they did to Cobie."

They divided the boat among them. The two men left Polly sifting through Cobie's few personal possessions in the cabin. The chief went forward to the hatch leading to the engine, and Pete climbed out onto the open deck. He looked around. Except for the remains of an old winch, a wooden bench, and the mooring line, the deck was bare. Pete circled the boat, peering over the rail. There was still no wind and the water was clear. Pete could see straight to the bottom, to the tip of the cement piling that served as Cobie's mooring.

No anchor.

Pete opened the door to the wheelhouse and went in. There was no wheel anymore, and any electronics had been removed long ago, probably by Joss Finch when he abandoned the boat, but Cobie had used the wheelhouse as a storage shed for his shellfishing equipment. Pete sorted through burlap bags, wire baskets, buckets, rakes, waders and assorted boots, a length of rope, a couple of buoys. No anchor there, either.

Willy appeared in the door. "Not much left in the way of engine down there. It looks like it's been used as the local parts supply store."

"And no anchor?"

"No anchor. No anything else, either. Whatever it was they were looking for, I'd say it's not here."

And when Polly climbed out on deck to make her report, it was the same. No anchor, and nothing else of any value anywhere. "So what's the next step?" she asked. "Dragging the harbor? Or would divers be better?"

"Nobody's dragging any harbor," said Pete.

Polly turned to the chief. "You have to recover the murder weapon, don't you?"

"Nobody said anybody's been *murdered,*" said Pete, annoyed.

Polly raised her chin. "Oh, no? And I suppose you have a better theory?"

But that was the trouble.

Pete didn't.

Chapter
8

Bright and early, to be sure; and it's the early bird, as
the saying goes, that gets the rations.

Polly woke at the first gray light. A sound had wakened her,
but now awake, she couldn't identify what the sound had
been. The keening of the mourning dove? A sudden shiver
in the pine outside the window? The tick of the grandfather
clock she'd helped Pete move from the middle of the room
into the corner the night before?

Somewhere down below, a dish or a cup rattled onto a
hard surface, and in a flash Polly recalled the noise that had
disturbed her. Feet on the stairs.

Pete was up.

Polly started to throw back her covers, but stopped,
sinking deeper into the discomfort of the foldout couch.
What was the rush? Pete would be out the door and on his
way to the weirs by the time Polly got downstairs. She had
all day. All day to herself.

Somehow, the thought didn't excite her. She rolled over,
and the first thing that met her eye was a wall of cardboard.
Pete had told her this extra room was to serve in part as a
guest room. The only trouble was, they hadn't expected a
guest so soon. Pete had tried to arrange things more

47

suitably—the cartons had been heaped along one wall, the couch had been pushed back against the other, the floor lamp pulled close for reading in bed, but Polly didn't feel like reading. So what else could she do? She could go for a ride, she supposed—check out a few of her old childhood haunts. But that was the kind of thing that was only fun if you did it with your brother or your best friend, and her brother was out on the weirs, and her best friend had married and left the island long ago. Still, she supposed she could go visit somebody. Kay Dodd was still hanging around the island, wasn't she? But Kay would be at work. And Polly couldn't think of anybody else she felt like seeing.

But she *was* wide awake. She threw a leg over the side of the couch, and then another, and then slithered out from under the comforter. She shivered. Pete and his Yankee parsimony. He turned off the heat for the summer come May first, thermometer be damned. She scooted across the hall into Pete's room and rummaged around in his closet until she found an oversize sweatshirt. She pulled it over her nightgown, and when her head popped through the neckhole, she happened to be facing the new door that opened onto the deck over the porch. There was the marsh, in May still half-dead and prickly looking, and beyond the marsh, the dark, choppy water of Nashtoba Sound.

And staring at the ominous-looking sound, Polly remembered Cobie and the job the chief had given Pete.

That's what she could do.

She could find Esther Small for Pete. Or for Willy.

Or was it for Cobie?

Joe Putnam swung a dripping netful of fish past Pete's head and upended it over the fish tote. "The chief wants to do *what*?"

Pete swiped salt water out of his ear, and even that gentle motion set his biceps groaning. He'd thought he was sore the day before. Today his back, his legs, his arms, even his armpits were screaming. "He hasn't definitely decided to do it, he's just considering it. Either using scuba divers or dragging around the wreck for the anchor."

Joe snorted. "Good luck to him. It could be thirty miles from here."

"No kidding?"

"No kidding. Thing like that'll bump along the bottom forever. Either that or get buried two feet under in a day, depending on the weather. You saw what happened to Jake's Point after that storm last month."

Pete had seen, all right. The spit of land was no more. Not that Pete didn't know where to look for it. What the sea ripped out in one place it slapped down in another, and now the sand from Jake's Point was burying the jetty at the mouth of the harbor.

Pete leaned on his net and took a breather, casting his eye back toward the harbor. Yes, things had changed. When Pete was a kid, the harbor had been a lot narrower and had cut into the land much deeper. When he wasn't on vacation, one of Factotum's jobs was to read the paper to an old, half-blind woman named Sarah Abrew. Sarah had maps of the island from two hundred years ago, from the days before the relentless surf had disconnected it from the mainland. What would Nashtoba look like a hundred years from now, he wondered? And how many centuries would it take for it to wash away altogether?

Joe Putnam nudged him with his net. "Hey. Quit the sight-seeing. We got fish waiting."

Pete got back to work. It might have been his imagination, but it seemed to him that after six or seven more netfuls, his aching muscles felt better.

The house at the end of Paine Road jumped familiarly at Polly as if it were an illustration from one of her childhood storybooks, or, probably more accurately, one of her own more treasured, real-life memories. The spanking white clapboards, the Christmas green trim, even the red impatiens in the windowboxes and multicolored tulips lining the brick walk seemed unchanged in the twenty years since Polly had last been here.

Only the owner was new. Nancy Murchison was small and neat, like her house. But when she opened the door to Polly she opened it only halfway, and she blocked the opening with her body. Polly wasn't surprised. She hadn't been gone *that* long from Nashtoba. She knew it wasn't fear of robbery or assault on her person that made Nancy Murchison act this way—the only thing Nashtobans guarded this fiercely was their privacy.

"Yes?" said Nancy.

"I'm Polly Bartholomew," said Polly. "I'm sorry to bother you. I'm trying to track down Esther Small. I think she used to live here?"

"Yes?" said Nancy warily.

"Do you happen to know where she is now?"

"No." Nancy began to shut the door.

"Oh," said Polly quickly, peering in. "What a beautiful place." At least it stopped the door from closing on her. She kept going. "Esther was right—it *is* a dream house. Did you pick that paper yourself?"

The door eased back a hair. "No, as a matter of fact, Esther Small did that. But I left it. I thought it suited the place."

"That's the hard part," said Polly. "It's easy when you start from scratch. But picking and choosing what to keep and what to scrap, that takes a knack. You bought the house from the Smalls?"

Nancy looked away. "No, we bought it from the bank."

"The bank?"

"The Smalls had financial problems, and the bank foreclosed on the house." Nancy Murchison stood back so Polly could see into the hall and the living room to the right. "That's their couch and their coffee table. And the lamps, too, now that I think of it. House and contents, that's what the papers said."

Polly peered into the room. It was airy and cozy all at once, the kind of room that made you want to linger.

And Esther had had to leave it forever.

"Not that any of the furniture was worth much," Nancy said, somewhat defensively, Polly thought. "But still, Esther must have liked it if she picked it out. I tried to give some of it back. I called her up and asked her. I wasn't going to charge her for it. But she said no. She said she had no room for it where she was staying."

"And where was that?"

Nancy's eyes narrowed. It was so easy to ask a Nashtoban one question too many. "Where was what?"

"Where Esther was when you called her. I gather from here she left the island?"

"And where'd you gather that? From here she went to Mooney's."

Mooney's Guest House. Twenty dollars a night and the bathroom down the hall.

But by now Nancy Murchison seemed to feel she'd answered enough questions and started asking them instead. It was another old Nashtoba trick. "What did you say you wanted Esther for?"

"To tell her about Cobie."

"Ah," said Nancy, nodding. "Funny what happened to him. And he was just here a week or so before that."

"Cobie? Here?"

"Maybe it was two weeks ago. He wanted to buy the house back. When Dick told him we weren't interested, he went wild. He told Dick we had no right to the place. Dick was as patient as he could be for as long as he could be, but he had to ask him to leave eventually."

"Did he say how he intended to pay for it?"

Nancy shook her head. "We neither of us took him seriously enough to ask about details like that."

"Why? Was he drunk?"

"He seemed all right to me. Until he lost his temper, that is. But coming in here out of the blue, trying to take back the house, I suppose he must have been drunk out of his senses."

Maybe, thought Polly.

But then again, maybe not.

Chapter
9

. . . you would have thought anyone would have been glad to get to land after being so long at sea . . .

It was, finally, a full day's work, and a full day's work meant a boat full of fish. And a boat full of fish meant that after hours of breaking his back out on the water, Pete now got to break it again by swinging hundred-pound fish boxes out of the boat and into the truck. When they were through, Pete collapsed onto a short piling to breathe.

"Beer?" asked Joe.

It sounded good to Pete. It sounded very good to Pete. But he was halfway to his feet when he remembered Polly. For all he knew, she'd been home alone all day, brooding on her misspent life. "I'll meet you. I think I'll pop by and see if Polly wants to come."

But when Joe walked away, Pete stayed where he was a minute longer, head down, hands dangling between his knees, too tired to move. He didn't hear the sensible crepe-soled shoes approach until he saw them.

"Hello, young man. Eunice Dipple. St. Louis, Missouri."

Pete looked up from the shoes and found a hand thrust into his face. He looked higher and saw the rest of Eunice Dipple—a pink nylon track suit hermetically sealing a middle-aged body, topped by a round, smooth smiling face that sported two dimples the size of quarters.

Pete stood creakily and shook her hand.

"And you're?"

"Pete." That was the rule around here—never give away anything you didn't have to.

But Eunice Dipple didn't seem to know the rule. "And you live here, don't you?"

Pete attempted a noncommittal nod.

"Me, I'm from St. Louis. Oh my, I think I told you that already. I'm staying here for two weeks. Right over there at the Whiteaker."

Pete followed the insistent finger. Not that he had to. He was well acquainted with the old Victorian hotel that sprawled along the sand at the far end of the pier.

"I've been watching you from my window," Eunice continued. "I'm curious to know what those fish are you're catching."

Pete decided it was easiest to answer one last question as he left. "Mackerel," he said as he set off down the dock.

To his dismay, Eunice came with him.

She walked along the dock by his side. "Ah. Mackerel. And you go there in that tiny little boat. Imagine. Now that boat over there, that looks much more substantial. But I've been here an entire week now, and it never goes anywhere. Why is that, I wonder?"

Pete followed the finger again, and this time it led him to Cobie's wreck. "That's not a working boat anymore. Someone lives on it." Or he did, anyway.

"Someone *lives* on it! Imagine that. And what does he do for a living?"

"Shellfisherman."

To Pete's surprise, the pink nylon beside him broke stride and shuddered violently. "Oh! You don't mean that offensive little man who walks the beach incessantly? Looking for clams, he says. Looking for *wallets*, more likely! A shriveled little thing with a crooked tooth and absolutely *filthy* trousers?"

"Could be."

Pete quickened his pace, but Eunice only adjusted her stride so she could fit two of hers to his one. "That man is a disgrace. A complete disgrace. Honestly, someone should do something about him. He took a perfectly good blanket right off my beach chair Thursday morning. And Mr. and Mrs. Donaldson in 14C, *they* lost their binoculars. We reported it to the hotel owner, Mr. Whiteaker, and he said he'd inform the police immediately, but that's the last I've heard of it. I spoke with the Donaldsons, and we've decided not to come back here again. We told Mr. Whiteaker that, too, and we told him the reason. It's a lovely place, but you can't allow that kind of thing, not if you expect to keep your better customers."

"You don't have to worry," said Pete, tiring of Eunice rapidly. "Cobie died last Friday."

"He . . . My goodness. Friday? But we weren't here on Friday. We went to Bradford for the $7.95 lobster dinner. Quite a bargain, really. Of course they were small lobsters, and we did have to pay to park. They never put anything about *that* in the paper, do they? Tell me, how did that horrid man die? Did someone finally catch him in the act?"

"No," said Pete. "He fell overboard."

It was the vindictive gleam in Eunice Dipple's eye that made him add, "And the lobsters ate him."

Polly stood on the steps of Mooney's Guest House, imagining she was Esther Small, arriving with all that remained of her worldly belongings in whatever bags she was carrying. She pushed open the door and looked around. To her left was the living room, looking much the same as it always had, and, it seemed, occupied by much the same people—the single elderly who enjoyed congregating in the one small, communal living area. But for Esther Small, coming from her own dear home with her own things around her, to leave behind her privacy . . . *and don't forget the bathroom down the hall,* thought Polly. She shuddered, and the door to her right opened, revealing a glimpse of the communal dining table and a woman Polly recognized as Harriet Mooney. She had the same orange hair, the same orange lipstick. And the same housecoat? Unlikely, surely.

Polly stated her business, and the minute she mentioned Cobie's name, Harriet Mooney pursed her lips. "He didn't stay here for long, I'll tell you that for sure and certain. Can't have it, you know. Not with all these old dears looking to me to keep a decent establishment. It wasn't a full month before I told the Smalls they had to go, and I felt plumb awful about it. But that Esther, she just put up her chin, paid up, and packed up. No argument."

"But do you know where she went?"

Harriet Mooney's face turned from something sure and certain to something slightly uncomfortable. "Can't say absolutely."

"But you suspect a possibility? It's awfully important, Mrs. Mooney." And it was, to Polly anyway. But why? She couldn't say, exactly.

Harriet Mooney looked down at her slippers. "Heard tell they might have gone to Skid's."

Skid's. The name plummeted to the bottom of Polly's stomach like last year's fruitcake. Skid's was the unaffectionate island nickname for Sid Pierce's dilapidated, three-story, Victorian monstrosity, located directly opposite the causeway that connected Nashtoba to the mainland. It was considered a port of last resort, and not only because it was the last stop before the mainland.

Polly thanked Harriet Mooney and left, suddenly so depressed it frightened her. What was it about the Smalls' downhill slide that affected her so intensely? Was it *there but for the grace of God go I?*

Polly didn't know. But if this was what happened to people's dreams, it was just as well she didn't have any.

Chapter
10
_____

"By the power! But this tops the stiffest
yarn to nothing."

When Pete got home he did indeed find Polly brooding,
but not over her own life. Polly was brooding over Esther's.

"*Mooney's,* Pete. After Paine Road she and Cobie lived at
Mooney's. Can you imagine it?" Polly sniffed. "You're
awfully smelly, you know that?"

Pete pulled off his rubber boots, crossed the kitchen, and
tossed them onto the screen porch. It didn't help much.
"Connie's not here?"

"No," said Polly.

"Did she call?"

"I don't know. I wasn't here, I told you."

Pete went to the phone and dialed the house. No answer,
of course. He tried the hospital and finally got through to
Connie's mother's nurse's station, but all they would tell
him was that she was stable and that neither Connie nor her
father was around. Pete hung up and picked up the pile of
mail on the counter. Three catalogs, four bills, a sweep-
stakes offer, a sample box of soap.

"But that's not the big news," said Polly. "The big news
is, two weeks ago Cobie showed up at the Murchisons and
tried to buy back the house."

Pete turned. "With what?"

"He didn't say. But he got mad when they wouldn't sell."

Pete thought, *Buying a house is a far cry from buying a few drinks. But when Cobie dreams, he dreams big.* "So did the Mooneys know where Esther went?"

"It gets worse. Skid's. I didn't go to Skid's. I couldn't bear it. Not after seeing that beautiful little house. Mooney's was bad enough. Think about it, Pete. They didn't even have their own *bathroom*."

Pete remembered Polly had always had a thing about using public restrooms. Now she sank her hand onto her fist and gazed morosely out the window. Yes, she was brooding all right. Still, when Pete suggested going out for a beer, she was more than ready to join him—but not, as it turned out, for the same reason.

Or even in the same place.

"Not Lupo's," said Polly. "Knackie's. If we want to find out where Cobie's money came from and how much there was of it, we have to retrace his steps. We already know what happened at Lupo's on Friday. Let's try Knackie's."

"I hate Knackie's," said Pete. "Besides, I told Joe I'd meet him at Lupo's."

So why, ten minutes later, was he walking through the door of Knackie's? Pete looked around. Yes, he really did hate this place. Part of the reason was that it had no windows, or none you could see out of, anyway. And part of the reason was the clientele. But most of the reason was his own personal history—Pete had made a fool of himself once by punching somebody in the face in Knackie's. It was that kind of place.

But then again, so was Lupo's, as of last Friday night, anyway.

Polly hopped onto a bar stool and ordered an extra dry martini on the rocks with an olive.

The bartender, Leon Price, shot Pete a look. "No olives."

"A twist will be fine," said Polly.

"No lemon."

Polly leaned on her elbows. "Then I'll tell you what. Why don't you just give me a large gin over ice?"

Leon grinned at her, and Pete shuddered. Leon had the kind of face that looked like it got hit twice a night. Leon gave Polly a glass full of gin. Pete wished, again, that Connie were here. He ordered a Ballantine.

"Have you seen Cobie Small in here lately?" asked Polly.

"Not since he croaked." Leon guffawed loudly.

Polly laughed politely. "When *did* you see him last?"

"Just *before* he croaked."

"Friday night?"

"Afternoon, more like. Bought us all a drink."

"He did?" Polly shot Pete a look of triumph. "You and who else?"

"Let's see. It was me and Hoochie, and Al Rawlins, and Jean Louise over there." He jerked his head at the old woman at the end of the bar. Other than two vaguely familiar men, one in rolled-down hip boots and one with a ponytail, there were no other customers in the place.

"Did he say where he got the money?" asked Polly.

"What money?"

"The money for the drinks. Didn't it strike you as a tad peculiar, Cobie buying all those people drinks?"

Leon shot another look at Pete. "Sure it did, at first. But he rattled on about Esther and some Colonel somebody-or-other who gave him the loot. Sounded like Esther got hitched up again and talked the guy into bailing out Cobie."

"A colonel?" asked Pete. "Or a general, maybe?"

"Colonel, general, what's the difference?"

"Not much," agreed Pete. Out of his peripheral vision he saw a flash of an elbow and turned to see Polly downing the last of her drink. And it was hot on the heels of the first of her drink. Pete decided it was time to get out of there. He pulled out his wallet and thumbed through the few bills remaining.

"I don't suppose anyone around here saw anything funny out on Cobie's wreck on Friday?" asked Polly.

Leon snorted. "You're asking in the wrong place. Ask over to Lupo's. Dave Snow's the one who's building the big fancy restaurant with the big fancy windows. Too bad Cobie's dead. Come laundry day, they'd get a nice view of his boxer shorts flying in the breeze." Leon guffawed again.

Yes, it was time to go. Pete paid up, but in the short space of time it took him to do so, Polly had eased herself down the bar and settled onto the stool next to Jean Louise.

Pete sighed. It was going to be a long night.

"I guess I missed all the action," said Polly. "Cobie Small buying free drinks for everybody."

Jean Louise looked up through cords of lifeless gray hair. "It was my birthday," she said. "Me an' Jane Fonda. We're the same age. Betcha din' know that."

Polly didn't. And she wouldn't in a million years have guessed it, either. She decided to get back to her original subject. "Kind of funny, wasn't it? Cobie Small with all that money?"

"Not funny at all, once you know how to work it." Jean Louise leaned over her mug of Southern Comfort and peered into its depths as if it were a wishing well. "Luck'll come. Trick is bein' able to sit tight an' wait for it."

"I'll tell you what Dave Snow needs," said Leon. "Luck. Either that or a lot of money. Sunk every cent he owns and borrowed to the hilt on top of it. I heard from reliable sources these first few months are make-or-break time for old Dave. Sink or swim, as they say. And if you ask me, it's gonna sink."

"Oh," said Pete, but he wondered as he kept one eye on Polly if Leon wasn't just full of sour grapes. Leon and Dave had started out even, both bartenders at Nashtoba's rival drinking establishments. Then, overnight it seemed, Dave Snow bought up Chester's Chicken Shack, knocked out the wall facing the harbor, replaced it with glass, and was busy turning it into an elegant restaurant.

Elegant when Cobie wasn't home, at least.

"Biggest pearl you'd ever wanna see," said Jean Louise. "Right there, sitting in the middle of Cobie's oyster. And you know what he did? Took it to Sorensen's and had a beautiful ring made out of it. Gold. Fourteen carats. And he gave it to Esther."

"Oh," said Polly, but it made no sense. How did finding a pearl in an oyster and turning it into a beautiful ring for his wife leave Cobie with money in his pocket? And how could he afford to have the pearl made into a ring in the first place?

Jean Louise reduced the level in her wishing well by an inch, turned to Polly and blinked. "I were him, I woulda *killed* old Esther. Called her up. Told her he had something for her, and she came quick enough. He give her the ring, and guess what she did? Threw it in his face."

Ah, thought Polly. "And Cobie sold it, and that's where the money came from."

But Jean Louise was off on her own tack. "So he tipped the elbow a little. So what? It was a cause for celebration, wasn't it? But old Esther, she just couldn't ever make allowances. Kinda stuck up, was Esther. If he'd give it to me, things woulda turned out a heap better." And Jean Louise flung back her hair for all the world as if she *was* Jane Fonda.

Now what the hell was Polly doing? Pete wondered. She had eased away from Jean Louise, and settled in next to the man in the hip boots. Pete tried to concentrate on what Leon was saying, something about Cobie trying to sell him four lobsters out of Pit's traps, but something the ponytailed gentleman said to his sister captured his ear instead.

"Aw c'mon. Be a sport. I'll even change my sheets."

Okay, it was *definitely* time to go. Pete slid off his stool and moved down the bar.

God, he hated this place.

* * *

"Gee, thanks, but no thanks," said Polly. "But you get some interesting offers around here, don't you? Like Friday. Free drinks. From Cobie Small, of all people. I wonder where he got the bucks?"

"Where I get mine is hard work," said the ponytail. "Where Cobie got his is dumb luck. Bought the ticket that very Friday morning. Never bought a ticket before in his life."

"No kidding?" said Polly. "How much?"

Pete moved up next to Polly. Now what was she doing, negotiating the price? "Okay, Pol. Time to call it a night."

"Wait a minute," said Polly. She turned back to the ponytail.

Pete wanted to leave her there. He really did. "Polly," he said.

"Hey, piss off," said Ponytail. He slid out of his seat.

Swell, thought Pete. Was he going to have to throw his second-ever adult punch in the very same place? He started to move around Polly and experienced a ridiculous sensation of triumph when Ponytail stepped back.

"Oh, for God's sake," said Polly. She grabbed Pete by the elbow, yanked him out the door and back into his normal self.

Chapter
11

"You're all in a clove hitch, ain't you?"

Connie squeezed her eyes tight shut when she heard Pete's voice. She was supposed to be there, dammit. This was supposed to be their big second chance. This was supposed to be their *vacation*.

"Where are you?" said Pete crossly. "I thought you said you were coming back."

Connie's eyes flew open. "Yeah, well, I'm having such a great time I decided to stick around another week."

"Oh."

This time Connie was able to hear in the one word not the reproach she'd heard before, but the misery behind it. "What's happening? How's Polly?"

"Oh, swell. Couldn't be better. She's now eaten everything in the house and has generously offered to go pick up a pizza for dinner. With my money. And other than getting me into a bar brawl at Knackie's—"

"Oh," said Connie.

Somehow the word seemed to work its magic in reverse.

"Look," said Pete. "I'm sorry. It's been a long day. Let me start again where I should have started in the first place. How's your mother? How are *you?*"

Connie exhaled. "Not good." And to her horror, she felt her eyes fill up. She squeezed them shut again and swallowed. "She's got a fever and she's vomiting everything. The doctor says it's from the medication. They've taken her off it, and now we're just sitting around waiting for things to level out before they try something else. Dad's a wreck. And you may have noticed I'm not doing so hot either."

"I think you're doing great."

"I don't know, Pete, she looks so awful."

"So would you if you were spewing up everything. So would I. So would everybody."

True, thought Connie. She perked up. "So," she said. "Any news on Cobie?"

"Case still closed. Unless, of course, you ask Polly."

"What does Willy think?"

"He's getting talked down the river by Rosie."

"What?"

"You know. *The African Queen.* When Hepburn talks Bogey into going down the Ulanga to blow up the Germans. Only in this case, Willy's getting talked into dragging the harbor. For the anchor. Polly's sure somebody murdered Cobie with it."

Connie thought about it and had to admit she kind of agreed with Polly. But Pete didn't seem to want to hear that. He said something about drinking gin out of the bottle next and not holding out for clean sheets, but before Connie could ask him what the hell he was talking about, he was onto Cobie again. Pearls. Lottery tickets. Lobsters. Then, just as suddenly, his voice changed from something somewhat peevish to something that forced her to jam her eyelids tight shut again.

"Hey, enough of that. You've got enough to worry about. *We've* got enough to worry about. But let's not worry until we have to, all right? If they say it's just the medicine, the odds are it's just the medicine."

"Yeah. I guess."

There was a small silence. "I feel like I've lost a dimension since you left," he said finally.

Yes. That was what it was like. Still, Connie noticed he didn't offer to come down this time.

And this time, she just might have said yes.

Polly's route to Beaton's Pizza wasn't exactly what you'd call direct. But then again, neither was her train of thought. She started out thinking about Cobie. Then about Esther. Then about her own messy life. And somehow it all led back to Cobie, and the next thing she knew, she was driving along Shore Road, heading for his wreck.

It was almost dusk, but the last light bouncing off the water seemed, conversely, to help brighten the sky closest to it. The beach stretched cold, bare, and silver until the raw shingles of Dave Snow's new restaurant rose into view. Polly's foot eased off the accelerator. What had Leon Price said when Polly had asked if he'd seen anyone around Cobie's wreck that Friday night? *Ask over to Lupo's. Dave Snow's the one who's building the big fancy restaurant with the big fancy windows* . . . Polly pulled over.

It was fancy, all right. Or at least it would be. The building itself sat high on pilings, with a dropped deck around three sides, the same three sides of the building bulging with bay windows. But inside, Dave Snow had warmed up all that cold glass by framing it with yellow pine, tiling the floor in brick. The walls were already painted a color that reminded Polly of old, mellow silk.

But Dave Snow was nowhere to be seen.

Polly stepped out onto the deck and looked around. Yes, Cobie's wreck did dominate the landscape. The only other distraction was the sight of two men walking toward it along the sand. As they drew closer, Polly could see them more clearly. The thin one with the rakish hair looked like Dave Snow. The big one with the red beard could only be Pit. As they drew level with the wreck they stopped, facing the water. Dave Snow planted his feet and crossed his arms. Pit Patterson cocked a knee and rested his hands on his hips. Their heads twitched front to side as they talked. Once in a while one of them pointed out to sea toward Cobie's wreck. Finally, Pit reached into his pocket, pulled out a shiny coin, and flipped it into the water. It skipped like a rock. Polly was so busy watching the rippling rings, she didn't see the third man approaching until she heard the whistle. *Danny Boy*. She stepped off the deck and walked down the beach.

They heard her, or felt her, when she was still ten yards off. All three men looked up, but it was the whistler, the one with the thick auburn hair that dipped over his forehead like a Kennedy's, who spoke.

"Hello." He flashed Kennedyesque white teeth, and suddenly Polly remembered him. The owner of the hotel, Jack Whiteaker. As she recalled, his bank account was also Kennedyesque.

Dave Snow turned to Polly, scratching what looked like a two-day-old mustache on his upper lip. "What are you doing down here all by your lonesome at this time of night?"

"I didn't know there was a curfew," said Polly. "I came to ask you if you saw anything weird out there around the wreck Friday night."

Suddenly it was as if there *was* a curfew.

"Gotta go," said Pit Patterson. He jammed his hands into his pockets and moved down the beach.

"Me, too," said Jack. He jogged off to catch up with Pit.

Only Dave Snow remained. "Wasn't here," he said. "I was working at Lupo's. Till this place opens, I still have to eat."

"When do you open?"

"Memorial Day."

Polly turned to face the restaurant. "It looks nice."

"Yeah," said Dave.

But when Polly looked back to Dave, she saw he was staring at Cobie's wreck.

Pete had just finished picking up pizza boxes and sub wrappers and listening to Polly hash over Cobie ad infinitum, when Willy showed up, this time in jeans and a new wool shirt Pete had seen in Hansey's Clothing Store and knew for a fact had cost him sixty-eight bucks.

They settled in around the kitchen table. When the upstairs was finished and empty of overnight guests, would they usher their callers up there instead? Pete tried to picture it. He couldn't. He supposed they'd be hunkering down in his kitchen for the rest of his life. Somehow, though, the thought didn't bother him.

Suddenly Pete realized the conversation had begun without him. They were talking about Cobie, of course. The missing anchor. The missing money. And now Willy was rubbing a large hand over a long face and doing something Pete didn't hear him do too much—gripe.

"I told Collins. I told him about the anchor, I mentioned the money, and you know what he said? He said considering the party involved, a couple of allegedly missing items didn't justify spending any more time and money on the case."

"And what did you say?" asked Polly.

Willy looked slightly chagrined. "Nothing that helped anything much. I said you mean the investigatory budget for a penniless drunk is less than the budget for a drunk governor?"

Polly giggled.

"And he said, a bit frostily, I thought, that someone with my experience should know better than to put too much weight on the unaccounted-for belongings of a homeless alcoholic. He said as for the money, he probably went back out and bought another bottle."

"For a hundred and thirty-two bucks?" asked Pete.

"Just what I said."

"And what did Collins say?"

"He said most of the drunks he knew didn't make change so great."

"And how did he get to shore? We left the dinghy on the beach."

"I mentioned that, too. And Collins said Cobie could have swum in if he was desperate enough. And he reiterated that the case was still going down as an accidental death. And he added that if I felt differently, I was free to look into it further. On my own time, of course."

"He's not your boss! He can't tell you that!" Polly looked so outraged, Pete almost laughed.

"He can tell me anything he wants. And I can do anything I want."

"Okay," said Polly. "So it's up to us."

Suddenly Pete lost the urge to laugh. Polly was launched.

First she reviewed the things that were as yet unresolved—the anchor and the money, of course, but also Cobie's visit to the Murchisons, the rumored lottery ticket, the pearl, the lobsters. Then she set forth a course of action that sounded at best, dubious, and at worst, ludicrous, but as Pete looked across the kitchen table, he saw that Willy watched her intently, absorbing without a qualm her every harebrained thought.

Again Pete's mind wandered. Did Polly know this wasn't a normal thing, Willy stopping by all the time like this? Did she know about the shirt? And if she did know, what did she think about it? Pete had no idea. For that matter, what did *he* think about it? Not that what he thought mattered. Not that he could do anything about it if it did. Not that he *would* do anything. Okay, maybe he could tackle that old Renault all right, but if there was one thing he'd learned when it came to Polly and men, keep out of it.

"Hey, beautiful dreamer," said Polly. "Wake up. We're talking to you. Did you ask around the harbor today? Did anyone see anything out on Cobie's wreck Friday night?"

"No," said Pete, "but I talked to a woman who doesn't like Cobie much." He told them about Eunice Dipple.

"And she accused Cobie of stealing?" Polly's amber eyes flashed like a cat's. When she appropriated somebody as her own personal cause, even if it was a dead somebody, it was best to watch out.

"She reported him to Jack Whiteaker." Pete turned to Willy. "And Jack said he reported him to you."

Willy shook his head. "First I've heard of it."

"But you don't think Cobie's a thief, do you?" asked Polly. "I mean you've never proved anything about Pit's lobsters, right?"

"I never tried."

Polly pulled her feet under her and sat up straight. "You mean someone accused Cobie of stealing his lobsters and you didn't do anything? You didn't even ask Pit where he got his so-called facts?"

The chief met Polly's eyes head-on—cool gray on hot amber. "It may look like there's a lot of me," he said quietly. "But it wears pretty thin covering the length and breadth of this island. Pit Patterson never made anything official out of his complaints about Cobie. I heard about them the same way you two did. And as far as I'm concerned, it's nothing more than a bunch of name-calling."

"And you're probably right," said Pete, for no good reason that he could think of at the moment except to cool Polly out.

It worked, at least temporarily. She settled back in her chair, hunched up her knees, and pulled her sweatshirt over them. Pete's sweatshirt. The sweatshirt he'd wasted ten minutes looking for that very morning.

"All right," said Polly. "So what do we do first?"

Pete stood up, yawning. "Go to bed. I have to be out on the weirs at daybreak." His muscles may have begun to shape up, but with the early rising and the long hours of physical labor, he didn't have much steam left by night. He moved toward the door, but it didn't seem to rattle his guests any. They bade him good night with barely a pause, and as Pete walked upstairs, he could hear them still talking. *Esther. Lottery. Pit.*

After he cleaned up, Pete paused at the head of the stairs. Yep, still at it. He could just hear their voices, making plans to meet in the morning.

To blow up the Germans, no doubt.

Chapter
12

He . . . sometimes put his nose out of doors
to smell the sea . . .

But in the morning Pete found himself standing on the dock next to Joe Putnam, gazing at the small craft warning flag flying from the harbormaster's office. Pete could see white froth and black troughs out past the mouth of the harbor. He knew they'd be crazy to go out there, and he knew Joe knew it, but since Joe had more at stake, it was going to take him longer to admit it. So Pete stood on the dock and waited and looked around the harbor.

There were no boats on the water and no hotel guests on the beach or even on the veranda. It was truly miserable weather. Cobie's wreck swayed like a metronome in the chop. Not far beyond the boat, Pete could see Dave Snow's nearly completed restaurant, and beyond that, four sprawling stories tiered like a wedding cake—the summer "cottage" of Seline DuBois. As he watched, a white-clad figure moved down the long steps and began to walk the beach, facing into the wind.

"There goes Seline," said Joe. "Crazy lady. Walks the beach every day she's here, come wind, come rain, come any kind of crazy, stinking weather. And the uglier the

weather, the uglier the snarl on her puss. Like somebody did
it to her out of spite."

The weather wasn't the only thing she fought tooth and
nail. As Pete recalled, she'd managed to build four stories
on a parcel of land with a two-story restriction by calling the
bottom story the basement and the top story the attic. She'd
encroached on the fragile dune with an illegal set of stairs.
And she refused to accept anyone traversing the beach in
front of her house, contrary to right-of-access laws that
dated back to the time of King James. Still, she had an up-
front and personal view of Cobie's wreck. And she was
walking in this direction.

He set off to intercept her.

Polly rested her head against the back of the seat in the
chief's Scout and said, "So much for Cobie's lucky number."

They had hit every lottery vendor on Nashtoba island,
but no one had cashed in a winning ticket for Cobie Small.
At the last stop, the liquor store on Cove Road that Cobie
most often frequented, they ran into Polly's ponytailed
friend from Knackie's, picking up at least fifty dollars'
worth of tickets. He looked like he might have tried his luck
with Polly again, too, but for some reason, when he saw the
chief with her, he changed direction.

And now they were on the trail of Pit Patterson.

The chief pulled off the road beside a fringe of beach
plum bushes, alongside a spit of sandy beach that curved
into an outcrop of rocks. The rocks, in turn, stretched out
into the harbor to form a small point beyond which Polly
could just see the top of Cobie's wreck. Along the rocks
bobbed a field of buoys. On top of the rocks stood Pit.

The chief and Polly scrambled out of the car, over the
beach, and onto the rocks. There was a good strong wind
and plenty of surf. The rocks were slippery, Polly wasn't
wearing the right kind of shoes, and she was relieved when
the chief, apparently never having heard that you were
supposed to let women fend for themselves these days,

extended a hand and pulled her over the largest gap. But Pit stood his ground, arms folded, staring down at his pots, making no move to meet them halfway. When they reached the lobsterman, Willy said something that was lost to Polly in the wind, but Pit only shrugged.

"Cobie Small," Willy yelled, louder this time. "Heard he was stealing from your traps."

Pit Patterson's watery blue eyes rolled first toward the chief, then toward Polly. "Where'd you hear that?"

This time it was Willy who shrugged.

"Cobie never stole any lobsters. If he'd asked, I'da given him some."

Polly raised her voice against the wind and waved an arm at Cobie's wreck, not far from the rocks. "You never saw him poking around your traps?"

Pit's eye traveled over Polly a second time. "I got no quarrel with Cobie."

And that was that.

Seline DuBois would have strode right past Pete, white canvas jacket clutched tight around her, head ducked against the wind, if Pete hadn't moved across her path.

"Ms. DuBois?"

She nodded but didn't stop.

Pete swung in beside her.

"My name is Peter Bartholomew."

Her face remained blank.

"I wonder if I could ask you a couple of questions about Cobie Small. That's his wreck right over there in the harbor."

"I'm well aware whose wreck that is."

"And that he's dead?"

She glanced sideways, and platinum hair flattened around a smooth face. Still, Pete figured she was at least in her sixties.

"Are you with the police?"

"No," said Pete. "But I am trying to find out if anyone saw anything out at the wreck late Friday night."

"I try not to look at the wreck. And if you'll study the geography, you'll see it isn't always easy."

"But you were here on Friday?"

"I was."

"And did you see any—"

Seline DuBois stopped walking. "I'll tell you what I've seen on that wreck. An intoxicated, unkempt, unclothed, offensive individual trespassing on my beach and fouling the waters of my harbor. That he's dead, I'm sorry. That he's *gone,* I consider nothing but a cause for celebration. This is where I'll be turning. Good morning."

She about-faced and left Pete standing alone in the sand. It was just as well. If she'd lingered, Pete might have had to straighten her out on whose beach, and whose harbor, it really was.

Joe still stood where Pete had left him, staring out to sea. He saw Pete and jerked his head after the striding white figure. "What the hell do you want with her?"

"I was asking her about Cobie. She wasn't too crazy about him, I guess."

Joe laughed. "I could have told you that. So could the harbormaster. She's been raising holy hell, in and out of his office twice a day trying to get him to yank Cobie's mooring permit. He's wrecking her view. He's polluting the harbor. He's annoying her guests. He's a danger to children and small animals. Got to the point she threatened Freeman's job if he didn't kick Cobie off that mooring."

"How could Seline DuBois threaten the harbormaster's job?"

Joe shrugged. Then he looked out to sea and at the sky and, finally, at the flag in front of the harbormaster's office. "Oh, the hell with it. Meet me back here tomorrow at the crack." He turned on his rubber-booted heel and clomped down the dock to his truck.

Jack Whiteaker was no shrimp, but as Polly stood between him and the police chief on the steps of the Whiteaker Hotel, she couldn't help noticing that the chief was a good three inches taller and maybe half again as broad. *He's so big, he should be scary,* she thought. *Why isn't he?*

But they fared no better with Jack than they had with Pit. He ran his fingers through that hair, smiled at them through those teeth, and denied flat out that any of his guests had ever complained to him about Cobie stealing. Or about Cobie doing anything, as a matter of fact.

Polly and Willy returned to the chief's Scout. "What next?" asked Polly.

"I drop you off and get back to work. This isn't my case."

"Right," said Polly. "I suppose you've got a couple of other murder cases waiting at the station?"

The chief turned. "No," he said calmly. "But what I do have is a staff of two, one of whom is on vacation, and a list of calls that will keep me busy till dusk."

"Like what?" asked Polly, suddenly curious. "What kinds of calls do you get around here, anyway? Help, my cat's having kittens?"

Willy grinned. When he grinned, his face creased all the way into his distant hairline, and the result, for Polly anyway, was that she hadn't felt this entertaining in months.

"The kittens were yesterday. Today it's a snapping turtle that seems to have strayed from Myer's Pond onto Fergy Potts's front lawn. And a suspicious package at the post office. And a loud radio on—"

"But don't you miss your old life? The big city, the important cases?"

The chief stopped smiling. "You mean cases that don't involve lonely old ladies or penniless drunks?"

"No," said Polly quickly. "That isn't what I meant. Only—"

Willy grinned again. "I didn't think so." They were almost at the house now. "I'm meeting the scuba club at two-thirty at Cobie's wreck. If the weather settles down, they're going to search for the anchor. Stop by if you want."

"Oh, Seline DuBois didn't scare me any," said Freeman Studley.

And not many people did, thought Pete. The harbormaster was young and small and spare, but as cocky as a pit bull. Pete had decided since he now had the day off, he might as well finish what he'd started, and he'd popped into the harbormaster's office, an old ice storage shed on the dock, to see if there was any truth to Joe Putnam's rumor.

"Oh, she fussed around here throwing names in my face," said Freeman. " 'I'll speak to so-and-so. I'll write a letter to the honorable la-dee-da.' You go ahead, I told her. And while you're at it, why don't you put in a call to the Dalai Lama? So she shoved off in a pretty good snit. Back again, two hours later, wanting to know who hired me. I told her I was appointed by the board of selectmen. She said fine, count on being unappointed real soon."

"And this was all over Cobie's wreck?"

"More over Cobie himself. Cobie and his colorful personal habits. She might have been able to take the sight of that old wreck if it didn't come with Cobie attached. But she knew if she got rid of the boat, she got rid of Cobie."

"Or if she got rid of you?"

Freeman grinned at Pete. "Not a prayer."

"She didn't have as much clout as she thought?"

"Oh, she's got plenty of clout up high, but around here, that kind of clout doesn't count for much. So she calls the president and the president calls the governor and the governor calls the chairman of the board of selectmen. So what? The chairman says nice to hear from you, buddy, hangs up, and goes out fishing."

"Still, she gets away with a lot."

"Not as much as she thinks. Those stairs of hers are coming down next month. And I know a few people who make it a point of walking to work along her beach a couple of times a week." And Freeman Studley, Jr., saluted in the direction of Seline DuBois's summer cottage.

With one finger.

It was still a long way till two-thirty, but Polly had thought of something else she could do on her own account. She could visit Earl Sorensen, the jeweler who had made the pearl into a ring for Esther.

The only trouble was, he hadn't.

"Cobie Small? Coming in here with a pearl? *Paying* us to make a ring out of it?" Earl Sorensen tipped an elegant profile to the sky and started to laugh. It took Polly a few tries before she could successfully interrupt him. "Didn't Cobie bring you a pearl?"

"In his dreams," said Earl, still laughing. He picked up a chamois cloth and wiped the glittering glass showcase that housed other rings, rings made up of emeralds, amethysts, rubies.

And pearls.

"Didn't he come in at all? Even without a pearl? To ask you about rings?"

"Cobie Small, thank the good lord, has never set foot inside this establishment." Earl Sorensen straightened a snow-white shirt cuff, for no other reason than to show off his fancy gold cuff links. At least that's how it looked to Polly.

So she decided to look at his ladies' wristwatches. She asked Sorensen to remove them from the showcase one at a time for her inspection. There were seventeen of them.

Unfortunately, there just wasn't one she liked.

Chapter
13

. . . The two gentlemen leaned forward and looked
at each other, and forgot to smoke in their
surprise and interest.

As Pete left the harbormaster's office, he happened to look
down the dock and spied the pink nylon form of Eunice
Dipple approaching. He turned, hunting for an escape
route, and on the far side of the harbormaster's office he saw
it—Captain Cobb's Fish Market. He ducked in.

Captain Cobb, whose real name was Steve Perez, was
behind the lobster tank, sweeping the floor. When he saw
Pete, he stopped sweeping and grinned. "Hey, Pete."

"Hey, Steve." Pete peered into the tank. Several dozen
greenish black lobsters crept around the bottom in slow
motion. "Tell me something, Steve. Do you get any of your
lobsters from Pit?"

"I get all my lobsters from Pit."

"Did you ever buy any from Cobie Small?"

Steve shook his head emphatically. "If I did, Pit would
have shot me."

"Why, because they were stolen from Pit's traps?"

"Not likely," said Steve. "If they were, Pit would have
shot *him*. Haven't you heard what's going on up the coast?
They've got guys riding shotgun around their traps. You

78

don't mess with a lobsterman. Everybody knows that. Even Cobie."

"Did you do much other shellfish business with Cobie?"

"Not much. At least, not lately. I need to know what's coming in when, and you never knew that with Cobie. Oh, I'd buy a bag of chowders from him once in a while."

Chowders. Those were the bigger quahogs, some of them the size and toughness of a clenched fist. "How much do you shell out for a bag of chowders?"

"This time of year? An eighty-pound bag would get you ten, fifteen bucks."

Ten or fifteen bucks. It wasn't even enough to set up the bar. It certainly wasn't the "fistful of twenties" Connie had seen in Lupo's on Friday.

Pete said good-bye to Steve and wandered out of the fish market, thinking. So Cobie should have known better than to mess with Pit's traps. The question was, did he? Steve seemed to think so. But why? Because Pit hadn't shot Cobie. But had he bashed in his head with an anchor?

Maybe.

Or maybe not.

Polly left Sorensen's dragging her feet. She knew what came next on the list, but she dreaded it. It was back to the hunt for Esther, and that meant a trip to Skid's.

As she crossed the porch at Skid's the floorboards sagged under her. She scanned the slots for nameplates over the mailboxes and found most of them empty. There was one for Sid Pierce, however. Polly found the bell next to it and pushed fast before her gumption left her.

The door to Polly's immediate right swung open. Polly had never met Sid before, and she stared. The man was squat and square with short black fuzz all over him—head, face, wrists, knuckles, ears.

"Full up," said Sid. He pointed at the No Vacancy sign tacked to the pulpy shingles.

"I see it," said Polly. "That's not why I'm here. I'm looking for Esther Small."

"Not here." He started to close the door.

"I know that. But this was her last known address."

"You think I buried her under the floorboards? I don't have her. I don't have her sot of a husband, either. After she disappeared, I kicked him out. That was fifteen, sixteen years ago."

Polly was surprised he remembered the episode so clearly. "She disappeared?"

"That's what I'd call it. Here one day, gone the next. I remember it didn't seem to surprise *him* much."

"Do you suppose you'd have a forwarding address in your files someplace?"

Sid Pierce bared his teeth. Polly half expected to see short black hairs on the teeth, too. "People who leave here don't leave a forwarding address. Not when they stiff me for two months' rent. How she paid the first month on that measly salary Fred Underwood paid her beats me—the sot was no help. But if you're looking for the sot, look on the wreck in the harbor."

"He's not there," said Polly. "He's dead. And I thought his widow ought to know about it."

Sid Pierce shrugged. "Nobody's seen her for fifteen, sixteen years. Odds are she's dead, too. Happens faster when you're down there."

"Down where?"

Sid Pierce aimed a blunt, hairy thumb at the floor. "Bottom."

As Pete left the fish market he was so busy thinking, he forgot about Eunice Dipple and nearly walked straight into her.

"Hello, again," she said. "Fancy meeting you here. Not fishing today, I see."

"No," said Pete. "Not fishing." Then he looked closer at Eunice. Under her arm was a fuzzy blue blanket. "You found it."

Eunice opened her mouth into an O, the dimples flattening. "Why, no," she said, and then clamped her lips together, her face turning as pink as her suit. "That is to say, actually . . . " she looked away and mumbled something.

"I seem to recall you thought the beachcomber who lived on the boat had stolen your blanket."

"Oh, no," said Eunice. "No, I was mistaken. You see I have my blanket. Good afternoon." She held out the square of thick blue stuff toward Pete, then tucked it under her arm, and walked away quickly.

But not so quickly that Pete missed the price tag still attached to the corner.

By two-thirty the wind had shifted around to the south, and although there was still a crusty black chop out past the entrance to the harbor, the harbor itself had calmed considerably. Polly and the chief stood on shore and watched the scuba club spread themselves out along a knotted rope and wade into the water.

Polly filled the chief in on the middle of her day—the trip to Sorensen's and her fruitless search for Esther. Then somehow, slowly, their conversation crept off into other things. Why Polly left Nashtoba. Why Willy came here.

Dreams, thought Polly. When she'd had them, it hadn't seemed possible that this small island could fulfill them, but Willy's dreams went well here. To be part of a place. To be able to help the people who lived there. To have a few friends. One special one, maybe.

An hour slipped by. Two hours. Longer. The divers worked methodically, stretched out along the rope, criss-crossing the harbor. They started at the end near Cobie's wreck and worked their way toward the mouth of the harbor.

And came up empty.

There were two more establishments with bird's-eye views of the harbor and Cobie's wreck—one was Dillingham Bait and Tackle, the other was Hillerman's boathouse. Both held mixed memories for Pete—the former of a cantankerous old coot named Ozzie who had about as much use for Pete as he had for a pair of bunions, the latter of a lost lady love.

Pete opted for the bunions first.

Dillingham Bait and Tackle, the sign said. Boats to Rent. Charter Fishing. Crawlers, Sea Worms, Squid, Sand Eels, Shiners.

The minute Pete opened the door he was greeted by a smell and a voice he hadn't much missed. "What are you doing traipsing around the beach annoying us hardworking folks? And here I thought you'd finally got a decent job for once."

Pete paused at the door. What was he doing? Did he really need this?

But the disembodied voice kept right on. "Why aren't you out shoveling fish? Can't Joe Putnam take a little breeze in his britches?"

Pete stepped into the shop. "Guess not." He walked steadily toward the back, talking as he went. It wouldn't get any better if he did it any slower. "Friday night. Cobie's boat. See anybody, anything?"

By now Pete could see the top of Ozzie's head—steel gray hair that looked like it had been cut with a lawn mower. It didn't look up.

"Nope," it said.

Pete about-faced.

"Don't suppose you care what I heard, either."

The trick was to slow down and not look like you did. Pete decreased the length of his stride, gauging the distance to the door against the length of Ozzie's average sentence.

"Two splashes. One big. One little. Then nothing. Then oars slapping water fit to kill."

No matter how slow he walked, it was no good. Pete reached the door at the *slapping water* part. He turned around. "Time?"

"Eleven o'clock. Thereabouts."

"And you didn't look out?"

"What for? It was dark. I figured it was Cobie tossing his

empties or lighting out for shore to make last call. Whoever it was, he *rowed* like a drunk."

"Did you tell the chief this? Or Lieutenant Collins?"

"Now why would I talk to them when I knew if I sat tight, I could tell it to a nice, nosy chap like you?"

"Gee, thanks," said Pete.

Ozzie didn't answer. He launched into an off-tune chorus of *Fools Rush In,* instead.

Pete's sojourn to the boathouse was as brief. The Hillermans rented out the boathouse in the summer and off-season on those rare occasions when they could find someone desperate enough to face up to the wind through the cracks.

Pete's lady love had been desperate, all right.

And so, it appeared, was the current tenant. He had an unemployed look—too young to have amassed much of a résumé and too wasted to have been eating right. His eyes bored through the tiny glass pane on the door and straight past Pete—when he saw there was no one else out there he seemed to calm down a bit. He opened the door.

"What do you want?" he croaked.

Either he was nervous or his voice had just changed. Pete shot him a grin. "Nothing as disastrous as your money or your life. Pete Bartholomew." Pete held out his hand. His new acquaintance started to raise one to meet it, saw it was shaking, and jammed both hands into his pockets instead.

Pete tried again. "You're—?"

The eyes flitted away. "Sam. Sam Smith."

"Sam. Okay. I see you've got a good view of that old wreck. I used to know the fellow who lived on it, and he met with some sort of an accident Friday night. Were you around here then?"

The eyes flicked back. "Around when?"

"Friday. Friday night. Did you see anything? Or hear anything?" he added fast. He didn't *usually* make the same mistake twice.

"No. I . . . I wasn't here Friday night."

Pete was almost relieved. The kid was making *him* nervous. "All right," he said. "Sorry to bug you."

He raised a hand and retreated down the steps.

Polly found the disappointment close to shattering. For the past few hours she'd been counting on one of those divers leaping out of the water and waving an anchor at her. So why was the police chief acting as if the anchor were nothing more than a misplaced coffee cup? Polly tried to get him to divulge his next step, but he didn't seem to have any.

Polly gave up. She said good-bye and started down the beach toward her car, but she hadn't gone far when his broad shoulder appeared beside her.

"I'm all out of leftovers. I was planning to eat at Lupo's tonight. Care to join me?"

Polly looked up, surprised. "Well, sure. I mean, I guess so. I'd better check with Pete."

"You check with Pete. If I don't hear otherwise, I'll swing by around seven."

They were at her car. Willy reached down and opened her door. Somehow, the old-fashioned gesture seemed to suit him. "Good-bye," he said.

"Good-bye," said Polly.

Chapter
14

"We'll sit you down if you please, and talk square like
old shipmates."

Pete walked into the police station just as Willy was
walking out. The chief would have kept going, too, if Pete
hadn't caught his elbow and said "Hey!"

"What now?"

"Oh, nothing much. I've just found you your first eyewit-
ness, that's all. Or an earwitness. And an overly edgy kid
who could use some checking out." He told the chief about
Ozzie Dillingham and his new friend, Sam Smith.

"That it?"

Pete peered at him. "Yeah. That's it."

"Okay." The chief started out of the station and stopped.
"I asked Polly out to dinner. She said sure, but she wants to
check with you first."

"Check with me for what?"

Willy shrugged. "Maybe she was afraid you'd booked her
a table at the Ritz."

"I didn't book any tables."

"Good."

They walked out of the station together, but once outside,
the chief didn't turn in the direction of his Scout. Neither

did he turn in the direction of Ozzie Dillingham's bait shop or Hillerman's boathouse.

"Hey," said Pete. "Aren't you going to check out my leads?"

"Eventually," said Willy.

Pete watched him walk down Main Street and turn into Hansey's Clothing Store.

Of course.

Pete got in his truck and headed for home. *So now what?* he thought. He could go home, but if he went home, his sister would be waiting for him, ready to talk him to death about a dead shellfisherman.

Instead of turning right at the end of Main Street, Pete turned left, and he didn't stop until he'd reached Lupo's.

There were three people at the far end of the bar, but they were people Pete could wave to and ignore without feeling criminal. It didn't help him any. Dave Snow brought him his Ballantine, leaned on the bar across from him, and began complaining in his ear. The plumber working on the new restaurant was two weeks behind schedule. The electrician was already five thousand dollars over bid. The linen tablecloths he'd ordered in a color called burnt caramel arrived looking more like singed pink.

"At least now you don't have to worry about Cobie," said Pete.

Dave Snow raised an eyebrow. His mustache, a new one, Pete noticed, twitched. "Cobie?"

"You know. What you were complaining about the other night. The whizzing off his deck in front of your new patrons."

Dave Snow laughed loudly. "You think I meant that? Come on. All the tourists love something like old Cobie. You know what he was? Local color, that's what he was. What every restaurant needs. It's a sure draw, something like that."

"Oh," said Pete.

Dave Snow gave him another beer. "Here. On the house."

Free beer? That was a first. Pete decided he must be hanging around the bar too much. But he wasn't ready to leave. Not yet. "Last Friday night. How'd it go in here after we took Cobie out? Did the crowd hang on till closing?"

"No way. Pit took off right after you three did. Everybody was sore at him for shoving Cobie like that. Matter of fact, the whole place kind of wound down once Cobie stopped buying. Joe hung around for a while, cracking sick jokes about Kay and Cobie till I told him to pipe down, but even he left early. I was talking to myself by ten-thirty."

"Did you happen to see Cobie with some money?"

"Did I see Cobie with some money. Everybody saw Cobie with some money. He flashed it in everybody's face."

"How much?"

Dave Snow shrugged. "He was buying. I was busy. But if you forced me to guess, I'd guess he had a couple hundred bucks."

A couple hundred bucks. So he'd set up the bar and been carted home with a hundred and thirty-two left.

Pete stood up. "Thanks."

"Hey," said Dave. "What's all this about Cobie, anyway?"

"Cobie? Nothing much."

At least, thought Pete, *I can still* hope *it is nothing much.*

The sign hadn't changed in thirty years. *Garret Gold— Antiques—Collectibles. You're welcome to browse—leave your children in the car.* One day the town nurse approached Fred Underwood, the shop owner, and tactfully suggested he rephrase his message—after all, said Dotty Parsons, we don't really want small children left unattended in a hot car, do we?

"Why ever not?" Fred Underwood had asked her.

And the sign remained.

The funny thing about Fred was that while he seemed anxious to keep children out, he filled his windows with the very things most likely to lure them in.

Dressmaker's dummies in antique clothes. Shadowbox scenes of cozy Victorian parlors. Indian clubs. Mechanical banks. A Civil War sword. And Polly's prepubescent favorite—a white rabbit's-fur muff. She even spied something she was sure Pete would like—a marble chess set, just like the one their grandfather once had. She remembered Pete used to play cowboys and Indians with the knights and the bishops for hours on end.

Fred Underwood heard the door and came trotting from the back of the shop, his eyes wide and swimming behind magnifying lenses. "May I help you?"

"Hi, Mr. Underwood. It's Polly. Polly Bartholomew."

The eyes grew wider. "Why Polly. For heaven's sake. I haven't seen you in ages."

Polly smiled. He *almost* sounded like he'd missed her. "I'm visiting my brother. I'm trying to help him find Esther Small. Sid Pierce told me she used to work here. I guess I'd forgotten about that."

"Oh, that was some time ago. But why on earth would your brother want to find her?"

"Actually it's the police chief who wants to find her. About Cobie. You know."

Fred shook his head from side to side so vigorously his glasses drooped. "A shame. That's all I can say about it. A waste and a shame."

"Do you know where she is now?"

Fred removed his glasses and rubbed his eyes. "Esther? Do you mean, do I know where Esther is right now? Why, no, no I don't. But why in the world would the police chief want Esther?"

"She's next of kin. As least as far as anyone knows."

"I see. The arrangements, you mean."

"That, too, I suppose. But she'd want to know what happened to him."

"Would she?"

"I'm sure she would."

Fred Underwood looked doubtful. He placed his glasses

firmly on his face and checked the earpieces. "I'm sorry I am unable to help."

Pete stopped on the way home to restock his refrigerator. He decided he'd make a batch of spaghetti sauce. It was cheap and it was filling and it would last them a week. If Polly stayed any longer than that, she'd get bread and water. And besides, it was one of Pete's favorite meals. Since he was eating alone tonight, he might as well eat something he liked.

But when Polly walked in and saw the simmering pot she said, "Oh, shoot. Spaghetti. I *love* spaghetti. But Willy's run out of food and wants us to go out to eat."

Us? Somehow Pete hadn't got the impression the invitation was for *us*.

"You go," said Pete. "I'm pretty bushed."

Polly's eyes flew wide. "*Me* go? With the chief? And what will you do, sit here eating spaghetti all by yourself? No, we'll ask Willy to eat here."

"Willy hates spaghetti."

Polly's eyes darted anxiously toward the stove. "Isn't there something else he could eat?"

"No," said Pete.

But when Willy arrived, in chinos and a navy blue sweater that still had the fold marks in the sleeves, she gave it another shot.

"You have to talk to Pete. He says he's tired and he's not coming. We can't let him sit here all alone and eat spaghetti."

The look on Willy's face confirmed Pete's suspicion that the idea of him coming at all was a new one. "Do you want to sit here all alone eating spaghetti?" Willy asked.

"Yes," said Pete.

"I thought so," said Willy. He turned to Polly. "This will work out much better. We can talk about him behind his back."

Polly laughed.

Willy touched her on the small of the back, guiding her to the door. The door opened and swallowed them.

She'll be okay, thought Pete.

Won't she?

Polly ordered a sirloin steak with salad and baked potato and a glass of merlot. Willy ordered the fisherman's platter and a Rolling Rock. Somewhere between the end of the first merlot and the beginning of the second, Polly felt something untwist inside her. It was just Willy. He was just telling funny stories about her brother.

And this was just dinner.

Of course, sooner or later the conversation took that deadly turn toward Cobie Small.

And of course, it was Polly who steered it there.

"Tell me something," she said. "Do you think Cobie was murdered?"

"Yes."

Yes. That was it. No ifs or ands. Not even a but.

The waitress cleared their plates and brought dessert menus. Polly ordered cheesecake and Kahlua. Willy ordered coffee.

"So what do we do about it? We can't find the weapon. We can't trace the money."

"Now we keep our eyes and ears open. Sooner or later someone will say something."

"If someone knows something."

"Oh, someone does."

"The one who did it?"

"That one, maybe some others."

"Or maybe the murderer will confess. Mine did. I mean, the man who murdered my fiance confessed."

"Yeah," said Willy. "Lucky."

It sounded offhand. He returned to drinking his coffee. But suddenly, for the first time in months, Polly felt like talking about the mistake she'd almost made, about the man she'd almost married, about the murder that had freed her.

So she talked.
And Willy listened.

Pete sat down at the kitchen table and reached for the old black rotary phone he'd refused to relinquish over the years. He stretched out till his feet rested on the chair opposite, and dialed the hospital. He got cut off again and misdirected twice, but this time he didn't give up. Eventually he heard her voice on the other end of the wire, and the minute he heard it, he knew things were better.

"She stopped throwing up right after I talked with you," said Connie. "And you were right. She looks *great* this morning. They've started some new medication, so now we're just sitting around waiting, but so far so good."

"Great," said Pete, and then, realizing for the first time how worried *he'd* been, he said it again. *"Great."*

"So tell me about you," said Connie. "How's Polly? What's up with Cobie?"

"Polly's out to dinner with the chief. Cobie's still dead."

"You're kidding," said Connie.

Pete was pretty sure it was in reference to Polly. But he didn't want to think about Polly. She'd be okay. Willy would make sure of it.

Wouldn't he?

"About Cobie," he said quickly. "Something's funny. First Dave Snow accuses Cobie of ruining the chances of his new restaurant, then Pit Patterson accuses Cobie of stealing lobsters, and a guest at the Whiteaker accuses him of stealing a blanket. *Now* Dave Snow has decided without Cobie to draw in a crowd, it's hardly worth opening up, Pit's insisting he offered to *give* Cobie lobsters, an old blanket reappears with a new price tag on it, and Jack Whiteaker apparently never heard a word about any of these thefts. And I have no clue where Cobie got his money, or where the anchor went, or who went out to the wreck. Add to that the one night I shouldn't have to worry about Polly and that's what I'm doing. Worrying."

"Hey," said Connie. "Polly's a grown woman. And she's out with the last of the good ones."

"Oh, really. You sound kind of stuck on him yourself."

Connie laughed. "At least Joe Putnam loves you."

Joe Putnam. And what did Pete care about Joe Putnam? And suddenly all his previous thinking seemed to reverse itself. What was he doing up here all alone, shoveling Joe Putnam's stinking fish and making sure his grown sister didn't get mauled by the chief of police while his wife— okay, his ex-wife—was equally alone in New Jersey with a mother who was possibly near death?

"Seriously," he said. "It sounds like you might be there for a while. Maybe I better come down after all."

Connie laughed into the phone. "Don't be crazy. What for? We're doing okay down here."

Sure, thought Pete, *but what about the rest of us up* here?

Chapter
15

"She'll lie a point nearer the wind than a man has a right to expect of his own married wife, sir."

And now what? thought Polly. Despite a needle-fine May drizzle, Pete was out on the weirs again, and Polly had taken one look at the running windowpane and gone back to sleep. When she finally got up, she ate a leisurely breakfast, piled the dishes in the sink, and roamed around the house, but she couldn't seem to settle down anywhere. The whole first floor was full of Factotum's junk. The whole second floor was full of Pete and Connie's junk, most of it still in boxes.

So she found herself back in the kitchen. She spied the dirty dishes in the sink. She could do the dishes, she supposed, but wasn't it almost time for lunch? So Polly ate lunch. She thought of doing the dishes, but by then it seemed to make more sense to wait till after dinner, when they could do all the day's dishes in one big lump.

She went upstairs and, since it hadn't warmed up any, went into Pete's room to find something warmer to wear. She found a flannel shirt and pulled it on over her jersey. And now what? Esther Small was a dead end, and they'd exhausted everything they could exhaust about Cobie, unless Willy had come up with a new angle overnight.

Willy.

All of a sudden her chest felt funny. Something was in there, restricting her breathing. What was the matter with her? It was just Willy. It was just dinner.

Polly crossed the hall to her bedroom, or what passed for her bedroom. She looked at the books in the shelves, glanced at the spines still poking out of boxes. That's what she could do—curl up on the couch with a book, assuming she could find one that had been written in the last ten years.

She couldn't. That was Pete for you—everything, books, movies, even Connie, recycled from a previous decade.

But a book still sounded good. Polly returned to Pete's room, grabbed his leather jacket off the hook on the door, and left for the library.

Except for some new books, the Nashtoba Ladies' Library hadn't changed much in the one hundred and fifty years since it had been founded by a group of sea captains' wives. It was because the wives founded it that it was called the Ladies' Library, but men could use it, too, assuming they were brave enough to face down the librarian.

It seemed to Polly that Eva Chase could have expressed a little surprise at seeing her—after all, she'd been about eighteen the last time she'd been in there—but no. When Polly walked through the door, Eva peered at her only long enough to identify her and to register her relations. One particular relation.

"Polly Bartholomew. Just the person I wanted to see. I understand your brother is involved in this Cobie Small business."

She made it sound as if Pete were responsible for the Cobie Small business, and Polly found herself jumping in to set the record straight. "Pete just put him to bed."

"*And* fished him out, I hear." Eva Chase beckoned Polly closer to the teak desk that had come across on one of the whaling ships. She was a big woman, square-rigged, and when under full sail, hard to resist. Polly moved closer.

"I want you to speak to your brother about this book."
She waved a file card in Polly's face.

"Pete forgot to return a book?"

"Heavens no, not Pete." So she could almost accuse Pete
of killing Cobie, but not of forgetting to return a library
book? "I'm talking about Cobie Small. Cobie Small failed
to return the very first book he borrowed from this library. I
must assume the book is still out there on that musty old
wreck. The book is a beautiful one, a large one, with many
illustrations and photographic plates. It would be a costly
item to replace. I would like your brother to look for it."

Polly examined the card. *Shipwrecks of New England.*
"I'll speak to Pete."

"I *would* appreciate it." Eva said it as if she'd expected
Pete to have thought of this sooner, the minute Cobie's
body floated into his net, say. "I must tell you, I was most
disappointed in Cobie. He had never used the library
before, and I spoke with him at length on this very subject,
on the importance of proper care and timely return of any
borrowed books. I spent a great deal of time with him. I
showed him our collection of books on the subject of
shipwrecks and I sent him to see Hugh Platt."

"Hugh Platt?"

"The president of our historical society. He's quite an
expert on shipwrecks, and I suggested to Cobie if the library
were unable—"

"Why was Cobie so interested in shipwrecks?"

"I have no idea. I don't grill people as to their purpose in
borrowing a book. Unless, perhaps, if they are of a tender
age, and the material is inappropriate. For example—"

The last thing Polly wanted to get into was a discussion of
what material Eva Chase considered inappropriate. She
said good-bye and hurried out, only realizing as she shut the
door behind her that she'd forgotten to look for a book for
herself.

But right now she had other things to worry about. Cobie
with a book on shipwrecks. It could mean nothing. On the
other hand . . . she got into her Renault, and after the usual

three tries, it started. She drove along Shore Road until she reached Cobie's stretch of beach. The rain had let up, but the sky hadn't lightened. The rain would be back. She got out of the car, walked through the darkened sand, and stopped in her tracks.

The dinghy was gone. Well, not gone, exactly—she could see where it was, bobbing alongside Cobie's wreck.

Someone was out there.

Polly ran back to her car and drove to the dock.

Pete saw her when they were still halfway out. A chocolate tootsie pop with arms, jumping up and down on the dock. And as they got closer, Pete could hear her hollering.

"Who the hell is that?" asked Joe.

"I think it's my sister. Something must be wrong. Connie must have called. Can you open this thing up?"

They were riding low in the water due to the full totes, but Joe advanced the throttle until the wake billowed even with the transom. They pulled into the dock just about when Polly ran out of breath.

Pete vaulted over the rail and onto the dock. "What's the matter? Did Connie call?"

"Cobie," breathed Polly.

"Cobie?"

"Someone's out at the wreck. Dinghy's tied up alongside. Have to go out there."

"Did you call Willy?"

"No time. Let's *go*, Pete."

"Hop in," said Joe.

Before Pete could think of a better idea, Polly duplicated Pete's leap in reverse, catapulting from the dock into the boat. Pete didn't have much choice but to follow suit. Joe pulled away from the dock and cut a wide arc toward Cobie's wreck.

The dinghy was alongside the wreck, all right. Joe pulled up on the opposite rail, and Pete pulled himself up. "You two wait here."

One of them waited. One didn't. Pete was halfway to the gangway when he heard Polly behind him. He held up a finger to keep her quiet, but they'd already made enough noise—whoever was down there must know he or she was no longer alone. Still, no one appeared.

"Stay here," Pete whispered to Polly. He lowered himself down the gangway. "Hello?" he called. "Anyone home?"

No sound.

He saw the hands first, lying pale and blue-veined on the table, knuckles like pine knots. Next he saw a blue plastic raincoat, and finally, as he dropped below the level of the hatch, he saw the heart-shaped face, also pale, and as empty of emotion as if an eraser had rubbed it out.

Esther Small was back.

Chapter
16

"There's only one man I'm afraid of . . . you . . . for
you cannot hold your tongue."

Polly, of course, had barreled down the gangway after him.
When she saw Esther, she said, "Oh!"

Pete felt it lacked a little something in the line of
introduction. He told Esther who they were and what they
were doing there. Sort of.

Esther turned to Polly first. "You're the one who bothered
Fred."

"I didn't mean to bother him. I just thought you should
know about . . . about this."

"Apparently so did Fred." Esther ran dulled eyes around
the mess in the cabin. "Cobie did all this?"

"No," said Pete quickly. "At least I don't think so. I think
someone was looking for something. I don't know who it
was or what they were looking for, but I don't think it was
Cobie."

Still, before he finished talking, Esther seemed to have
lost interest. She transferred her gaze to the porthole. "Do
you know, when Fred called me, I said I wasn't going to
come. I meant it, too."

"We'll help you clean up," said Polly. "We meant to

98

before." She stooped to collect a stray boot, but Esther raised a hand to stop her.

"Don't. Please." She stood up. "Where is he? Where is Cobie?"

"The funeral home," said Pete. "They've been—" he stopped. *They've been holding him for you* didn't sound just right.

Esther moved toward the gangway. "I've taken a room at the Whiteaker. I'll stay until I've buried him and cleaned up his mess. What's one more time? I've done it often enough, and this is the last of it. This time, when I go, I won't be back." She smiled grimly. "Of course I've said that before. It's harder to disappear than I thought."

"So Fred knew where you were all along?" asked Polly.

The heart-shaped face turned toward her. "Yes. But I made him promise to tell no one else. After the first slip, he stuck to his word."

"You didn't want Cobie to find you?"

"No, I didn't. I wanted to be done with it. But Cobie figured it out. He knew I must have left word with someone, and he knew it most likely was Fred. And he figured out how to get around Fred, too. Cobie was smart. Don't let anybody tell you he wasn't smart."

"So Fred gave Cobie your address?"

"Fred gave Cobie my phone number. My old number, that is. I've changed it since. But in the meantime, Cobie called me."

And Esther came running? Somehow Pete didn't think it had gone just like that. "Cobie asked you to come back?"

"Not in so many words. Not at first. At first he said he needed to see me about something important. He said—" Esther looked out the porthole again and cleared her throat. "What does it matter what he said? Just that I believed it. Again. And I came. And it was more of the same. Bigger, but the same. I'd have a house again. And a car. And a new wedding ring." She looked down at her misshapen fingers. "I sold my old one to pay for the bus."

"So what did you do?" asked Polly.

"What do you mean, what did I do? I left, of course."

Polly looked puzzled. "Was he drunk?"

Suddenly Esther looked puzzled, too. "Do you know, I don't believe he was. I'd gotten to the point where I would smell it when it wasn't there, and I wouldn't smell it when it was. I think I've talked myself in and out of Cobie's being sober more times than I can count. But, no, I don't think he was drunk."

Polly looked even more puzzled. "And this time he really did have money. If you'd only known that."

For the first time Esther smiled. "You don't understand, do you? I hope you never do. Now I must be going."

She moved up the gangway. Pete followed. It mustn't have been easy for Esther to drag the dinghy to shore, row herself out, and clamber onto the wreck. Despite her bluff talk, it must have meant something to her to make this trip.

"Care for a lift back?"

That clean slate of a face was suddenly filled with relief. "Thank you. That would be easier, yes."

"Joe," Pete called. "Run Polly in and pick me up on the beach."

He settled Esther in the stern of the dinghy. She clutched her raincoat tight. "I don't remember being this cold here," she said. "It must be the damp." She pointed down the beach. "And I don't remember that."

Pete looked. "Dave Snow's new restaurant."

Esther twisted around once to look from the restaurant to the old boat, but she said nothing else.

They were almost on the beach before Pete broke the silence. "I think you should know there's some question of foul play regarding Cobie's death. He was struck on the head."

"I see." Esther said it so calmly, Pete wasn't sure if she'd heard him right. "And the state of the cabin would contribute to your concern?"

Oh, she'd heard him, all right.

"It contributes to Chief McOwat's concern. The state

investigation is over. They concluded it was an accident. The rest is unofficial speculation at this point. But before you go, I'm sure the chief would like a word."

"I'm sure he would," said Esther.

But it sounded more like *I'm sure he can go hang* to Pete.

Polly lagged behind as Pete and Esther left Cobie's cabin. She'd been distracted from her original purpose, but she hadn't forgotten it, and once she was alone, she made a thorough search for the missing library book, picking up as she went. It didn't take long—once in their proper place it was even more obvious how sparse were Cobie's possessions—but Polly found no book.

She returned to the deck and dropped over the side into Joe's skiff.

"Who was she?" asked Joe.

"Cobie's wife, Esther."

Joe turned to Polly, his eyes above the thick beard wide. "No shit? Didn't recognize her. She staying out here on the wreck?"

Polly shook her head. "She has a room at the Whiteaker."

Joe said nothing else. The silence seemed awkward. Polly and Joe had known each other in school. She'd been good friends with Kay. Shouldn't they have more to say to each other than this? "How's Kay?" asked Polly finally. "I thought I might stop by and see her later."

"Not tonight. We're going out tonight."

"Oh," said Polly. So she'd have to go back to the library for that book.

The silence returned. Polly's unease increased. What was it about Joe Putnam that spooked her? Was it the black beard? No. Polly liked beards. But that stocky body was not unlike her dead fiance's. Of course, that was it. When they reached shore, Polly was relieved to get out.

Pete looked just as relieved to get in. Polly could see Esther, already halfway down the beach, walking toward the Whiteaker. She looked less seedy from here—you couldn't see the split in the raincoat or the worn heels on the shoes.

And this was a woman who had just walked away from riches, thought Polly. Not just a four-hundred-dollar lottery ticket, either. And not a single pearl. Cobie had offered Esther a house and a car. He'd gone so far as to talk to the Murchisons about buying the house back. He *must* have had money. But where did it come from? Polly didn't know. All she knew was that Cobie had recently gone to the library for the first time in his life to take out a book on shipwrecks.

What the heck. Polly decided it couldn't hurt to pay a visit to the local shipwreck expert, Hugh Platt.

Chapter
17

Certainly I did not know her way. She turned in every direction but the one I was bound to go; the most part of the time we were broadside on . . .

Hugh Platt wasn't six feet tall, Polly guessed, but his gauntness made him look taller. Or maybe it was the way he walked toward her like a great blue heron—neck extended, elbows akimbo, tuft of hair blowing in the man-made wind.

"Good afternoon," he said graciously, holding the door wide. "May I help you?"

He must have been from somewhere else.

"Yes, you may," said Polly. "At least I hope so. I'm here about Cobie."

The great blue heron blinked. "Cobie?"

"You know. Cobie Small. He lived on the wreck in the harbor. It's actually his library book I'm after. It was never returned. Eva Chase said she sent him to talk to you about shipwrecks, and that's what the book was about. Shipwrecks. Did he leave it here, by any chance?"

"Ah, yes. Cobie's shipwreck. Now I see. Come in, why don't you?" He retreated down the hall. Polly followed, and when she turned left behind him, she sucked in her breath.

The room was full of books. Some of them were in bookshelves vertically. Some were crammed horizontally on top of the vertical books. Some were on the floor in piles.

Some were on the desk in piles. And there were books scattered individually on couches, chairs, windowsills. There were other things in the room, but Polly noticed them only after she'd recovered from the sight of all the books. Still, once she noticed the other things, she found them intriguing in their own right—model ships, funny round-bottomed bottles, a cannonball, and a foot-long brass spike lying on the desk.

Hugh Platt removed several books from one of the chairs and offered Polly the seat. She sat down. Hugh fumbled with the books on the divan under the window and also sat.

"Now let's see. You say you're after a library book that Cobie Small seems to have lost?"

"Shipwrecks of New England. A big thing with lots of pictures. Eva Chase seems to think if she has to replace it, she'll break the bank."

A pucker of flesh appeared between Hugh Platt's eyebrows. "And she asked *you* to try to find it?"

"Sort of," said Polly. "It's a long story. My brother Pete was the one who put Cobie to bed that last night, and he was the one who fished him out of the water the next day. Somehow Eva figures this makes him the one who should go out to the wreck to look for the book. But Pete's busy fishing, and since I'm not doing anything, I looked instead. It wasn't there."

"I see," said Hugh. "Well, I can tell you he didn't leave it here, either."

"Oh," said Polly, disappointed. Still, since Hugh Platt didn't look like he was about to kick her out, she decided to keep going. "I was kind of curious what he wanted with the book in the first place."

"Now that I *can* tell you. Cobie found an old coin on the beach."

Something in Polly's throat started thrumming. She knew it! She knew Cobie found something. A coin. A valuable coin. It fit. It fit everything. She leaned forward in her chair. "An old coin?"

"A 1775 British guinea. Gold. He brought it to Ben

Hopkins. Are you acquainted with Ben? No? He runs the coin and stamp shop over in Arapo, on the other side of the harbor. Ben appraised the coin, but he apparently told Cobie that the worth might vary depending on its history. For example, if it could be documented that the coin came from a shipwreck, its value would double." Hugh smiled. "People are such fools for souvenirs from the deep. So Cobie came to see me in hopes that I could pull a colonial-era British shipwreck in Close Harbor out of thin air." He chuckled. "I'm afraid I was forced to disappoint him."

"But wasn't the coin worth anything as it was?"

"A negligible amount. Hardly worth the trouble. But as I said before, as to the book, I can't help you."

"No," said Polly. "Well, thank you."

She must have sounded as disappointed as she felt. It was almost as if Hugh Platt suddenly decided to try to cheer her up. He leaped to his feet, walked to the desk, and picked up the heavy brass spike. "Do you see this? Do you see the stamp on the end, 'U.S.'? This spike was made by Paul Revere. It was used and reused in the construction of several ships, the final one the USS *Concord,* a 196-foot battleship that served in the Civil War and was struck by lightning and sank in 1906. This spike was recovered from the wreck of the *Concord* by divers in 1958. Quite some life, wouldn't you say?"

Polly crept up to the desk. "I guess! And what are these funny bottles with the round bottoms?"

"Ships' bottles often had rounded bottoms. They were suspended in racks so they wouldn't tip. Now look over here. This is the *Concord."* Hugh led Polly to the shelf containing the model ships.

Polly examined the model of the *Concord,* but soon her eye was caught by another model. "And this?"

"That's the *Explorer,* a New Bedford whaler that crashed ashore at Naushon in 1886. Hugh pointed to a frame on the wall, in the middle of which was a small, dark splinter. "This is a piece of the *Explorer*'s deck."

And pity those poor fools who went crazy over souvenirs

from the deep! But Polly could see how easy it would be to get hooked. When she finally moved to the door, it was only because she remembered what her grandfather always said—there was nothing worse than an uninvited guest who'd forgotten his watch.

Pete paused mid-forkful of spaghetti to watch Polly happily dispatching a meatball in one bite. Maybe it was the food, but Pete thought there might just be something else rekindling the spark in her eye tonight. He decided to find out. "When's Willy coming by?"

Polly chewed and swallowed and wiped her mouth daintily. "Who says he is?"

"He always does. At least since you've arrived. Haven't you noticed?"

Polly paused on her way to spearing another meatball. "What are you talking about?"

"Nothing. I just wondered how it went last night. I could tell he didn't want me there. I figured you two would—" he stopped.

Polly's amber cat's eyes looked like they'd just seen a Doberman pinscher. She set down her fork.

Pete decided to change the subject fast. "So, congratulations. You found Esther."

At first Polly didn't answer him. She looked like she was listening to her breathing. "I didn't find Esther," she said finally. "Esther found us."

"No, you found her. You flushed her out. You convinced Fred Underwood to call her."

Polly said nothing.

Pete tried again. "What else did you do today?"

"Nothing."

"Come on. It was a long day." And it wasn't getting any shorter. "You must have done something."

Slowly, reluctantly, Polly unleashed a few words. "I looked for the book. That's how I found Esther."

"What book?"

"Cobie Small's missing library book."

Pete prodded more, like a farmer with a stubborn ox.

Polly talked more, one slow step by one slow step.

Why in *hell* was it so hard for him to talk to her?

But when Polly finished explaining about the book, she told him about Hugh Platt. And not far into the subject of Hugh, she picked up her fork. By the time she'd hit the 1775 gold coin, she was eating again.

So this was what it took, thought Pete—Cobie. And what was the harm? It might just get her over this slump of hers. It would at least get them through this visit. "So why give up now?"

Polly looked up.

"I seem to recall that Hugh Platt's pretty well fixed. A negligible sum to him might not be a negligible sum to someone else. If I were you, I'd stop in on Ben Hopkins. Find out how much that coin was really worth."

Pete couldn't help feeling pleased when Polly shot him a half grin from across her empty plate of spaghetti.

But it didn't last long. A perfunctory crack of knuckles on wood, the creak of the wrought-iron latch, and all the light left her face along with the wind that ushered the police chief into the kitchen.

She pushed back her chair and scrabbled for the empty plates.

Pete waved at the chief and then at the pot on the stove. "Spaghetti?"

The chief shook his head, eyes on Polly. Polly's eyes were on the plates. She walked to the sink, dropped the plates on the counter, fussed with the drain.

"Hey," said Pete. "Come back here. Tell Willy who you found today."

"You were there," said Polly. "You tell him."

Pete looked at Willy. Willy didn't see him. His eyes were fixed on the back of Polly's head.

"We found Esther Small," said Pete. "She was out on the wreck. I told her you'd want to talk to her. She's staying at the Whiteaker. And there's a missing library book." Pete waited for Polly to chime in.

She didn't. But, Pete was interested to note, she did fill the sink with water.

"And Polly found out something else, didn't you, Polly? Cobie found a gold coin. A . . . what was it, Polly?"

"A guinea." The dishes clattered into the sink.

"A guinea?" said Willy. "Gold? That must be worth a few drinks."

Polly moved from the sink to the table and collected the glasses and silverware, crossing in front of Willy still without looking at him, dumping more dishes into the sudsy water.

"What about this book?" Willy asked.

Nobody answered him.

"Polly?" said Pete. "It was about shipwrecks, right?"

"Yes," Polly said to the suds.

Finally Willy looked at Pete. Pete noticed there were two vertical lines between his eyebrows now.

"Did you talk to Ozzie?" asked Pete.

Willy nodded. "You were right. No help there."

"And the kid?"

"You were right there, too. He's too nervous. I'm running a check on him." He looked at his watch. "I'd better get moving if I want to catch Esther Small at a polite hour. I'll talk to you both tomorrow."

"Okay," said Pete.

Polly said nothing.

"Good-bye, Polly," said Willy.

"Good-bye," said Polly.

As soon as the chief left, she barreled the last plate into the drain, announced she was tired, and went upstairs to bed.

Pete was alone.

He expected it to feel good. Why didn't it? But when the phone rang and he heard Connie's voice, he expected it to get better.

It didn't do that, either.

They started out all right. Her mother was home and

108

feeling better than she'd felt in months. Connie was in high spirits.

Until Pete happened to ask when she was coming back.

"I don't know. Mom just got settled in, and they'd kind of like me to stick around. I haven't been here in a while. I was thinking I might take a week—"

Pete couldn't believe his ears. "A week? You mean the entire rest of our vacation?"

"What vacation?"

"What do you mean what vacation? The vacation we've been counting on for—"

"You mean the vacation you decided to spend weir fishing? The one you invited Polly along for? You call that a vacation?"

Pete said nothing. He listened to all the blood pounding into his temples instead. *High blood pressure,* he thought. *I'm giving myself high blood pressure. Settle down.* He breathed in and out deeply. Twice. When he finally spoke, he was pleased at how calm he sounded. "That's not exactly fair. I have certain responsibilities that—"

"Oh," said Connie. "And I don't, is that it? Or is it that mine don't count?"

And all of a sudden there they were again, close to that old ledge. The thing to do was to back up. But Pete was tired and aggrieved enough in his own right. "I'd like to know when you're coming home."

"Oh, really. I didn't know I was on the clock."

Pete hung up.

He tried the breathing trick again, but it didn't work.

Chapter
18
***

*. . . the sea breeze was rustling and rumbling
in the woods, and ruffling the gray surface
of the anchorage . . .*

Polly drove over the wooden causeway the next morning, hoping the trip would do her good, finding even before she reached the other side that it did. She'd gone to bed last night with her chest in a vise, and it was only now, as she expanded the distance between them, that it started to come loose.

So it wasn't just dinner. It wasn't just Willy. It would turn into what it always turned into, and even as she thought about it, the viselike hold on her lungs grew worse.

The causeway rumbled under her. If she had a brain in her head, she'd keep going right now, away from Nashtoba, back to Southport. She tried to remember what it had felt like the first time she'd taken the trip. No, not the first time, but the last time. The time she'd left the island for good. It hadn't felt like this, she knew that. When she left her island home to begin her life in the real world she'd been full of . . . full of what? Excitement. Hope. And now? Now she was full of nothing but a donut from Mabel's Coffee Shop.

And what had Esther Small felt when she'd made this trip? What had Connie felt? It was pretty clear why Esther had left. And unlike some others, Polly hadn't had much trouble figuring out why Connie had done it. But nobody had asked Polly. At least there was this to be said for herself—she wasn't the only Bartholomew who kept lousing things up. Some of it had to be genetic. Perversely, the thought cheered her up. What the heck, she decided. She might as well stick around long enough to find out how much Cobie's coin was worth.

It was 10:30 when Polly took her first step into Ben Hopkins's coin shop, but it took her another minute to take a second step. There was too much to look at. She didn't know what she was seeing, exactly—all she knew was there was a lot of it.

The shop itself was tiny, maybe fifteen feet square, but every inch of it seemed full of something. The walls were covered with framed coins and bills, and certificates that were either awards, licenses, or diplomas. The shelves and every single horizontal surface were covered with coins in rolls, coins in plastic pouches, coins in boxes, even a few coins lying loose on the desk. The desk also housed an assortment of magnifying glasses, jeweler's loupes, pens, pencils, and paper.

Ben Hopkins sat behind the desk examining a coin with a magnifying glass. He was probably sixty, but he could have been seventy. He was nattily dressed in a rust-colored cardigan and flannel slacks, with a bushy gray mustache and sideburns projecting below a flat tweed cap. He looked up, saw Polly, dropped the coin and glass, and rose courteously to his feet. "Help you, young lady?"

"I hope so," said Polly. "It's this business about Cobie Small."

"What business about Cobie?"

"Well, he's dead."

"I know that. Toppled overboard. Drunk."

"There's a little more to it than that."

Ben Hopkins picked up the coin and the magnifying glass. "Do tell. Like what? Thought the whole thing was pretty clear-cut."

"Well," said Polly. "He seemed to have come into some money."

"Sure he did. Two hundred and fifty bucks. I gave it to him. For a gold coin. Tried to buy it off him the first day he came, but he wouldn't sell it. Thought it was gone for good. Then he came back the next day and sold it to me."

For two hundred and fifty dollars. Polly's spine slumped. It accounted for the drinks money, but not for the house and car for Esther.

"May I see the coin?"

"Nope. Sold it already. You don't come across many like that. Fine condition. Every detail preserved—the shield and crown, the motto, George's face."

"George?"

"King George III. Dei gratia. Thanks to God, that's what it says. Thanks for what I'd like to know? Stamp Tax, Tea Tax—"

"Oh," said Polly. "That George. Did Cobie tell you where he found it?"

"Found what?"

"The coin," said Polly patiently.

"'Course. The coin. Found it on the beach around Close Harbor someplace. Not surprising—that April storm took out a good big bite."

"But that's all he found, one British guinea worth two hundred and fifty dollars?"

"That's all he brought me."

"He was interested in shipwrecks."

Ben Hopkins chuckled. "Who isn't? Come summer you should see the people swarming around the chapel."

"The chapel?"

"Now don't tell me you've never been to see the Mariner's Chapel. Last stop before shipping out, third stop after hitting home. First stop was the tavern, of course. Second was the wife." Ben Hopkins chuckled, but he soon cut it short. "And if you didn't come home, you got a fancy stone or a brass plaque." His face grew dark. "There's a slew of plaques and a whole field of stones. Oh, it's a gloomy enough place, but interesting, for all that."

"Where is it?"

"Right across from the harbor, a mile and a half down on your left."

Polly thanked Ben Hopkins and left.

Joe Putnam's boat stank. So did Joe Putnam. So did Pete. A fourteen-foot, dead and rotting basking shark had floated into the weir, and the two men had spent the past hour struggling to shove it back out.

Now they were collapsed on upended fish totes, drinking Cokes. Pete could vaguely remember when the thought of a Coke this early in the day had turned his stomach to acid. Now, it tasted like gold. Which reminded him . . .

"Hey," said Pete. "Did you hear what Cobie found on the beach? A gold coin. An English guinea. From 1775."

"No shit?" Joe ripped off his cap and wiped his face. "Worth much?"

"Not a fortune, at least not according to the early reports. But Cobie apparently promised a house and a car to his wife. Polly's checking it out."

Joe Putnam laughed. "Tell her not to waste her time."

"Why's that?"

"What do you mean, why's that? Because I knew Cobie. He could dream up more useless schemes than Congress. That coin'll turn out to be a token from a video arcade, you watch."

Now that Polly had actually gotten off the island, she found herself looking back at it with more respect. Not that it was a long look—as she drove along the harbor from the Arapo side she could still make out the glistening white of Seline DuBois's house, the raw yellow of Dave Snow's restaurant, the majestic sprawl of the Whiteaker Hotel at the end of the dock, even the ducklike blob that was Cobie's wreck. As she watched, the wind swooped down and ran over the surface of the water, giving it a washboard effect. Cobie's wreck swung gracefully around on its mooring until it faced west. The flag in front of the harbormaster's office stiffened and snapped. Polly had to admit, it was a scenic sort of place.

And so was the chapel. It was right where Ben Hopkins had said it was—a mile and a half down the road on the left. It didn't look like much—a small, white clapboard building with clear windows and something that looked more like a widow's walk than a steeple on top. It was nestled in the middle of a row of pines so thickly green they seemed almost black. And behind the chapel a forest of ancient, kilted gravestones overflowed the wrought-iron fence and climbed up a gentle slope.

Polly pulled to a stop, got out of the car, and picked her way up the uneven stone steps. *Mariner's Chapel*, the sign read. *Established 1806*. The heavy green door closed with nothing but an antiquated latch. Polly lifted it and crept in.

The chapel was empty. Polly looked around her. The floors were badly scuffed, the ancient pews worn and nicked. The pulpit was nothing more than an oblong box. The walls were plain white. And yes, they were covered with a slew of plaques. Polly began in the rear left corner and walked in a clockwise direction, reading as she went.

In loving memory of Captain Ely Bangs, lost at sea by drowning en route to the West Indies November 14th, 1840—aged 38 years.

Sacred to the memory of Captain James Clark, died of black water fever, Prince's Island, Africa, 1819, in the fifty-eighth year of his life.

This tablet commemorates Captain Foster Berry, buried at sea 1886, aged about forty-four years.

* * *

In loving memory of Captain Charles Winslow, lost at sea during typhoon, Indian Ocean, 1863, Aet. 32 years.

In memory of Captain William Sears, killed by gunshot, Basein, India, 1864, aged 28 years, 5 months.

And so on.

Most of the tablets inside the chapel commemorated captains, but outside in the graveyard, among the wobbly stones, it was a different story. Here were the young boys, simple seamen. A few stones, like the one for Jonathan Pease, marked actual graves. *Here lies buried the Body of Jonathan Pease, beloved son of Samuel and Mary, departed this Life while at sea Jan. 8.th, Anno Dom. 1826 in the 15.th year of His Age.* So Jonathan's body had come home, but the vast majority of stones weren't actual grave markers but memorials to a more distant, watery resting place. Joshua Sears, lost at sea in 1810. Isaiah, beloved son of Rachel and John Fates, lost with ship and crew in 1868. Franklin Small, drowned at sea. Joseph Nickerson, died at sea. More Jameses and Davids and Samuels and Benjamins lost at sea to drowning or disease or causes unknown, fates unknown. Polly wandered from stone to stone, stopping to read verse, examine the art, do the math. You died young when you died at sea.

Polly ran out of iron fence and kept going. Soon the ground began to rise beneath her feet. She looked up and saw a gleaming white obelisk in the center of the rise. She drew closer, read, sank to her knees, and started over.

Here lie the bodies of the seventy brave men who died aboard the General Newcomb, wrecked in the storm off Close Harbor December 25th, 1778. May their souls rest in eternal peace.

And at the bottom, in smaller print, *This monument erected by the citizens of Arapo, September 19, 1858.*

Chapter
19

It began to be chill, the tide . . .
rapidly fleeting seaward . . .

They had circled almost half the island in Pete's old truck and still Polly hadn't stopped talking.

"It has to be," she said for the sixteenth time. "Don't you think so, Pete? What else could Cobie have meant? He said the drinks were on the general. He showed up at Ben Hopkins's shop with a gold coin from 1775. The *General Newcomb* went down in 1778, right there in the harbor. It said so on the monument. The coin *has* to be from the ship. And you aren't going to find one solitary gold coin on a ship, you're going to find an entire *hold* full of it. Or at least a big chestful. There has to be more treasure. And Cobie Small has to have found it. It's what made him stop drinking and send for Esther and promise her a house and a car and a brand new wedding ring. Isn't it?"

Pete refused to agree with her. Still, here he was, driving her to Hugh Platt's to ask him about the 1778 wreck in the harbor. He supposed if he had anything better to do, if the alternative were something other than picking up the phone and attempting to sort things out with Connie, he wouldn't have gone along with any of this. But he *had* gone along with it. He was as bad as Polly. Anything for a distraction.

And he had to admit this was a pretty good one. Despite himself, Pete found his mind traveling back to his childhood and the tales of gold doubloons and Long John Silver. *Treasure.*

It took Hugh Platt exactly seven and a half minutes to disillusion him.

Polly held out a little longer.

They were sitting in Hugh's library, Hugh on the divan in front of the window, Pete and Polly in the stuffed chairs facing him. Polly had told Pete about the great blue heron, *and the description was right on the money,* thought Pete. Hugh blinked and jerked as he listened to Polly pour out her story about Esther Small arriving at the Whiteaker, her visit on the wreck, Cobie offering her a house and car.

"You see? There has to be more gold somewhere. And it has to have been from the *General Newcomb.*"

It was when Hugh Platt smiled regretfully and shook his head, even before he said the words "I'm sorry to disappoint you," that Pete gave up on Polly's theory. He didn't have to wait to hear the rest.

But Hugh Platt elaborated. "They would never have carried King George's gold on the *General Newcomb.* The *Newcomb* was an American brig. You recall what was going on in 1778? We were at war with England. The colonists hated King George and they hated his money. They spurned the British coinage and minted their own, each colony with its own design. Some of the coins were quite unique. But no, I'm afraid the most likely explanation for Cobie's guinea is that it fell out of the pocket of a British soldier."

"A British soldier?" asked Polly. "On an American ship?"

"Not on the ship, on the King's Highway. In 1775 Nashtoba was still connected to the mainland, and that road along the harbor was part of the King's Highway. The British soldiers traveled it frequently."

So that was that. Pete tried to catch Polly's eye to suggest they get going, but Polly apparently still wasn't convinced.

"I don't know," she said. "Cobie mentioned the *General*

to several people. He said 'the drinks are on the general.' It was wrecked right there in the harbor. It *must* fit."

"It doesn't," said Hugh. "I'm sorry. But it's an interesting story, the story of the wreck. Perhaps you'd care to hear it."

"I don't—" began Pete, half rising.

"Yes, please," cut in Polly.

Hugh Platt stretched out his legs and rested his hands behind his head. Something told Pete the story wasn't going to be short. He dropped back into his seat.

"It was Christmas Eve, 1778," began Hugh. "The *Newcomb* was on its way from Boston Harbor to the Carolinas with a detachment of soldiers. The British were planning to chop the colonies in two at the Carolinas, and the *Newcomb* soldiers were on their way to help fend off the attack. But they were hardly out of the bay, heading for the open sea, when the wind picked up, and the next thing they knew they were caught in the middle of a good old New England northeaster. The captain of the *Newcomb,* Captain Jeremiah Harvey, decided his ship would best weather the storm anchored behind Jake's Point, but—"

"*Our* Jake's Point?" Polly interrupted.

"Yes, our Jake's Point. But the winds were fierce and the anchor didn't grab. The *Newcomb* began to drift toward the harbor."

"Our harbor," said Polly. "Close Harbor."

"Yes," said Hugh. "Close Harbor. Harvey did everything he could. He furled the sails and struck the topmast, but the heavy seas crashed over the bow. The anchor cable snapped, and that was it for the *Newcomb*. It bumped backward onto a sandbar and stuck, a mile from shore in a blinding northeast blizzard."

Hugh Platt paused to clear his throat. Pete snuck a look at Polly. She was leaning forward in her chair, hugging her arms, probably holding her breath.

"Harvey cut down the masts in an effort to lighten the ship and float her off the bar, but the hull had cracked on the first contact, and she was rapidly filling with water. He directed his crew to the quarterdeck, where they huddled in the few remaining feet of dry space. That's when things began to get ugly."

"Didn't they have longboats?" asked Pete. "Couldn't they at least have tried for shore?"

"They launched one boat. The boat and its crew disappeared into the rough seas and were never seen again. Their only hope was for rescue from shore to reach them. Harvey fired off a signal gun and settled down to wait. But the temperature kept dropping. The wind, waves, and snow beat at them. Some men actually suffocated from the snow, some were swept overboard and drowned. Most froze. They wrapped themselves in the sails, but the sails afforded little protection. Finally a few men made a mad dash below to salvage the ship's store of brandy. Harvey saw them drinking and ordered them to desist, but they ignored him. He pleaded with them if they wanted to make good use of the brandy to pour it into their boots instead of their gullets—"

"Their boots?" said Pete, not sure he'd heard correctly.

"Their boots. Harvey knew if they drank the brandy, not only would their mental and physical capacities be compromised but their blood vessels would open up and they'd freeze to death in an inkling. But alcohol doesn't freeze as fast as water. Alcohol in the boots would ward off frostbite."

"I like this Captain Harvey," said Polly.

"He was a smart man," said Hugh. "And the men who obeyed him lived. Those who didn't were dead by morning."

Polly shuddered. "What about the folks on shore? Couldn't they see there was a ship in trouble?"

"Certainly," said Hugh. "But they were in the middle of a raging blizzard, remember? As soon as there was a break in the storm, the folks over in Arapo launched a dory, but they couldn't make it past the breakwater. They had to give up. The men still alive on the *Newcomb* piled the dead bodies around them for further protection from the storm and spent a second agonizing night on the wreck. In the morning the survivors looked to shore, and guess what they saw?"

"What?" said Polly.

"The townfolk building a road of ice floes out to the sandbar. They worked all night and the entire next day. Meantime Captain Harvey ordered his men to their feet and made them march around in the small space to keep their blood flowing. They were so frozen they could hardly stand, but Harvey drove them, never giving up. He saved their lives."

"But how many?" asked Pete.

"When the townfolk finally reached the wreck, they found seventy dead bodies frozen in grotesque positions, still clinging to shrouds and spars. Thirty were alive but unconscious. One frozen soul barely managed to avoid being left for dead by blinking his eyes when the rescuers came near. Ten of the men they removed from the *Newcomb* died soon after. Six more underwent extensive amputations due to frostbite and lived as cripples for the rest of their lives. Fourteen men survived unharmed."

"And Captain Harvey?"

"He was among the survivors."

Polly sighed. "But the ship. Nothing is left of the ship?"

"Even by the time the townfolk reached it, the hull was buried ten feet in the sand and the superstructure was knocked to pieces. Almost immediately afterward the wind swung around and carried everything out to sea."

"And there was no treasure."

Hugh Platt smiled sympathetically. "The *Newcomb* was a Revolutionary War brig. Its cargo was soldiers. I'm sorry."

"Oh, well," said Polly. "You were right. It *was* an interesting story. Thank you for taking the time to tell it."

"My pleasure," said Hugh, standing.

Pete followed suit.

Eventually, so did Polly.

Chapter
20

*. . . and you cannot imagine a house in such
a state of smash . . .*

They must be eating faster, thought Pete. This time he was
finished with the dishes and just passing out the coffee when
Willy walked in. Pete got Willy a coffee, but while he did
so, he kept one eye on his sister. She said hello with her
nose in her cup and drank her coffee so fast her gut must
have blistered. When she was through, she pushed back her
chair.

"I'm going out. I'm meeting Kay Dodd tonight."

She was? This was the first Pete had heard of it.

When she was gone, Pete looked at Willy. He should say
something. But what? He was relieved when the phone rang.
As he snatched it up, Willy turned for the door, which was
tactful and all that, but it only meant Pete had to call him
back.

It was the station.

Willy spoke briefly and hung up. "Esther Small just called
from the Whiteaker. Her room's been ransacked." He
strode to the door.

Pete thought fleetingly of the phone call he'd just about
decided to make tonight to Connie. He was the one who'd
hung up, he was the one who should call back.

121

Then he grabbed his jacket off the back of the chair and followed Willy.

It seemed worse than the job on the wreck, maybe because Esther Small was sitting there in the middle of it, not crying, not yelling, just clasping and unclasping her hands. And shivering.

"I was downstairs eating dinner," she said. "I came back and it was like this."

Willy looked around. "I'd say it was just as well you weren't here."

Jack Whiteaker, who had led them upstairs, exhaled loudly through his teeth. It wasn't exactly a whistle, but it was close. "We've never had any trouble here. Nothing like this."

Willy turned to him. "Someone was on duty in the lobby?"

"I was. I saw nothing unusual. It's a quiet time of year."

"And you were at the desk the entire time Mrs. Small was at dinner?"

"Just about. I took one phone call in the office. Wait. I remember that call. The phone rang, I went into the office to answer it, and there was no one there."

"I'll need the names and room numbers of the other guests," said Willy.

Jack nodded, and left.

Pete looked around the room. The bedding was ripped apart, the drawers flung open, Esther's suitcase upended on the bed, sheets and clothes strewn all over the floor. In the bathroom towels had been flung in the tub, Esther's few toiletries swept into the sink, some opened and emptied.

"Is anything missing?" asked Willy.

"I don't know. I didn't stop to look. I called the police."

"That was just right," said Willy. "But I'd like you to look now. Please don't touch anything. Try to picture how it looked before."

"Except for the things in the bathroom, I'd left everything

in my suitcase. I didn't plan to stay long. I brought very few clothes. A pair of slacks and a blouse. There. There they are." She pointed to the floor. "And my nightgown." That was flung on a chair. She made a move to pick up the underwear scattered across the dresser top, but Willy stopped her. She turned away, embarrassed. "My skirt and sweater. I don't see my skirt and sweater anywhere."

"Aren't you wearing them?"

Esther looked down at the clothes she had on. "How silly. Of course I am." She pointed to, but was careful not to touch, a cheap best-seller so frayed it must have been read many times or, what seemed more likely as Pete looked at the ridiculously garish cover, discarded in a secondhand shop. Esther moved around the room and ticked off on her mental list a manicure kit, a heating pad, a travel alarm.

"And in the bathroom?" asked Willy.

She walked into the bathroom, examining the contents of the sink. A comb, toothpaste and toothbrush, deodorant, soap, an empty shampoo bottle, a large jar of cold cream that had been scooped out into the sink. "I think everything is here. Why wouldn't it be? I have nothing, nothing that anyone would want to steal." She looked up at the chief. "Why would anyone do this?"

Willy met Pete's eyes. "Mrs. Small, did your husband ever talk about acquiring a large amount of money, discovering something of great value?"

She smiled bitterly. "Every day of his life."

Pete stepped in. "Wasn't there some specific talk more recently? You told us he was going to buy you a house and a car."

"I told you no such thing. I told you he *promised* me these things, which is something else entirely."

"And you didn't believe him?"

Esther raised her chin, eyes snapping. "It didn't matter what I believed. It was what he believed. Why can't any of you understand that?"

"Mrs. Small," said Willy. "Your husband was seen

around town with an unusual amount of cash in his hands. He talked of there being more. We're trying to determine if this is related to his death in any way."

Esther Small peered tiredly at the chief. "Frankly, I can't see that it matters."

Pete left the chief to do his job. When he reached the lobby, he looked around. He could just see Jack Whiteaker's profile through the office door behind the desk as he jotted down the names and numbers Willy had requested, but there was no one else in sight. The dining room was empty. So was the half circle of rattan chairs in front of the fireplace. So were the two wood-paneled phone booths along the far wall.

Phone booths.

Pete crossed the lobby and peered through the glass panels in the doors. It was just like in the movies. The receiver in the second booth dangled two feet from the floor, whooping loudly.

Polly found Kay Dodd on her own doorstep, just fitting the key into the lock. She ushered Polly in with her, and the minute Polly stepped inside, she was consumed with jealousy. It was so clearly the home of a person at peace with herself.

Kay was a newspaper photographer by profession, and the evidence that she enjoyed what she did and felt competent at it were all over the walls—framed black-and-white photographs of people, places, events that she had covered with her camera.

And then there was the rest of the place. It was crammed with furniture she must have culled from the dump. No two pieces matched, but every single thing somehow belonged there, served a purpose, made a statement of some sort.

And then there was Kay. She seemed never to have heard of the word *fashion*. Her hair hung to her waist in a thick, frizzy braid, her eyebrows ran from temple to temple in one straight line, she was dressed in sweater and pants Polly's mother might have worn, and still, if you stuck her on the cover of *Vogue*, she'd sell a million copies. Polly couldn't understand it.

They hugged and said they were glad to see each other, then drew back awkwardly, smiles straining. It had been too long. To fill the gap, Polly moved to examine one of Kay's pictures—Cobie Small, clad in waders, leaning on a clam rake, beaming at the photographer. "Nice shot."

"It was hard to miss with Cobie," said Kay, something wistful edging into her voice. "He was so . . . Cobie."

They looked at each other.

"It's good to see you," said Polly.

Kay's answering smile came easier this time and stayed longer.

"So, all in all, I guess you've had better years," said Kay two hours and the better part of a bottle of wine later.

"You could say that. But what about you? Pete says you and Joe are moving in together."

Kay's eyes rounded. "We are?"

"Aren't you?"

"Joe and I aren't doing anything together. Not anymore. Not since a few weeks ago when he began waving threats in my face."

"Threats?"

"You move in here *or else*. You stop going out to that boat *or else*." Kay unwrapped herself from her chair and went to stand in front of Cobie's picture. "We got sort of friendly, Cobie and I. Ever since I did that bit for the paper. Once in a while I'd meet him at sunup and we'd walk the beach together. He checked it first thing every morning, looking for any valuable flotsam and jetsam. We'd walk and talk. He told some good stories. But you had to catch him early before he got too much liquor into him. Still, everything was fine until that idiot Pit Patterson began making cracks about it. I told Joe if he didn't react, that would be the end of it. I guess he managed to hold back in public, but that only made him explode all the more in private. So I got sick of it. I told him to shove off."

Good for you, thought Polly. If only she'd been that smart, her life would have had one less mess. "And you kept seeing Cobie?"

"Yes, I did. Why shouldn't I? And these past couple of weeks were such a gift with him not drinking. One night we sat out on that old boat and shot the breeze till three o'clock in the morning."

"What did you talk about?" These days Polly couldn't imagine talking to anybody till three o'clock in the morning, much less Cobie.

Kay returned to her chair and dropped into it, her body fitting comfortably. "We shared our dreams of glory. Winning the Pulitzer Prize. That was mine. Finding a million dollars. That was Cobie's."

A million dollars. Polly's palms prickled. "Something tells me you had more of a chance at yours."

"You wouldn't think so if you'd listened to Cobie. He acted like he had it already. He'd even mapped out how he was going to spend it."

"How?"

"Oh, most of it was for Esther. I think that was his one big regret in life, that he hadn't provided any security for Esther. He wanted to fix it so she'd never have to worry about money. He wanted her to have a place of her own that no one could ever take away from her. He wanted her to have some fun, finally. There was only one problem with his plan."

"That Esther wouldn't take him back, even if he came with a million dollars?"

Kay laughed. "That was the second problem. The first problem was, he didn't have the million dollars. He didn't have anything."

"You're sure about that?"

Kay had been about to drain the last of the wine into Polly's glass. She stopped with the bottle half-cocked. "What are you saying?"

Polly shrugged. "Not much. Probably nothing. It's a strange tale with lots of dead ends. Still . . ."

Kay filled Polly's glass and pushed it toward her. "Come on," she said. "Start talking."

It was late when the chief reappeared in Pete's kitchen, but Pete was still up, staring at the phone, telling himself for the twentieth time it was too late to call Connie. Pete opened the refrigerator and took out two Ballantine Ales, sliding one across the kitchen table to Willy. Willy opened it, took a hit, grimaced, and pushed it back into the middle of the table.

"I don't know why you buy this stuff."

"Neither do I." Pete looked guiltily at the clock. But it was too late to call Connie. Really.

Suddenly Pete noticed the chief, too, was looking at the clock, and the two vertical lines had again wedged themselves between his eyebrows. "Where did she say she was going?"

"Kay Dodd's. They used to be pretty friendly."

"Oh," said Willy. "So anyway, I'd say it's pretty clear what happened at the Whiteaker. Somebody called Jack from the lobby phone, and the minute Jack left the desk, he dropped the phone and ran up the stairs."

"Unwitnessed."

"Unwitnessed."

The chief said no more. But he did look at the clock a few times.

Pete shifted uncomfortably. It was none of his business, this thing with Willy and his sister. If he was smart, he'd stay out of it. "Listen," he said. "About Polly."

"Yeah," said Willy. "What got into her? We were getting along all right. Now she won't look me in the eye."

"I might have messed it up. I guess I kind of kidded her about you coming over. I think I made her nervous."

Willy rolled his eyes. "You mean now *I* make her nervous." After a minute he said, "This fiance of hers. Not so nice, I gather."

"He was a jerk," said Pete with feeling. "But she actually

figured that out and tried to dump him before he got killed. The only trouble was, he wouldn't let her out. Whatever threats he used, they worked. I guess in a way they're still working. If you ask me, I think she just needs some time to dig herself out from under."

"You think I don't know that? I'm not stupid. I'm not sixteen, either. I just wanted to have dinner and talk. She's easy to talk to."

Polly? Easy to talk to?

Willy looked at the clock one more time and rose. "And do me a favor. Keep your big yap shut in the future."

"Don't worry," said Pete. It was the last time he'd talk to Polly about a man.

Any man.

Ever.

Polly left Kay's with her head spinning. She'd told Kay about her treasure theories, and Kay had laughed at her. Okay, maybe not *at* her, but she'd had a good chuckle over it. And it sounded like Kay probably knew Cobie better than anybody else around here. So if Kay thought it was all a pipe dream . . . Well, it had been fun while it lasted.

Polly pulled down the dirt road that led to her brother's cottage and braked sharply. *Damn.* Willy's Scout was still in the driveway. She backed up till she hit Shore Road, and began to drive aimlessly.

The weather seemed to be picking up—at least the clouds had left enough room so Polly could see a fair representation of stars and the half moon between them. She drove along Shore Road, circumnavigating the island, her mind finally slowing down, but when she reached the beach near Cobie's wreck, she saw something that reversed the process entirely.

She pulled down the road far enough so the car was out of sight, and returned on foot to the beach, keeping well behind the scrub. The dinghy that she had seen in the moonlight, returning from Cobie's wreck, had now reached the shore. A slight, dark figure shipped the oars clumsily, splashed out, and pulled the boat in short jerks and hops up the beach. When the dinghy was once again resting where it had been found, the shape stepped back, dusted off its hands, and tossed a long, thick braid back over its shoulder.

Chapter
21

He went in with a sounding plunge.

The second time Polly swung down the road, the coast was clear. Pete was still sitting where she'd left him, at the kitchen table, looking from the clock to the phone and back again. The minute Polly got within earshot, she set in. "Guess who I just saw out at the wreck. Kay Dodd. I told her about Cobie, and I hadn't been gone fifteen minutes when she must have taken off to go look for the treasure."

"Did she look at the Whiteaker, too?"

Polly peered at Pete.

"Esther Small's room got wrecked."

Polly pulled out a chair.

Pete added details.

"Don't you see what this means?" asked Polly finally. "Somebody's still looking for something. Whoever killed Cobie and trashed his cabin didn't find what he was looking for. The minute he heard Esther went out to the wreck, he became convinced she found it."

"But found *what?*" asked Pete. He sounded irritable, but that didn't surprise Polly. He'd sounded irritable since morning. "Even Esther Small refuses to admit there might be something. She implied the same thing Joe Putnam did about Cobie. That he had one harebrained scheme after another, and none of them ever amounted to anything."

"Oh, Joe Putnam," said Polly. "What does he know? Kay believed there could be treasure, and she *knew* Cobie."

Pete didn't answer.

Polly studied him with some concern. It was late, and a shadow of his morning's beard had already started to form on his chin, but that wasn't the only shadow in his face. "Tired?"

Pete looked up. "Tired? Yeah. I guess."

She sat down. "I haven't heard much about Connie lately. Her mother's still doing all right?"

"Great."

"Good. And when's she coming home?"

"She's home."

"I mean Connie. When's Connie coming home?"

"Oh. I don't know. A week, maybe."

A week, thought Polly. And how many days did a week make? Not enough if it was all that was left of your vacation. Or too many if you were waiting for someone to come home, someone you'd already waited for long enough. Something told her all **was n**ot well in paradise. But then again, the Bartholomews didn't appear destined to dwell much in paradise, did they?

Polly tossed and turned most of the night, dreaming fitfully about an assortment of men—Cobie Small rising out of her bathtub to ask her if she'd like a drink before dinner; Joe Putnam leering at her from her closet, where he had just tied up Kay Dodd with the film he had ripped out of her camera; Pete calling to her as he pulled out of the driveway with his truck full of old black telephones that he was moving to New Jersey; and, finally, her murdered fiance coming at her with a flyswatter. Through it all, Willy McOwat seemed to alternately loom and recede, and each time he drew close, Polly grew smaller. She awoke with the conviction that it was time to give up on it all, to give up on men, Cobie included. But if she gave up on men, what did it leave her? Kay Dodd?

Kay Dodd. Suddenly Polly remembered where she'd last seen her. She scrambled out of bed, showered, dressed, ate, piled the dishes in the sink, and set off to find her.

She tracked her through the newspaper. The laundromat was installing a new, recycling water system, and Kay was on location, taking pictures.

When Polly got there, Kay was pointing her camera at the tiny, run-down building that housed the island's only laundry. "Working on that Pulitzer Prize–winner?"

Kay stuck out her tongue. "What are you doing here?"

"I've got a better question. What were you doing out at Cobie's wreck in the dead of night? Looking for his treasure?"

Kay lowered her camera. Her expression was more than half sheepish. "You saw me?"

"Did you find it?"

Kay shook her head, and her long braid undulated. "I went over **that** wreck splinter by splinter. Nothing. But I couldn't help it—I kept thinking about what you said. I decided you might be right, that there might be something out there. But I didn't find a thing. Not even an old penny in one of his pockets. So I've decided you're nuts." Kay turned her attention to the laundry.

Polly turned her attention along with her. The pictures on Kay's wall had been nothing like this. "This is what you do, then? Things like this?"

"Sometimes. Most of the time."

"And you like it?"

Kay straightened. "Sometimes I like it. Sometimes I hate it. And once in a while, I love it."

"And if you never win the Pulitzer Prize?"

Kay grinned. "I look at it this way—if I keep trying till I die, I'll never know I didn't get it. Hey, I have an idea. Why don't you talk to my boss, Ada Frey? Didn't you used to want to be a reporter?"

Yes, she had. But that was a million light-years ago. And

now? To return to Nashtoba? The idea gaped like a canyon before her, a canyon it would take too big a leap to cross.

Too big a leap backward.

The promise that had hovered in the sky the night before was fulfilled by morning. Pete knew better than to actually expect sun, but the temperature had risen by a good ten degrees, and the skiff puttered toward the weirs over calm waters.

Joe eased back on the throttle as they slipped into the trap, reaching for his dip net at the same time. Pete was about to grab his net likewise, but as he looked over the side, he realized there was no need. The water was still and clear, and there was nothing in the monotone sky to reflect off its surface. Pete could see straight through to the sand.

And that's all he saw—sand.

There wasn't a fish in there. It didn't take long to see where the fish had gone, either—there was a gaping hole in the net the size of Cobie's dinghy. And in another second Pete saw what had created the hole—twisted in the softly undulating twine was the anchor Pete had last seen swinging from the ceiling in Cobie's cabin.

"Joe," he hollered. "Cobie's anchor!" He leaned over the side, peering into the deep, and something clipped him smartly on the back of the skull.

The next thing Pete knew he was over the side, plummeting downward through the wintery water.

Chapter
22

---

*. . . paddle as I pleased, the tide was still
sweeping me down . . .*

As Polly headed home she spied the Nashtoba Ladies'
Library. She slowed. She never had reported back to Eva
Chase about her unsuccessful search for Cobie's book.
She'd never even taken out a book for herself. She parked in
front of the library and went in.

This time Eva Chase didn't even say hello. "Well?" she
asked. "Do you have it?"

"I'm sorry, I don't. I searched Cobie's boat myself, but no
luck. I even checked with Hugh Platt."

Eva wasted no further time on her. She sailed off into the
fiction stacks, her spine mast-straight. It was no big accident
that Polly decided to go the other way. *Biography.* She
passed over Lindbergh and Truman and Kate Hepburn and
kept moving. *History.* Wars seemed to figure prominently
on this shelf: Civil, Spanish-American, 1812, Revolutionary . . . Polly stopped. Revolutionary. She'd been fasci-
nated by Hugh Platt's tales of the *General Newcomb,*
intrigued by the idea of the colonists spurning the king's
money. She could stand to learn more about the Revolutionary War. She pulled a book off the shelf.

* * *

By the time Joe Putnam had hauled Pete back on board, he was so cold his inside organs were aching. He couldn't feel his outside organs at all. He opened his mouth to swear at Joe Putnam, but he couldn't get the words past his chattering teeth.

"Jesus," said Joe, whipping off his own jacket to hand to Pete. "Man, I'm sorry. When you hollered, I swung around and caught you with the net handle. You okay?"

"Ca-ca-ca-ca-ca-ca," said Pete.

"Here." Joe handed him his jacket. "And there's a blanket on board here somewhere."

"Ca-ca-ca-ca-Cobie—" said Pete. "Anchor."

Joe pulled a filthy wool blanket out of the storage bin in the bow and tossed it to Pete. "Hunker down in this. I'll get you on shore in a jiffy."

"No," said Pete. "C-C-C-Cobie's anchor. It's d-d-down there. I'm already wet. Let me g-g-get it."

"Are you crazy? You'll freeze to death. I'll get you in and come back out with a couple of divers."

Since by now Pete couldn't feel his inside organs, either, he had to admit it made sense. "And the ch-ch-chief. G-g-get the ch-chief."

"Okay. I'll get the chief."

When they reached the dock, Joe offered to drive Pete home, but Pete assured him he could manage.

"Okay," said Joe. "Don't get in the tub. It'll let the rest of your heat out. Dry off, get under a pile of blankets, jack up the heat, drink something hot. You got that?"

Pete got it, but he was kind of sorry he did. He'd been dreaming of a hot tub all the way to shore. But when he got home, he followed Joe's instructions to the letter.

He woke some time later to the sound of dishes rattling.

The minute Pete came through the kitchen door, Polly could tell something had happened to him. He was wrapped up in a quilt. He was a funny color. Polly felt that old lurch of panic somewhere in her esophagus. "What's the matter?"

When he told her she couldn't believe it. "That *idiot!* He could have killed you!" She rushed to fill the kettle with hot water. "Are you sure you're all right?"

"Sure," said Pete, but he didn't convince her. He looked shriveled. Pinched.

"I think you should see Hardy Rogers. You could have chilblains."

"Chilblains are cold feet."

"Oh," said Polly. "Well, you could have chilblains going on frostbite. And you know what happens when you get frostbite. Remember the men on the *General Newcomb?* Things got amputated. They lived as cripples."

"I don't have frostbite. But I could use that cup of coffee." Pete started to get up, but Polly rushed over and pushed him into a kitchen chair. "Sit." She poured him coffee, then wrapped the hot kettle in a towel and put it on the floor in front of his stocking feet.

"Put your toes on that. And if you die of frostbite, I'll sue Joe Putnam for you. I never did like him, anyway."

Pete looked up. "You didn't?"

"At least I don't like him now," Polly amended. "Not since I talked to Kay."

"Why? What did Kay tell you?"

Polly launched into the whole story. Joe's objecting to Kay's visits to Cobie, Joe's threats if Kay didn't cease and desist, Kay's decision to break off the relationship with Joe and keep the one with Cobie.

When she finished, Pete looked skeptical. "Joe says things are going great. He says they're moving in together."

"Well I'm telling you they aren't, and they aren't." She checked the kettle at his feet to see if it was still hot.

There was a knock on the door. Polly straightened, alarmed. Willy? Was it Willy? If it was Willy, he'd walk straight in.

Nobody walked in.

Again, Pete started to get up, but Polly beat him to it. She went to the door. It wasn't Willy. It was worse.

Joe Putnam.

He walked into the kitchen with one of those rolling struts that made her want to trip him. She was surprised at how suddenly and strongly she loathed him.

He wouldn't sit down. He stood over Pete, face flushed, eyes dark. "You okay, man?"

"Yeah," said Pete. "Did the chief get the anchor?"

Joe shuffled in his boots. "He got it. He got it because I went back and hauled up the twine with the anchor hooked in it. I need to patch it anyway."

"What did you do with the anchor?"

"I dropped it off at the station."

"You touched it?"

"Of course I touched it, what do you think? What do you . . . Oh," he said, his face reddening. "Evidence, is that it? Christ, Pete, it's been swishing around underwater for days. I don't figure I messed it up any. Listen, I came by to tell you I probably won't have that twine patched by morning. So you've got tomorrow off, anyway. Just as well, huh? Give you a day to dry out."

"Yeah," said Pete.

"You sure you're okay?"

"Yeah," said Pete again.

Silence descended.

When Polly spoke up, her conscious intentions were good—to ease the atmosphere. It was the subject matter she half-unconsciously selected that was the problem. "I saw Kay yesterday."

Joe Putnam's eyes flicked to her face, to the floor, to the ceiling, and, finally, to the window. "Yeah?"

And it was the arrogance, the insolence, the *who gives a damn?* in his voice that pushed Polly in deeper.

"As a matter of fact, I saw her twice. Once at her place and once coming in from Cobie's wreck. I guess she misses him."

The eyes locked on Polly's and burned.

Bingo.

He turned to Pete. "Gotta go. I'll call you when I'm patched up."

"All right," said Pete.

But after Joe left, Polly decided it wasn't all right. It was time for her to assert herself around here. She didn't like Joe Putnam, and she didn't like the way Pete looked—dragged down, hollow-eyed. She didn't like the idea of him going out on the water again with that creep. She decided when Joe called she'd answer the phone and tell him Pete had lumbago. She had no idea what lumbago was, but she figured it would serve the purpose.

As long as it wasn't another word for cold feet.

Pete gave himself an extra two hours in the sack the next morning. He was tired. Maybe that dunking had knocked some of his stuffing out. But whatever it had done, it had left him feeling unable to cope with a phone call to Connie last night.

And this morning?

This morning Polly didn't give him the chance. When he stumbled into the kitchen, she charged him.

"My *God,* I thought you'd never wake up. Come here." She grabbed his elbow and yanked him toward the table. "Look at this."

Pete looked and saw a pile of French toast surrounded by crinkly bacon. Suddenly he was starving.

"Not the food, the book. Will you look at it?"

Pete tore his eyes away from the breakfast of his dreams and finally noticed a thick book lying open beside the plate. He flipped it over to read the cover. *The History of the American Revolution—1775 to 1783.* He looked back at the plate. "You made French toast."

Polly shrugged it off. She pressed Pete into his chair and slid the plate in front of him. She pushed butter, syrup, and juice toward him, went to the stove for coffee, and filled his cup. She sat down across from him, reached across to the book, and pointed halfway down the left side of the open page. "Read it."

Pete looked at the heading at the top of the page first. *The Impact of the Colonial Navy.* He looked up at Polly.

"Just read it."

Pete cut a double wedge of buttered and syruped French toast, shoveled it into his mouth, chewed, and read.

But pretty soon he stopped chewing.

"See? Didn't I tell you? The *General Newcomb* wasn't just some staid old Revolutionary War brig. She was a privateer, Pete. That's what our navy was back then, a bunch of pirates, mostly. And just before the *Newcomb* was wrecked, she plundered a British ship. The *Royal Arms,* fresh out of Portsmouth on its way to the colonies. And see what the *Royal Arms* was carrying?"

"*Rumored* to be carrying."

"She was carrying *gold.* A great big chest full of King George's gold, gold that was supposed to pay off his loyalist spies in the colonies. And look what happened to the gold."

"The *alleged* gold."

"It wasn't *alleged* when it left England! And the only reason it was *alleged* when it got here was because it never *did* get here. It was never accounted for at all, was it? Of course not. Because the *Newcomb* plundered the *Royal Arms* and took it. The *Newcomb* got caught in the storm and was wrecked right here in Close Harbor. Incidental to our purposes is the fact that the spies never got paid, vital information never reached the British forces, and they ended up losing the colonies. But that doesn't concern us. What concerns us is that the gold went down with the *Newcomb,* and as Hugh Platt said, the *Newcomb* was half-buried by the time the rescuers got there. So the gold was buried with it. And it wasn't until that big storm in April that it got unburied. And guess who found it? The guy most likely to find it. A miserable little alcoholic shellfisherman and beachcomber who just happened to walk the entire beach looking for treasure the very first thing every morning." Polly beamed at Pete.

And she kept on beaming no matter how hard Pete tried to play devil's advocate.

"Admit one thing," she said finally. "It's worth another trip to Hugh Platt, isn't it?"

Pete had to admit it was.

Besides, it wasn't like he had anything else to do.

Except, of course, to call Connie.

Chapter
23

"There's a strong scour with the ebb," he said.

The minute they mentioned the plunder of the *Royal Arms*, Hugh Platt's tuft of hair began quivering.

"Could I see the book, please?"

Polly handed over the *History of the American Revolution*. Hugh sat on the divan under the window again, but this time his pose was less relaxed—he sat hunched over his knees, his face hardened into a cementlike image of concentration, his long fingers creeping into his tuft of hair and twisting, twisting, his eyes darting back and forth over the close print.

"It makes sense, doesn't it?" asked Polly. "It means there has to be more gold."

"I don't know," said Hugh. He didn't look too happy. Pete suspected he didn't get caught out in his field of expertise this way too often.

"There has to be more gold," said Polly. "And Cobie has to have found it. Ask anybody. He was buying drinks. He wanted to buy a house and a car for Esther. He sat around out on the wreck with Kay Dodd, plotting how he'd spend a million dollars."

"I don't know," said Hugh again. "I've never heard

141

mention of this chest of gold until this minute. It would require more research." He flipped to the back of Polly's book, checking references, no doubt.

"Granted, it's a wild shot," Pete tossed in. "But would you consider it a possibility?"

"I told you I would have to look into this," said Hugh crossly. "And I will do so, certainly. I have my resources. It will take some study. I'll borrow this book, if I may. It is not one I happen to have in my own personal collection."

He acted as if it were their fault.

Never out-expert an expert, thought Pete.

Polly spent the rest of the day driving Pete crazy. "There must be something we can do instead of just sitting here waiting. Okay. I have an idea. Let's start backward. Let's assume that Cobie found a chest of gold one morning out on the beach."

"It doesn't happen like that," said Pete. "You don't just walk along and stub your toe on a chest of gold."

"Sure you do. At least you could, couldn't you? Let's start at the beginning. The *General Newcomb* hits a sandbar off the mouth of Close Harbor, the boat breaks up, and the heavy chest of gold sinks to the bottom."

"Or bumps along the bottom for thirty miles. Joe Putnam said it could."

"Oh, *Joe Putnam.* What is it with him? Well, for our purposes, we're going to assume it sinks to the bottom. Then what happens?"

"The remains of the boat would act like a reef. The sandbar would get higher and higher, the chest would get buried deeper and deeper. And in a couple of hundred years—" Pete stopped. Suddenly he remembered the rest of that conversation he'd had with Joe Putnam. "Come on." He led Polly upstairs.

In lieu of more permanent decoration, Pete had tacked a map of Nashtoba to the wall in the other room. He waved Polly over to it and pointed to the harbor. "Look. This map was printed last year, and it's already out of date. There's Jake's Point at the mouth of the harbor. And Jake's Point isn't there anymore. Not since that storm in April."

Polly reached up to touch Jake's Point, then ran her finger off the map in the direction of Boston. "See? The *Newcomb* could have run aground on the point."

But Pete shook his head. "Come on," he said again. Pete unpinned the map, rolled it up, grabbed his denim jacket, and headed for the stairs. Polly grabbed Pete's leather jacket and caught up with him at the bottom.

Sarah Abrew heard the sound of tires and looked up from the large print book she was struggling to read. She hadn't expected him. Not really. She'd insisted he stay away. If anyone deserved a vacation, Pete did. It wasn't his fault he'd become the highlight of her day.

And just because she'd missed him so much, the minute he walked into the room, she said, "Go away!"

"Nice," said Pete. He took the book out of her hands and kissed her on the cheek the way he always did. "I hope you've at least got something pleasant to say to Polly."

Sarah held out her arms and Polly ran at her. Once they'd finished fussing at each other and Sarah had resettled her feathers, she peered up at the dark young man looming over her. "All right," she said. "You may sit, but you may *not* read one single solitary word out of that newspaper."

That was Pete's job, reading her the newspaper. At least that's what Sarah had originally hired Factotum for. How many other little things he'd ended up doing for her she couldn't possibly remember.

"Don't worry," said Pete. "I didn't come to read, I came because I want something out of you. Those old maps, Sarah. Of Nashtoba. Are they still in here?"

She could hear him, already behind her, opening up the cupboard under her hi-fi set. "What would I move them for? Now what are you up to? Searching for buried treasure?"

Polly's sudden shriek of laughter startled her.

"Come here," Sarah snapped at her. "Let me look at you.

Well, I've seen you look better. Now sit down and tell me what that fool brother of yours is up to."

The paper was thin, almost like parchment, and tied up in a roll. While Polly brought Sarah up-to-date on as much recent history as she could bear to tell her, Pete wrestled the old map out of its string, and spread the newer one beside it on the floor.

"What the devil are you doing over there?" asked Sarah.

Polly left Sarah's chair and knelt beside Pete. The two maps were so different that if they hadn't borne the traditional compass markers, Polly would have been tempted to turn one of them upside down. Polly touched the dried-out brown paper of Sarah's map. "How old is this thing?"

"Let me see," said Sarah. "It was Great-grandfather Jeffreys who had all the maps. That would make it early 1800s."

"Look, Polly." Pete pointed to the harbor. "See how much narrower and deeper it is? And Jake's Point isn't even there."

"Of course it isn't," said Sarah. "Jake's Point didn't fill in for another fifty years. And now where is it? Back to nothing. Let *that* be a lesson to you."

"So the *Newcomb* didn't run aground on Jake's Point," said Polly.

"Not on Jake's Point, no." Pete traced the line Polly had drawn earlier, the sea route the *General Newcomb* would most likely have taken coming from Boston, but this time his finger landed not on dry land but in the water. "According to Hugh Platt, the *Newcomb* ran aground on a sandbar, not on the shore, remember? But the road the islanders built out of ice floes had to rest on something. It had to be shallow water. So maybe this is exactly where it hit, where Jake's Point is now. Or I should say where it was up until a month ago. There was nothing there but a high bar when the *Newcomb* struck, but the wreck itself hastened the formation of a nice shoal. Eventually it built itself up until it connected to the mainland."

"Lordy, Pete, you make it sound like the lost continent of Atlantis. It's a measly old handful of sand with a bunch of beach grass on it. Or it was."

"I don't care if it was a lost continent or a bunch of sand," said Polly, "All I care about is that the wreck of the *Newcomb* was under it. Along with all that gold. Then somewhere along the line, the process began to reverse itself. Jake's Point got eaten away at, instead of added onto. And then along came that April storm that ate it right down to the treasure."

Polly looked hopefully at Pete, but Pete's expression remained neutral. He refolded Sarah's map, returned it to its cupboard, and sat down on the couch.

"So if all this is true, where's the treasure now?"

"You say you think Cobie found it?" said Sarah. "Then it's at the bottom of the cash register at the nearest bar."

"No it isn't," said Polly. "Willy checked."

"Not the actual gold doubloons, you ninny. Nobody walks around with gold doubloons in their pocket."

"These aren't gold doubloons," said Polly. "Gold doubloons are Spanish. These are British guineas. With the head of King George on them and everything."

"King George, King Cole, what's the difference? You don't want to be looking for the head of King Anybody. If Cobie were in his right mind, he would have cashed in the gold for good old United States currency and slapped it in the bank."

Polly and Pete looked at each other.

The bank.

They started laughing.

Chapter
24

"You'd be as rich as kings if you could find it . . ."

Polly fidgeted at the door as they were leaving Sarah's. It was Saturday. The bank closed at noon. But Pete kept asking Sarah questions. Had Anna Pease come by to do the cleaning? Had May Winslow taken her grocery shopping? Had she remembered to put her bottles out for the Boy Scout bottle drive on Thursday?

Yes, yes, yes, said Sarah.

But still Pete fussed around, emptying her mailbox, sorting out bills from advertising, until Sarah winked at Polly, jabbed a knotted finger into Pete's spine, and pushed him out the door.

As they drove off, Polly said, "If we find a million dollars, let's give some of it to Sarah."

"She wouldn't spend a cent. She'd put it in the bank and leave it to us in her will."

Polly laughed. "You're right." After a minute she said, "Seriously, Pete. What if you did find a million dollars? What would you do with it?"

"Who knows."

"Oh, come on."

"I mean it. I'm not going to get it. Why waste my time thinking up how to spend it?"

"Okay, so forget the million dollars. I'm talking about your dreams. What do you want more than anything?"

This time he didn't hesitate for a second. "One hour of peace and contentment a day at home alone with Connie."

"Oh, come on. That's too easy."

"Right," said Pete so bitterly, Polly looked over in surprise. They'd reached the end of Sarah's street, where it intersected with Main Street, and Pete would take a right turn to head for the bank. Instead, he sat there, staring straight ahead.

"You know," said Polly, "it just might help if you talk to me. I've got lots of experience on how *not* to do things. You could learn by reverse example. Come on. What's the matter?"

She didn't really expect him to tell her. He never had. He probably never would.

But now he sighed as if his ribs would break. "I don't know what's the matter. It's just that there's always something. If it's not Connie, it's me. If it's not me, it's her mother. If it's not her mother, it's—" He didn't finish the thought. But then again, he didn't put the truck in gear, either.

Polly snuck a look in the side-view mirror. There was no one behind them. What the heck. She decided to give it a shot. "So why does this surprise you? When have things ever been easy with you and Connie? And I think by now you can safely assume they aren't going to be."

"Thanks. That's helpful."

"All I'm saying is, I think you should stop waiting around for this idyllic life to begin. It isn't going to. So why don't you work on rolling with the punches a little?"

Polly had to admit she was surprised when Pete looked at her thoughtfully. After a minute he said, "So what about you, Pol? What's your big dream?"

"I don't know. I can tell you what it used to be before it

went bust. A husband, a home, a couple of kids. Pretty boring."

"There's nothing wrong with that dream, Polly."

"There isn't? Then what happened to it?"

"Maybe you're in too much of a rush. Maybe you tried to jam the wrong people into it."

"No," said Polly. "It's me. I'm just no good at it. I've decided to give up on it."

Pete eased the car into gear and turned onto Main Street. "I can see why right now you might want to take a break from it, but why do you have to give up on it forever? Can't you take a . . . a sabbatical?"

Polly snorted. And she would have said something more and plenty of it if she hadn't just noticed where Pete had parked—in front of the police station. "What are you doing?"

"I'm getting Willy. No one at the bank is going to tell us anything about Cobie's money. But they might tell the police chief."

Polly yanked her door open. "I'll see you later. I'm meeting Kay at the newspaper."

"Polly," said Pete. "Will you cut this out? You can talk to him. He's not sixteen. He's not stupid, either. It was just dinner."

"It's *never* just dinner."

It had made so much sense in Sarah's living room. You found a bunch of gold coins, you cashed them in for ready money, and you put the money in the bank.

The only trouble was, Cobie didn't.

Cobie had no bank account. He had no safe deposit box. But according to the bank manager, Del Farber, he seemed to have some money *somewhere*.

Del allowed Pete to accompany the police chief into his office. It was no corner office on Wall Street, but it had enough chairs for the three of them, and enough leg room so that Pete could stretch out. Del himself looked pretty relaxed for a banker—he wore a jacket and tie, but the top button on his shirt was unbuttoned, and his hair looked like it had seen a lot of wind since it last saw a comb.

"Cobie came to see me," he said, "about buying back the house on Paine Road. But he seemed to have little knowledge of how the financial world works. He assumed since we foreclosed on the property, we still owned it. I explained to him that the bank doesn't retain reclaimed property, the bank sells it. We're not in the real estate business. We're in the business of making money. But Cobie became quite angry. He felt we had no right to dispose of something he still seemed to consider as his own personal property."

"But he implied he could afford the down payment to buy the house back?" asked Willy.

"He *implied* nothing of the kind. He stated flat out that he had the wherewithal to buy back the house in toto. In cash."

Pete shot a look at Willy. "No mortgage?"

"No mortgage," said Del Farber. "He had a few things to say about that, too. He wasn't going to let us talk him into signing any more papers that would let us steal his house out from under him the minute he hit a little slump. I believe those were his words exactly."

"Did he say where the money came from?" asked Willy.

"No, and I didn't ask him. I suggested his only recourse was to talk to the Murchisons on the off chance they might be interested in selling, but I warned him that I knew the Murchisons, and I knew they were happy in the house. I mentioned one or two other properties, but Cobie wasn't interested. He told me that was the whole trouble with people like me. They thought a house was just a house. He said there was only one thing that was *just* anything, and that was money. Money was just money."

And Del Farber shook his head as if Cobie had told him the month of May on Nashtoba was just cloudy.

Kay Dodd wasn't at the newspaper. There was a big celebrity in town, and Polly had read about it and would have known where to look for Kay immediately if she'd only remembered.

Gary Moorehouse, the author of the best-selling how-to book, *Dying without Crying,* was speaking at the Ladies' Library. Polly had no interest in listening to Gary. She hoped when she died there would be at least one person standing around her grave sobbing his bloody eyes out. But Kay would have to be there to take Gary Moorehouse's picture. Polly wandered toward the library.

Slowly.

Still, she had to walk around outside for fifteen minutes before Kay came bolting down the library steps, leading the less avid Moorehouse fans who hadn't lingered for their signed copies.

"What are you doing here?" asked Kay.

"Looking for a lunch partner. Are you off? Want to eat?"

"Let's go to my place. I have to pick up a lens, and I have homemade chicken salad in the refrigerator."

Polly hopped into Kay's minivan and they drove to her apartment.

But they never ate any chicken salad.

When they opened the door, Kay's apartment looked much the same as Cobie's wreck.

After he'd been murdered.

Chapter
25

*It was such a scene of confusion as you
can hardly fancy.*

The upholstery on Kay's mismatched chairs was ripped open. The blanket chest she used as a coffee table was empty and the contents tossed on the rug. The desk drawers were pulled out and upended. Even Kay's pictures had been taken down. Kay raced through the three small rooms, then returned to stand in the living room, trembling. Polly pushed her into what was left of the nearest chair, went to the telephone, and called the police station.

She told Jean Martell what had happened, but somehow before she'd gotten to the part about where she was, she heard Jean whisper her name into the air somewhere on the other end, and the next thing she knew, she was talking to the chief directly.

"Polly. Where are you?"

"Kay Dodd's." It occurred to her he might not yet know where Kay Dodd lived. "Eleven Wood Road," she added. "Second floor."

"Get out of there. Now."

"No one's here. Nobody but Kay, I mean."

"You're sure?"

"I'm sure."

"Okay. Don't touch anything. I'm on my way."

He must have taken the crow's route. And Polly had to admit this time she was glad enough to see him. It wasn't just the sight of him, it was the sound of that even keel in his voice.

And this time he had a sunburned Ted Ball with him. Ted moved around the apartment doing the usual routine—pictures, notes, fingerprints—while the chief talked to Kay, but before Willy had gone three sentences, Kay stopped trembling. He sounded as if his only concern was Kay's well-being, but Polly noticed he got plenty of information out of her while he stood there chitchatting. *He's good at this,* she thought. Finally he asked Kay to look around, to make note of anything missing.

Kay walked through the rooms in a semi-trancelike state, but she seemed certain enough when she said, "Everything's here."

It took a while for anyone to remember Polly.

"Where's your car?" asked Willy.

"Home. I rode with Kay."

The chief said something to Ted, quietly, in a corner, then opened the door for Polly. He followed her and led her to his Scout. They got in and rode as far as Main Street without anyone saying anything.

"So," said the chief finally.

Polly cringed, waiting. What would he say? *Why are you running from me? Why can't you talk to me?*

"Cobie Small's wreck, Esther Small's room, Kay Dodd's apartment. What do you figure?"

"What do *I* figure?"

"Sure. You still have a feel for the place, don't you? You still know these people better than I do. What's this ransacker after?"

"Oh, that's easy," said Polly, relieved. "He's after Cobie's treasure. The chest of guineas from the *General Newcomb* that got uncovered in that big storm in April." She bit her lip and waited, but unlike Pete, he seemed to swallow this hypothesis hook, line, and sinker.

"So first he searched Cobie's wreck—"

"After he killed Cobie."

As far as Polly could tell without looking at him, the chief didn't balk at that hypothesis, either.

"Then he searched Esther Small's room. The wreck is obvious enough. But why Esther's?"

"Because she'd been out there. At the wreck. And she knew Cobie better than anybody. She might have an inside track on some secret hiding place."

"So our friend must have known she went out there. Who knew that, I wonder?"

"Me. And Pete." Then Polly remembered something, and a sensation that felt partly like the ice of a new fear and partly like the chill of an old certainty cut through her. "And Joe Putnam! Joe Putnam took us out to the wreck in his boat."

Willy shot a look sideways. "There must have been others. Anyone on the dock or driving by."

Polly said nothing. Joe Putnam had been *out* there.

"So what about Kay Dodd's apartment? *Why* Kay Dodd's apartment?"

"Kay went out to the wreck, too. I saw her. At midnight the very night I told her all about Cobie and the treasure."

"At midnight. So the number of people who might have seen Kay is most likely smaller."

True, thought Polly. And that time, Joe Putnam hadn't been with them. But that cold certainty stayed with her just the same, and in a minute it came to her why it had. She whirled in her seat. "It's not only who *saw* her go out there, it's who *knew* she went out there. And *he* knew. He knew because I told him!"

"Who?"

"Joe Putnam. I told Joe Putnam. I was standing right beside him in Pete's kitchen, and I told him Kay went out there. It's Joe Putnam who did all this! He cracked Pete on the head when he got too close to the anchor. He . . . oh, God. I should have known it the minute I saw him. They're all the same. Take what you want, and if there's something in your way, smash it to pieces. Pick your weapon. Words, an anchor . . ."

They had reached Pete's cottage. Willy pulled in behind Polly's car and turned toward her. There was something in his face that hadn't been there before. Was he angry at something? No, it wasn't exactly anger, but it was something, something she didn't want to meet head-on. She had to get out of there. She fumbled frantically with her seat belt.

Willy reached over, moved her trembling hands aside, and flipped the belt release. "One more question. When Kay walked into the apartment, what did she do?"

Polly paused with her hand on the door handle, flustered. "Do? What did Kay do?"

"Did she look around, did she search the place?"

"No, she just stood there. Wait a minute. First she ran into the bedroom, then the kitchen."

"Was she gone long?"

"A couple of seconds. Why?"

"Say she did find something out at Cobie's wreck. Say she hid it in her apartment. The first thing she'd do would be to check to see if it was still there."

Polly's eyes widened. "But Kay didn't find anything. She told me."

"You're good friends?"

"Yes." But the word didn't come out with the proper conviction. She tried again. "I *know* she didn't find anything." But that came out worse—too much protesting.

Still, for some reason, Willy seemed ready to leave it there. "Okay. So if she didn't find anything, neither did whoever searched the apartment. And that means he's going to keep looking."

"True."

Willy sat silent. Eventually he said, "Joe Putnam, huh?"

"Yes," said Polly. "And that's not all of it, either. He was jealous of Cobie. He and Kay fought over it, and she broke up with him because he tried to bully her into not visiting Cobie anymore. And then Joe lied about it. He told Pete he was moving in with Kay. Just last week he told me they were going out someplace together, and the very next day *Kay* told me they weren't even seeing each other."

Willy looked at the house. "Pete's home?"

"He should be." *He'd better be.* Polly opened the car door.

"One thing," said Willy. "Just for the record."

Polly froze.

"They aren't all the same. They aren't all looking to *take* something."

He was out the door before Polly could answer.

Chapter
26

"It's my old sea chest they're after."

Pete had just opened the refrigerator to see what it could do for him in the way of lunch when a car pulled into the driveway.

Willy.

With Polly?

She'd never taken his advice in *this* much of a hurry.

And she hadn't now, apparently. The chief came in first, looking a little tense around the jawline. Polly followed, face the color of a tomato.

But Willy pulled out chairs for both of them and slipped smoothly into a long narrative about the trashing of Kay Dodd's apartment. It seemed to Pete, Willy was uncharacteristically long-winded until he realized he was surreptitiously watching Polly. Was he giving her a chance to regain her composure? And regain it from what? Whatever it was, it was none of Pete's business.

"So it looks like somebody's still looking for something," Willy concluded finally.

"And too bad we don't know where he'll look next," said Polly, seemingly fully collected now. "We could get there first and lie in wait for him."

To Pete's surprise, Willy actually seemed to consider the suggestion. "Or we could pick his direction for him."

"Wait a minute," said Pete. "What are you talking about?"

"A trap," said Willy.

"A treasure hunt!" cried Polly.

Something told Pete he'd better sit down, too.

"We plant a rumor," continued Willy.

"Or a clue," chimed in Polly. "Maybe even a map."

"Wait a minute," said Pete again.

"A map's good," said Willy. "But a little obvious. A place like this, a rumor might work better."

"But it has to sound like it came from Cobie," said Polly. "It has to sound like he found the treasure, and he hid it, and we've only just come across this clue, whatever it is. But we have to act like it doesn't mean anything to us, right? We have to word it in such a way that only the guy we're after will know what it means. And he'll go after it, and we'll be right there, hiding."

"And then what—you jump out and arrest him for trespassing?"

"Nobody jumps out at all," said Willy. "Our purpose is to pinpoint a direction for this so-called investigation."

"A direction toward a particular person, is that it?"

"A direction toward Joe Putnam," said Polly.

Pete laughed.

Polly's chin came up, but Pete was interested to note it was Willy she talked to. "Okay, they aren't all the same. I guess I know that. But does that make Joe Putnam any less of a bully or a liar? And how far a leap is it from that to murder? We know that he knew Esther and Kay had been out to the wreck, that he was jealous enough of Cobie to threaten Kay over it, and to lie about it. *And* we know that when Pete found the murder weapon, he knocked him into the water."

"And fished me out and handed the anchor to Willy," said Pete, but he'd stopped laughing. He'd begun to remember other things. Joe eagerly supplying Pete with lists of

Cobie haters like Pit Patterson and Seline DuBois. Joe pooh-poohing all the talk about treasure and discouraging any efforts to find the anchor, but when the anchor finally appeared, making sure he disturbed any telltale evidence.

"Well?" said Willy, watching him.

No. It was crazy. All of it. And probably illegal. "Something tells me this isn't in the handbook of standard police procedure."

"Strictly speaking," said Willy, "this is no longer a police matter. We're all private citizens here. And that brings me to where you come in, Pete. You're the last person who spoke to Cobie."

"Second to last," said Pete. "Assuming whoever killed him spoke to him."

"Okay, second to last. Still it makes sense Cobie might have mumbled something to you. All you have to do is mention in passing that Cobie said something like—" Willy stopped.

"Right. Like what?"

"I don't know. Maybe something about Cobie digging."

"Oh, *good,*" said Polly. "Digging. Why didn't we think of that sooner? That's what they always do with treasure."

"Wait a minute," said Pete for what seemed like the tenth time. "I don't care who's searching for what where, who's moving in where, and what anybody did with any anchor. There still isn't a single, solitary piece of proof that there *is* a treasure. And there's nothing concrete to tell us Cobie found it if there is."

"It doesn't matter if there is or isn't a treasure," said Willy. "Or even, for that matter, if Cobie found it. All that matters is that somebody else thinks he did."

"Right," said Pete. "And there's no evidence of that, either."

"Someone has broken into three separate places," began Polly.

"Now there," said Pete. "Right there. Breaking and entering. And you say it isn't a police matter. You think Lieutenant Collins—"

"I don't think much about Lieutenant Collins," said Willy, *somewhat cryptically,* Pete thought. He looked from the police chief to his sister and back again.

"You really mean this."

"Of course he really means it. He's not stupid."

"Thank you," said Willy.

Pete looked from Willy to Polly and back again. That, of course, was the obvious explanation. Willy had gone temporarily brain-dead. Polly had cast some sort of spell on him. Well, Pete, for one, wasn't going to run around the island setting up some idiotic treasure hunt just because the police chief was stuck on his sister.

"No," he said.

He only had to say it three more times before Willy gave up and went home, but Polly kept at it. By the time the phone rang, Pete was getting pretty damned sick of it.

"Hello," he snapped into it.

"Excuse *me,"* said Connie.

"Sorry," said Pete. "Polly and I were arguing."

"So excuse me again. Call me when you're not so busy."

Polly was right, Pete decided. This was never going to be easy. "I'm not busy," he said evenly. "I've been trying to call you." Well, he'd been thinking about it, anyway.

Polly crept into his line of vision, pantomimed a punch with one hand and a rolling motion with the other.

"Get out of here," said Pete.

"What?" said Connie.

"Nothing," said Pete. "How are you? What's going on?"

Polly left, grinning.

Connie ignored his first question and answered his second. "What's going on? Let's see. The folks have decided to take advantage of my presence and drag me around to see all the relations. Tomorrow it's the Julius cousins. Monday it's the Fosters. Tuesday it's somebody they call Uncle Henry," but I think he's a counterfeit. I've never heard of him."

Pete had never heard of him, either. But then again, he'd never heard of the Julius cousins or the Foster family. What he had heard was the word *Tuesday.* So Connie wasn't coming home anytime soon.

They grew polite. How was her mother? Fine. How was he? Fine. Any more Cobie news? He told her about the *Newcomb,* the *Royal Arms,* the supposed treasure, he listened to the neatly packaged responses, he heard the strain grow thicker.

Enough. So Connie was going to stay in New Jersey for a while. So roll with it. "Okay, I have a plan. You stay through the cousins and the Fosters and the forged Uncle Henry and come home on Wednesday. That gives you four days to finish the world tour and four days for us to have some semblance of a vacation together."

Pause.

"Three and a half for the world tour," said Connie finally. "Today's half over." But now Pete heard something else, too. Something that sounded ready to come home.

"Wednesday," he said firmly. "It'll take you at least a half a day to get out of there."

"And half a day to get home. But that still leaves us a whole four-day vacation. With me visiting with Polly and you out weir fishing. Now that's the stuff my dreams are made of." But it was said with humor this time. Now that he thought about it, had it been said with humor *last* time?

But it didn't matter anymore. Suddenly there was something else he wanted to find out. "What *are* your dreams made of?" he asked her. He'd just now realized he'd been married to this woman for nine years, divorced from her for almost three, and he had no idea what she dreamed about. New Zealand, most likely. Was that why he'd never asked before, he was afraid of the answer? His first surprise was that she seemed to sense it was a serious question. His second was that she fudged the answer.

"What brought this on?"

"Polly asked me earlier."

"And you answered——?"

"I told her all I wanted was an hour of peace and contentment alone in my own home with you."

Silence.

"You mean it, don't you?" she said finally, softly. "Living on Nashtoba, doing what you do, us being together, that's all that's important to you."

"Wrong order," said Pete. "Us being together, *then* living on Nashtoba, doing what I do—"

Connie laughed. "I'd hesitate to put that theory to the test. But that's good, Pete. That's achievable. You won't die frustrated."

"Wanna bet? Wednesday's still a long way off. But no cheating, here. What's your big dream? Something tells me a loaf of bread, a jug of wine, and me beside you isn't going to do the trick. So what is?"

"Oh, I don't know. Nothing much. Curing the common cold. Being the first woman president. Maybe just seeing the world. But only if you come along, of course."

She spoke lightly. Pete answered in kind. "And I suppose you expect me to bring the jug of wine and the loaf of bread?"

She laughed again. "I'm no freeloader. I'll bring the bread." Then her voice changed. "I like your plan. I'll see you Wednesday."

Pete hung up feeling better.

And, somehow, lonelier.

Polly didn't just leave the kitchen, she left the house. It had been a long day—first the talk with Pete, then Kay's apartment, then seeing Willy. And it was a long way from over. She got in the car and drove without thinking. She was beginning to find that this aimless driving suited her, soothed her.

She was able to keep her mind detached until she was halfway down Main Street and her eye happened to light on the sign for the antique shop, Garret Gold. She thought about her last visit. Had Pete been right? Had she talked to Fred Underwood in such a way that Fred had actually listened to her, had sent for Esther? Suddenly Polly felt like visiting old Fred.

And Fred, it seemed, was glad enough to see her, until she tried to thank him for calling Esther.

His eyes misted over. "I doubt that Esther is as grateful. Still and all, I felt it was the right thing to do."

"It was," said Polly. "And Esther knows it was. Really."

Fred seemed to brighten. He grasped Polly's elbow and led her around the shop, showing off his newest treasures. Polly tried to look and listen attentively, but she had trouble focusing.

Until she saw the box.

It was not an impressive piece—about eight inches square, dull black, with pitted brass fastenings. Polly almost walked past without noticing, her eyes at the last second picking out the words on the tarnished plate. Even then she thought she was hallucinating. She pulled her arm free.

"Mr. Underwood!"

He jumped. "Mercy! What is it?"

"This box. Where did you get it?"

"Heaven's to Betsy, don't *startle* me. I thought something had broken. That box? Oh, dear. Perhaps I shouldn't have put it out. But I asked Esther if she wanted it. I told her it was rightfully hers, but she wanted nothing, she said. Absolutely nothing. So I thought, well then, why not? I put it out. But if you'd like to buy it, I'll send Esther the money. That's fair enough, wouldn't you say? Although she did *insist*—"

"Mr. Underwood," said Polly calmly, breathing deeply, "let me be sure about this. Why is this box rightfully Esther's? Who gave it to you?"

"Why, Cobie. Cobie Small. He said he needed to keep it somewhere safe. He said that eventually it would come in handy. And he specifically said, he most emphatically stated, that if anything happened to him, I should see that it went to Esther. I tried, as I told you. But she said she wanted nothing. She refused to even look at it. She wouldn't listen to me describe it. It's not an item of great value, it's in quite poor condition as you can see, but Cobie seemed to feel rather strongly about it."

I bet, thought Polly. She looked down and read the name etched into the brass.

HMS *Royal Arms.*

She opened the lid gently.

But, of course, it was empty.

Chapter
27
___

Their eyes burned in their heads; their feet grew
speedier and lighter; their whole soul was bound up in
that fortune, that whole lifetime of extravagance and
pleasure, that lay waiting there for each of them.

Pete stared at the unassuming square of dark metal sitting in the middle of his kitchen table.

"See? See?" said Polly. "It's the proof! You said there was no proof, and here it is right in front of you. It's the money box from the *Royal Arms*. Cobie found it. He gave it to Fred Underwood for safekeeping. Not only is this the proof that the treasure exists, it's the proof Cobie needed to tie the gold to a shipwreck. The proof that would double the worth of all those gold guineas!"

"One gold guinea. Stick to the facts here. So far we've come up with one coin."

"Oh, please," said Polly. "Will you look at this chest? It must have held millions of them."

"How do you know? For all you know, a guinea is the size of a hockey puck. It might have held five of them. It also might have held nothing. And if it's been kicking around in the harbor since 1778, wouldn't it be rustier?"

"Things don't rust until they hit the air, Pete. Oxidation, they call it. And this thing hit the air for the first time in April, remember? See how the lock was banged open? Those scratches are fresh. What more do you want me to tell you?

Cobie found the chest of gold, and he gave the chest to Fred Underwood for safekeeping."

"Right. And what did he do with the gold?"

The adrenaline that had lifted Polly's arms, eyebrows, spirits skyward for the last fifteen minutes drained out of her. She drooped. "That's the problem, isn't it? Now we *know* it's out there somewhere, and we're still not an inch closer to it."

"Maybe he gave the gold to Fred for safekeeping, too, only the minute Cobie died, Fred decided possession was nine-tenths of the law, and he kept it."

"I don't think so."

"You can think what you want," said Pete. "The fact remains—"

"The fact remains," said Polly, "that you no longer have an excuse. It's time to lay down that rumor."

Pete ground the heel of his hand into the knot of nerves between his eyebrows.

Polly eyed him with concern. "What's the matter?"

"Headache."

And why, then, did she suddenly decide to ask him, "How was Connie?"

"She's coming home Wednesday."

Polly's eyes flashed with pleasure. "Great. That's good news. It'll be good to see her."

Pete rubbed his forehead again.

Polly jumped up, opened the kitchen cupboard, and got down the aspirin. "Here. Stop being a martyr. Take two. *Then* will you call Willy?"

Pete eyed the chest. "I don't know. It's not a very big box. It—"

Tires swished in the gravel drive. Pete went to the window, looked out, and was surprised to see a taxi.

He was even more surprised to see Esther Small get out of it.

Pete met her at the door and led her into his kitchen. She was dressed in the same skirt and sweater she'd been wearing when Pete had last seen her at the Whiteaker. She walked in hugging her shoulders.

"Still cold?"

"Miserable." She looked around his kitchen, saw the chest on the table, and passed over it, apparently without interest, to focus instead on the view of the marsh from the window. She sighed softly. "This is lovely."

Pete offered her a chair, which she refused. He offered her coffee, which she also refused. Pete had to admit he was relieved—he wasn't sure he had any milk or cream left, and he was pretty sure all his mugs were in the sink, dirty.

"I can't stay," Esther explained. "The taxi is waiting. And I apologize for disturbing you. But I'd like to ask you a favor. Or perhaps *favor* is not the right word—wouldn't a favor imply something free? I fully intend to pay you for your services. To hire Factotum. It's not an enormous job, but it is one I find myself unable to tackle for a surprising variety of reasons. I'm preparing to leave the island tomorrow, but there remains one unfinished task. That boat. I would appreciate it if you would deal with it."

"Deal with it?" asked Polly. "What do you mean, deal with it?"

"I mean get rid of it. I leave it to you. Do what you wish—sell it, sink it, burn it, I don't care. If you sell it, the money is yours. If you find there is an expense involved in disposing of it—" She reached into her purse and extracted a small piece of paper. "You may bill me through this address."

Pete took the paper from her. Her name was printed carefully across the top, followed by "care of Beldon's Market." The address was an old mill town a hundred miles to the north. It wasn't an area known for its thriving economy. Pete looked up.

"I have a room above the store. I do the bookkeeping for the market. I am able to pay, I assure you."

Pete shook his head, embarrassed. "It's not the money. It's—"

"What about Cobie's things?" asked Polly.

"What things?" said Esther. "I don't want his things. Give them away. Burn them with the boat."

"Maybe if you waited a bit," Pete began, but Esther overrode him.

"Waited for what? This part of my life was over long ago. This time I would appreciate leaving here knowing I've left no loose ends."

"Okay," said Pete. "I'll deal with the boat." He felt like saying something else, something about Cobie, maybe, but the right words wouldn't come to him. And Esther didn't give him much time. She said thank you and good-bye and was out the door almost before the meter ticked over.

Polly wasn't far behind her. "Hey," said Pete. "Where are *you* going?"

"Ben Hopkins," said Polly.

Ben Hopkins listened to Polly's tale of the chest from the *Royal Arms* with interest. "Fancy that. The money box. And Cobie found it."

"Apparently," said Polly. She shaped a cube in the air. "It's about this big. How big is a guinea? How many would a box like this hold?"

Ben chewed his lower lip. "Hard to say. A few of 'em, I can tell you that. That guinea wasn't as big as a quarter. Bigger than a nickel, though." He studied Polly's hands, still suspended midair. "Hard to say," he repeated. "But I'll tell you this. I'd give you a week's wages for one look at a box full of 'em. Pretty sight."

Suddenly Polly wanted to see the coin. She wanted to see it desperately. "Who bought Cobie's coin?"

"Some fellow from over your way. Fellow from the historical society. Cobie showed it to him, sparked his interest. When he heard Cobie sold it to me, he came looking."

"Hugh Platt?"

"That's the fellow."

"What did he pay for it?"

Polly should have known better than to get personal, and

around those parts there was nothing more personal than the subject of money. It didn't matter if you were talking about a new pair of gloves or your annual salary. The subject of money was taboo. So Polly wasn't much surprised when Ben said, "Don't see as how that's any of your business, young lady."

But Polly didn't really care what Hugh Platt had paid for the coin. All she wanted was to see the thing. She left the coin shop and drove straight to the historian's.

It was amazing how quickly Pete's headache went away the minute the door closed behind Polly. The house was quiet. Connie was coming home Wednesday. And sitting on his kitchen table was an honest-to-goodness, real, Long-John-Silver-type treasure chest.

Maybe.

But Pete couldn't help indulging himself in one brief moment of fantasy. Maybe his own dreams didn't require heavy financing, but he knew better than to take Connie's light chatter about dreams in the spirit she intended. He hadn't been far wrong with his speculation about New Zealand, but she wasn't planning to stop there. She wasn't even planning to *start* there. And a million dollars would launch her nicely. Still, you didn't see the world or run for president or cure the common cold from the confines of a small cottage on a marsh on Nashtoba, did you?

The thought filled Pete with a dread so cold it drove him in search of his jacket and out of the house. Yes, there was his marsh, mostly drab grays and browns, but new green in spots, coming to life the way it did each spring, bringing Pete back to life with it. He'd seen places in the world that didn't die each year, didn't struggle to survive season after season against harsh, unfeeling odds, didn't leap to victorious joy each spring only to gather strength for the next battle, the next defeat.

How boring.

Pete zipped up his jacket and set off over the marsh for the beach. How many times had he walked this stretch of sand? How often did it rise and fall and bend and twist and reinvent itself in new shapes, new configurations? What was buried under his feet even as he trod over it? He was pretty sure whatever it was, it wasn't a million dollars.

But put aside what the chest may or may not have contained, the chest itself was a part of history. It had traveled across the ocean two hundred years ago. It had been sitting under the sand in Close Harbor for a couple of centuries. And what might it have contained?

It might have contained nothing.

But for some reason, after a few solitary minutes of quiet reflection under the leaden May sky, Pete was now inclined to agree that the small metal lockbox had probably contained *something*.

He began to walk faster. Okay. So what might it have carried? Not gold. If the chest had been full of gold, why would Cobie single out one lone coin to sell to Ben Hopkins? Because he needed some ready cash. Some drinking money. So why didn't he bring along the chest, show Ben Hopkins the proof that the coin was from a shipwreck, at the very least collect five hundred instead of two hundred and fifty dollars?

Because the coin wasn't from the chest. The coin had fallen out of the pocket of a British soldier. The chest was a separate find, a decided coup for a beachcomber, but unrelated to the George III guinea.

But the chest on the *Royal Arms* was reported to be full of British guineas. It was too much of a coincidence that Cobie would have found one coin dropped by a British soldier, and an empty chest that had once held the same coins from the same era.

Okay, so say the chest *was* full of gold coins.

So why didn't Cobie show the chest to Ben Hopkins?

Because he didn't want Ben Hopkins to know there was more gold. Because he didn't want *anyone* to know there was more gold.

And why not?

Because it was for Esther.

And because Cobie didn't trust banks. Cobie didn't *like* banks. And he stashed it . . .

Pete slowed. That was the question, of course.

Where had he stashed it?

Cobie had left the chest with Fred Underwood, the only person he knew would keep safe the proof that would double the value of the gold. Fred Underwood would do it for Cobie because Cobie was doing it for Esther. So wasn't Fred Underwood the only logical person Cobie could have trusted with Esther's gold?

No. Because if Fred Underwood knew the value of the chest as proof of the value of the gold, he'd never have put it out in the shop for sale. He'd never have let Polly have it. And he certainly wouldn't have let her have it if he actually had the gold. So Fred Underwood couldn't know anything about any treasure.

If there *was* a treasure.

And Pete was right back where he'd started.

Almost, anyway.

Polly may have been anxious to see Hugh Platt, but Hugh Platt didn't seem so anxious to see Polly.

"I'm quite busy," he said the minute he opened the door and saw her. "I'm preparing a lecture to be delivered in Bradford this evening. But I believe I told you I'd be in touch the minute I determined something, and I have as yet found no corroboration whatsoever on this matter of the *Royal Arms.*"

"Oops," said Polly. "I forgot you were looking. But you can stop now. We've got corroboration plenty. We found the chest. It says *Royal Arms* right on it and everything."

Polly doubted Hugh Platt could have looked more surprised if she'd just told him the Red Sox had won the World Series.

"You found it?"

Polly grinned at him. "In Garret Gold. Cobie gave it to Fred Underwood to keep safe for him. For Esther, really. But Esther didn't want it. So Fred let me have it. There's nothing in it, of course, but it proves our point all right, doesn't it? The *General Newcomb* raided the *Royal Arms,* just as that book said, and stole the spy money. And that's why I came here, Mr. Platt. Ben Hopkins says you were the one who bought Cobie's guinea. Could I see it? It won't take a minute."

Hugh Platt continued to stand there, frowning at her, looking one-upped.

"Could I see the coin?" she prodded.

Hugh came out of his trance. "The coin. Yes. It's in my safe." He left Polly standing in the doorway and disappeared down the hall. He returned carrying a small velvet box, the kind engagement rings came in. At least it was the kind Polly's engagement ring had come in, and the sight of it did something to her throat. She'd given the ring back. Thrown it back, actually . . .

But Hugh Platt had opened the box, and all bitter memories of engagement rings were forgotten.

There it was—small, delicate, shining brightly. King George III in solid gold. A two-hundred-year-old British guinea. And maybe it wasn't as big as a quarter, but somehow it seemed to fill the room.

"Thank you," whispered Polly.

When Pete returned to the cottage, the chest was no longer on the kitchen table. He wasn't surprised—Polly's car was back in the drive.

But when he found her on his bedroom floor with the big crockery jug he tossed his pocket change into, he *was* surprised. "What are you doing?"

"Robbing your till. But only temporarily. I saw the guinea. It's only a little smaller than a quarter. So I'm filling this chest with all your quarters to see how many it holds. To see what this treasure is really worth."

Pete felt it was greatly to his credit that this time he refrained from saying *what treasure?*

Polly didn't notice. She was flipping quarters and nickels out of the crock and into the box, her lips moving as she counted. It was a big crock. Pete accumulated a lot of pocket change. He sprawled on the couch and waited, and when the coins were still a hair shy of the lip of the box, Polly said, "One thousand!"

One thousand. So one thousand guineas, worth $250 apiece—no, $500 apiece, as long as the chest existed to prove they came from an honest-to-goodness, real-live ship-wreck . . .

Okay, so it was no million dollars.

But it could buy Esther Small a house and a car without flinching.

And it could get Connie a lot farther than New Zealand.

Chapter
28

"I could not doubt that he hoped to seize upon the treasure . . . cut every honest throat about that island, and sail away . . . laden with crimes and riches."

Pete called Willy. He had to admit he was starting to find the idea of the trap intriguing. Still, once they'd assembled around the table and shown Willy the chest, he couldn't resist his old role as devil's advocate one more time.

"So let me get this straight. We lay down a rumor that Cobie mumbled something to me that night when I tucked him in. Something that would pinpoint the spot where this treasure is buried. Then we sit around said spot for days, nights, even, waiting to catch whoever it is—"

"It should take about fifteen minutes," said Willy. "You think once you plant the idea, this fellow is going to sit around? What he's going to do is start digging."

"And that's another thing. I'm not sure about this digging. It's too corny. Besides, there's a lot of beach out there. We need to narrow this down to a precise location."

"Obviously, you don't know the first thing about treasure-hunting," said Polly. You have to give the coordinates. Twenty-five feet from the old elm. Ten feet southwest of the—"

"Right. Cobie in his drunken ramblings pinpoints exactly the location of his buried treasure. But I like the old elm,"

Pete added, despite himself. "There's a patch of scrub oak right there on Cobie's beach, and one nice big fat one that sticks out a mile. We could designate that tree somehow, refer to a hole in its trunk, find out how many paces it is from the water—"

"It has a hole in its trunk?"

"It doesn't have to have a hole in its trunk any more than there has to be a treasure. Just so long as this guy thinks it's there, he'll come looking. And we'll be hiding in the woods, watching. But first we need to go down to the beach and pace it off."

"And when and where do we lay down this rumor?" asked Willy.

"Beston's Store," said Pete.

"No, Lupo's, around happy hour," said Polly.

The three of them looked at each other.

Pete was dismayed to notice that he was the first one to start grinning, but Willy wasn't far behind him.

And Polly couldn't have looked more pleased if Pete had just served her an eight-course lobster dinner.

Pete and Polly stood on the beach in front of Cobie's wreck. It had stayed calm all day, but now a soft breeze crept up her neck, and the boat rocked as gently as a cradle. Polly pulled up the collar of the jacket she'd stolen from Pete and glanced casually left and right. She could see no one, but that didn't mean no one could see them. That's why they'd left Willy out of phase one. "How about that black rock over there?"

Beside her, Pete made a subtle twist in the direction of the rock. "Not bad. Come on."

They made it look like a meaningless walk, trailing along the water line, arching gently away, and as they passed the black rock, Pete began to count under his breath. "One, two—" They hit the edge of the clump of oaks. "Thirty-four, thirty-five—"

"There," said Polly. "There's the big tree you were talking about."

"Forty," said Pete. "All right. So that'll be our story. The hollow oak forty paces from the black rock." He looked around. "And we can hide behind that thicket of wild roses." His eye met Polly's. "Come on," he said. "Admit it. Don't you feel kind of dumb?"

Polly giggled. "Kind of."

"I can't believe Willy dreamed this whole thing up."

"No," said Polly after a minute. "Me, either. But you know what I think? I think he's enjoying this. It isn't his case. He doesn't have to act all official. He can play a little."

Pete grinned. He twisted his wrist so he could read his watch. "Happy hour has arrived. Time for Lupo's."

Pete escorted Polly into Lupo's with some trepidation. He'd had his fill of Polly and barflies. But at least he knew these barflies better. And apparently they knew Polly better.

"Polly!" Dave Snow cried more gleefully than Pete felt seemed warranted. "Sneaking out before curfew, I see. Glad to see you're still around. How long are you staying? What are you drinking?"

To Pete's surprise, she ordered a Ballantine. To his even greater surprise, she said, "Who knows how long I'm staying. I'm free as a bird. Which means I'm unemployed, actually."

"Unemployed?" said Joe Putnam. "Want to sling fish?"

"No, thank you," said Polly crisply.

"If you're looking for a woman to sling fish, try Eva Chase," said Pit Patterson from the stool on the other side of Joe. "I saw her out in the harbor spearing eels last Friday."

Polly swung toward Pit. "Eva *Chase?* The librarian?"

"Yep," said Pit. "Eva Chase. Said she fries 'em for breakfast. Ask me, the only thing an eel's good for is striper bait."

Polly shot Pete a look. "It's funny you mention Eva. I saw her recently. She was all upset about a missing library book of Cobie's."

Neatly done, thought Pete, as he slipped into the space

Polly had made for him. "The last time I saw Cobie, he wasn't worried about any library books. His big problem was oak trees." He chuckled.

"Oak trees?" asked Dave.

"Yeah, oak trees. The night Connie and I took him home. The night he died. The minute we pulled up to that stretch of beach by his wreck, he yelled something about a big oak and took off for the woods. You know that patch of scrub? It was all Connie and I could do to get him into the dinghy and out to the boat."

"A big oak?" said Polly. "I wonder what he meant by that."

"Knowing Cobie, not much," said Dave. "For all you know, he could have been hollering about a boat, not an oak."

"No," said Pete. "It was 'oak' all right. A hollow oak. He worried it to death. That's all he said the whole time we were packing him to bed. Well, it wasn't *all* he said, but not a word of it made any sense. Once he got through worrying about the oak, he started worrying about some rock. A *black* rock. On the beach. He was afraid it was going to get covered up."

Joe Putnam snorted. "'Course it's gonna get covered up. It's all gonna get covered up. If not by sand, then by water. Matter of fact, it'll probably be by water. That beach lost a good foot last year."

"True," said Pete. "Maybe that's what the forty paces was all about."

"What forty paces?" asked Polly.

"More Cobie jibberish. 'Forty paces from the rock.' Or maybe it was 'to the rock.' Maybe he wanted to remember where the rock was after it got covered up so he wouldn't hit it with the dinghy."

"Or maybe," said Polly, "the hollow oak was forty paces from the rock."

Pete winced. Wasn't she getting a little obvious?

"What would Cobie want with some old hollow oak?" said Pit.

"Maybe it was his pisspot," said Joe.

"No," said Pit. "Cobie pissed in a bigger pot than that."

Everyone at the bar guffawed except Dave Snow. His eye crossed Pete's and slid out the window to the water.

"Hey, Joe," he said finally. "Kay's all right?"

"Sure," said Joe. "Right as rain."

"Lucky she wasn't home, I guess."

"Wasn't home when?"

"Home when her place got torn up. This afternoon, wasn't it?"

"She's fine," said Polly. "I was with her. We got there after it was all over. Still, any attack's a scary thing. She was shaking like a leaf when she saw the place. She—" Polly's voice drained away.

Pete turned to see her staring at Joe Putnam.

Joe Putnam's face was bloodred. He drained his beer and left.

Pete and Polly, their work done, left shortly after.

Polly hunkered down between the chief and Pete and shivered. As dark neared, so did the cold. Out of her peripheral vision she saw the chief's arm rise halfway, but it came no further before it fell. She experienced a curious disappointment. But then again, she was *cold*. They'd been crouched behind a knot of wild rugosa rosebushes on the edge of the scrub oaks for almost an hour without a single sighting.

"Don't we—"

The arm rose again, but this time only to touch a finger to his lips. He pointed.

A dark truck swept along the road and slowed, then accelerated and was gone.

"Damn," said Pete. "Whose dumb idea was this, anyway? You said fifteen minutes—"

"Shh," said Willy.

A twig snapped. Leaves swished against cloth. Finally Polly heard a steady, measured tread, then a soft voice, a voice she knew. "Forty! Here."

A flashlight gleamed, combing the big oak in front of them. A second voice, also familiar to Polly, said, "You're crazy, you know that?"

Kay Dodd laughed deep in her throat. "I know. I can't help it. It made more sense when you told me about it earlier."

"There's no goddamned hole in this tree, Kay. Besides, if Cobie spouted it off to Pete, why didn't he spout it off to you? You were so all-fired buddy-buddy—"

"Don't start with me, Joe. I told you, I never hung around Cobie when he was drinking. He only gave it away to Pete because he was drunk."

"Okay, okay. But there's no goddamned hole in this tree."

"Right. So let's go home."

"Your place or mine?"

Kay's throaty laugh again. "Whose bed is smaller?"

If Joe Putnam answered her in words, Polly didn't hear it. There was a muffled rustling sound and then footfalls receding.

The three of them stayed where they were, silent, until they were sure they were alone in the woods again.

Polly straightened up. "I told you, didn't I? Joe Putnam."

"And Kay," said Willy. "Interesting."

"It sounds like he told Kay what he heard in the bar tonight."

"And they came out here together," said Pete. "Even though they supposedly don't get along too well these days."

"Interesting," said Willy again.

"Shhh!" said Polly, ducking.

The sound of swishing leaves was back.

Chapter
29

"Oh, shiver my soul," he cried, "if I had eyes!"

"Oof!" said the first voice.

"Dadblameit!" said the second.

Then, "Christ on a bloody raft, Ed!" The first voice again. "Move that bloody whale carcass. You made me lose count. Now we gotta go back to the rock."

"Sorry, Bert."

Polly's eyes strained in the dark, but it was her ears that confirmed her suspicions for her—the blundering, crashing, flailing sounds of a large person finding his way through the woods in the dark could only be Ed Healey, the three-hundred-some-odd-pound Ed Healey most often found on the steps of Beston's porch; the caustic "Christ on a bloody raft" could only belong to his fellow porch-sitter, Bert.

And here they came again.

"Thirty-*two*, thirty-*three*, thirty-*four*—"

"Watch out for that log, there, Bert."

"Thirty-*five*, thirty-*six*, oof!"

"I told you, Bert—"

"Thirty-seven, thirty-eight, thirty-nine, forty! And here's the tree. Christ, we made it. Okay, this is it. Now get on the other side over there and start feeling around for the hollow. Ow! Mother-a-God, if you don't get your thumb out of my nose by the time I count—"

"Now, now, Bert, haven't you done enough counting for one night? Heck, I don't find no hollow in this oak. Do you find a hollow?"

"No I bloody don't! And if you got me out here in the dank and the damp on some sort of sorry wild-goose chase—"

"*Me* got you out here? You were right there when Pit came strolling up and yacking about Cobie and the forty paces and the black rock. And it was you as started in about Fred Underwood and the chest Cobie found and Cobie's having all that cash sort of sudden like. And Evan telling you about all those busted-up 'partments—Cobie's wreck, Esther Small's room, and Kay Dodd's place."

"Oh, shut up," said Bert.

For a few seconds Polly heard nothing but the sound of heavy breathing, some sporadic grunts and groans.

"All right," said Bert finally. "That queers it. I guess I know when I've been suckered, all right."

"Yep," said Ed. "There's no hollow in this here oak. And not another decent size tree anywhere near. Yep, I guess you got suckered, all right."

There followed the sound of a hard palm coming to rest on soft flesh, a large gust of air being expelled, and an injured voice decrying the need for anybody to push.

The two men floundered out of the woods and down the beach.

Polly burst first. "Oh! Oh!" she said through gasps. "Ed! And Bert. Did you ever see such a sight? I've never seen them off that porch in my life!"

This time she felt, rather than saw, the arm as it rose, and this time, it made contact. A hand the size of a ham brushed as gently as a feather across her lips.

She should have figured as much. If the men on Beston's porch had cottoned on to it, so could the rest of the island. They'd laid a trap, all right, a trap for themselves. At this rate, they'd be here all night.

But this time the treasure-hunter hadn't entered the woods. It wasn't any crackle of undergrowth they'd heard, but those slow, haunting strains of *Danny Boy,* suddenly cut short. When the whistling resumed, it had moved off up the beach.

"Did he hear me?" asked Polly. "Did I scare him off? Is that why he didn't come into the woods?"

"I couldn't see him," said Pete.

"Danny Boy," said Willy.

"Jack Whiteaker," said Polly. "But that makes no sense. He's the one person around here who *doesn't* need Cobie's money."

"Maybe," said Pete.

The three of them sat around Pete's kitchen table, warming themselves over hot coffee, wolfing down the omelettes that Polly, much to Pete's surprise, had offered to whip up.

"That hotel has got to be a financial drain most of the year," said Pete. "It's an ark. It's always under repair. And even in summer it's not full up."

"But he's got money coming out of his *ears,"* said Polly. "You're the one who told me that."

"Money is a finite resource," said Willy. "He wouldn't be the first multimillionaire to go bankrupt."

But still, Polly shook her head. "I think we should be talking about Joe Putnam. He was the first one out. He was the one with the information, the opportunity—"

"What about Kay?" asked Willy. "She was with him, don't forget."

Polly snorted. *"Kay."* But suddenly her voice changed. "She told me the relationship was on the rocks. That's not my idea of a relationship on the rocks—whose bed is smallest. She sounded like she was ready to unzip right there in the woods."

"Please," said Pete. Call him a prude, but he didn't think that was any way for a sister to talk.

But it didn't seem to bother Willy any. "True," he said.

"And, Pete, Joe told you things were definitely on with Kay?"

"Yeah," said Pete. "But I've been thinking about that. Things aren't always on when they're on."

"Or off when they're off," said Polly. "Believe me, I know from whence I'm talking."

Suddenly Willy seemed interested in the ketchup bottle. He picked it up and studied the label closely.

"But I still don't see that it matters what Joe and Kay are or aren't doing," said Pete quickly.

"It matters if Joe killed Cobie out of jealousy," said Polly, "and tried to cover up by denying the motive."

"But where does that leave the money?" asked Willy.

"What money?" said Pete. "So far it's still one coin."

Polly said nothing. Instead, she pointed to the chest from the *Royal Arms*, still sitting in the middle of the kitchen table. "Willy's right. We have to focus on the money. At least we know that Kay and Joe knew Cobie found a bunch of money."

"No, we don't," said Pete crossly. "All we know is that you told Kay you *think* Cobie found a bunch of money and that Joe heard us talking a bunch of garbage in the bar tonight."

"But the question is, did they kill Cobie?" asked Willy.

Polly's head snapped up from her plate. "'They?' Who said anything about 'they'? We're talking about Joe, not Kay."

"I know how you feel about Joe Putnam," said Willy quietly. "But right now Kay Dodd appears to see him differently. There were two of them in the woods. And don't forget it was Kay who rowed out to the wreck."

"And trashed her own apartment?"

"Maybe. It would be a smart move. It might eliminate her from the list, at least temporarily."

"Wait a minute," said Polly. "What about Ed and Bert?"

Pete waved a hand. "Forget about Ed and Bert."

"Why?"

"Because I know Ed and Bert a little better than you do. Forget it, all right?"

"Like I'm telling you to forget about Kay! She did *not*—"

"But do we forget about Jack Whiteaker?" interceded Willy.

They never got to decide if they should forget about Jack Whiteaker. They were interrupted by a knock.

Polly jumped up. She came back with her eyes popping and rolling and Joe Putnam trailing.

When he saw the police chief, Joe Putnam stopped cold in the doorway. "Guess you're busy. Just wanted to say I got the twine patched. We're on for the morning."

"It's Sunday," said Polly.

"Yeah? Tell that to the mackerel."

"Okay," said Pete. "See you in the morning." He looked at Willy, half expecting him to say something.

Willy said nothing.

Joe left, mumbling something about sunup coming early.

True, thought Pete. Sunup did come early. He should go to bed right now. But before he could rise from his chair, there was a second knock on the door, and Dave Snow entered the kitchen without waiting for an escort, waving a fistful of something that looked like Monopoly money.

"Hey! How are you, old man?" He shoved the notes into Pete's hand. "Here. Coupons for free drinks. I'm making the rounds. We open Memorial Day." He nodded to the chief, grinned at Polly, shoved more coupons at them.

"Polly, do you know, it's good to see you around here again. I mean it. I got to thinking after you left today. If you're looking for a job, I could use some help in the new restaurant. Maybe we should talk about it. Get together, have a drink—"

The chief stood. "It's late. Guess I'll hit the road."

Pete watched Polly try not to look surprised.

"Good night," said Willy.

"Good night," said Polly.

The chief left. Dave Snow slid into the chair next to Polly.

"Are you hitting every house on the island with those coupons?" Pete asked.

Dave laughed loudly. It occurred to Pete that he might have used a few of his own coupons before he came. "I'm not that desperate. And I wouldn't have bothered coming here if I didn't have . . . what do you call it? Inferior motives." He winked at Polly. "Actually, I was at Whiteaker's trying to steal his dinner guests away with these free coupons and I ran into Esther Small. I've been wondering what was going to happen to that old boat. I think I told you, I like that boat. But Esther says it's in your hands now. So I'll give you a thousand dollars."

Pete stared at Dave. *A thousand dollars?* "It's got no engine. Not much of anything else, either. And a bilge full of water."

"Hey, who cares? So it's a piece of junk. I just want to make sure that piece of junk stays where it is. It'll attract business."

"Right," said Polly. "You could put a fountain on it with a spotlight. Or run the daily specials up the mast."

"Let me talk to Esther," said Pete.

"I told you, I already talked to her. She says it's yours."

Suddenly Polly chimed in. "I told you Pete, I was interested in buying that boat. I'll give you twelve hundred."

Pete stared at her.

"Jeez, Polly," roared Dave. "What are *you* going to do with it? Okay, Pete. Two thousand. Take it or leave it."

"I don't know," said Pete, still peering in amazement at his sister. "Let me think about it."

Dave Snow collected his stash of coupons and left. He'd been a lot happier coming than he was going, Pete noticed. When the door had shut behind him, Pete turned to Polly. He was afraid to ask. "You want that boat?"

"No, of course not. But aren't you curious why Dave does?"

"No." Pete yawned and stood up. "I'm going to bed."

"Pete?"

He stopped at the door.

"About Willy. Maybe it *was* just dinner."

"Maybe," said Pete.

She said nothing else. Still, Pete thought she might have looked a hair disappointed. He headed for the stairs. It was late. He thought Polly might follow him. But when he left her, she continued to sit there, staring at the chest in the middle of the table.

Chapter
30

[He] showed us at the end into a great library,
all lined with bookcases . . .

It seemed to Pete daybreak came specially early the next morning, but once his eyes were fully open, he saw why.

The sun was out.

He blinked like a mole. *Sun.* On Nashtoba in May. He jumped out of bed and looked at the thermometer. Fifty-six degrees. He decided he could look forward to another week on the weirs if this kept up.

But by ten o'clock he saw how wrong he was. At least you could fend off the cold by keeping in motion. All you could do in the heat was to shed layers. By eleven both men were stripped to the waist, their flesh glistening. By noon Pete wished Joe Putnam would send him for another dunk. And as Pete thought about that dunk, he looked over his shoulder at Joe Putnam. Was it possible Polly was right about this guy? Pete doubted it. He'd known Joe Putnam since high school. Then again, he supposed every murderer was known since high school by somebody. And Joe had been out in the woods last night, looking for Cobie's treasure. And it was funny about Kay.

Or was it?

Pete decided to try to find out. But how? Joe was one of

those macho types who probably figured baring his soul was more dangerous than stepping into a sinkhole in waders. So how could Pete get him to talk? By baring his own soul first? Maybe.

Pete set the end of his dip net on the deck and leaned on it. "Whew. Getting hot."

"Here." Joe parked his net, went for the cooler, tossed Pete a Coke, took one for himself, and sat down on the cooler lid.

Pete drained half his Coke, wiped his mouth, and sighed a sigh that somehow came out more heartfelt than he'd intended. "I tell you, Joe, I don't know how you do this. I'm falling asleep every night with my toothbrush still in my mouth. I don't even have the strength to fight with Connie long-distance. Of course, you're not wasting any energy fighting with Kay—"

Joe snorted. "I'm not? If I could tap the sparks, I'd light up half New York." He crushed his empty can and threw it into the bow of the boat. "I don't know, the rules aren't the same anymore, you notice that? It used to be you could expect certain things. Fair was fair and foul was foul. Now what are we s'posed to do, just sit around and let 'em do what they want? Let 'em make fools out of us in front of the whole damned town?"

"I don't care whether I look like a fool to the whole town," said Pete. "What do they know about it? I just don't want to look like a fool around the people I care about."

"So what's a fool, will you tell me that? Somebody who doesn't give a shit what she does? Who doesn't lift a finger when she's outta line?"

"I guess it depends where the line came from."

Joe leaped to his feet. "There *aren't* any goddamned lines anymore! Everybody's just goddamned good friends! And people can be friends with whatever kind of a goddamned bum they want!" He picked up his dip net and chucked it like a spear as far as he could throw it. It pierced the twine and hung suspended in midair. Then he kicked the cooler.

But it seemed to Pete, Joe's boot decelerated before he made contact. Nothing sprang a leak, anyway.

Joe slumped onto the cooler and stared down at his boots, eyes black.

"I tell you, she's got me doing some crazy shit."

"Yeah," said Pete.

"So we talked. Yesterday we talked. When I heard what happened to her apartment, I went tearing over there, and she was glad I came. She said . . . Oh, she said some stuff. But how it ended up, she said I should be able to respect her judgment. She says she respects mine and wants to hear what I think, but in the end she's gonna do what *she* thinks is right, and I have to respect that. She said I should look at it reversed. Like if she told me she didn't like something I was doing, she'd want me to weigh her opinion in with my own, but in the end I'd have to do what I figure I ought. I don't know, it kinda made sense when she said it."

"It makes sense now."

Joe looked up. "Yeah. Well, I told her I figured I could do that. I could respect her judgment and all that. And after I told her that, it went all right." He chuckled. "And the *reason* she was sucking up to—" Joe stopped short. "Hey, what is this, a ladies' sewing circle? We've got work."

He picked up an oar and paddled the boat deftly the few feet needed to retrieve his net. Pete watched him, his mind going ten times as fast as that makeshift paddle. What "crazy shit" had Kay got Joe doing? Why, and to whom, was Kay "sucking up"? But suddenly Pete remembered something else, something Ozzie Dillingham had said. *Oars slapping water fit to kill.* Whoever had rowed in from Cobie's wreck that night didn't know much about rowing a boat. When you knew what you were doing, the oars didn't slap the water at all. And if there was one thing Pete could say about Joe Putnam, it was that when it came to anything around the water, he knew what he was doing.

So who didn't?

Pete gave up and sweated in silence alongside Joe until they were done. It wasn't until they'd almost reached the dock and Pete looked down the beach and saw the wreck, with Dave Snow's restaurant just beyond it, that he spoke again. "Tell me something. I'm fielding offers for Cobie's boat. In your professional opinion, what do you think it's worth?"

Joe twisted at the wheel to stare at Pete. "You think somebody's going to give you money for it? More likely they'll charge you to haul it out."

"Who said anything about hauling it out? It can just sit there, can't it?"

"It won't sit there long. Not without somebody bailing and caulking."

"So it sinks. So that's the end of it."

"Not in Freeman Studley's harbor, it isn't. On top of the water it's just an eyesore. Underneath, it's a hazard to navigation, and the owner's liable for any damage it causes. And it's a hell of a lot easier to move her while she still floats."

As they pulled in to the dock, Pete looked down the beach again toward Dave Snow's new restaurant. If he were smart he'd go there now, take that two thousand dollars, and hand it to Esther. But that was assuming the offer still stood, and that was assuming a lot. By now, Dave Snow would have sobered up.

Pete drooped through the door an hour later to find a hopping mad Polly, dancing around and pointing a finger in his face. "Okay. Where is it?"

Pete kept going toward the porch, and he stayed out there until he'd shed his boots and his jacket and his sudden urge to pound something. When he returned to the kitchen he said calmly, "Where's what?"

Polly pointed at the kitchen table. "It's *mine*. You had no right to take it."

"Take *what?*"

"The *chest*. The treasure chest!"

Pete looked at the empty kitchen table. "I didn't touch the chest."

"Who has it? Willy?"

"Listen to me, will you? I didn't touch it. I didn't give it to Willy. It was on the kitchen table last night. It was on the table this morning."

Or was it? He'd eaten his Wheaties sitting at the table that morning. There was no box there that morning. Pete swiveled from the table to Polly. "Wait a minute. It was gone when I got up. What happened to it?"

"I'll tell you what happened to it. It was stolen. Whoever has that treasure needs to have that chest if he wants to double the treasure's worth. And I know who stole it."

"Wait a minute," said Pete again. It seemed to him he'd been saying that a lot lately.

"No, I won't wait," and she didn't. She went to the phone and picked it up. As she waited to connect she kept talking. "Joe Putnam was in this kitchen last night. He saw that chest. I bet you he came back in the middle of the night—"

Joe Putnam again. The man who had just admitted to Pete he'd been doing some crazy shit lately.

Someone on the other end of the phone had apparently picked up. Polly was saying hello, giving her name.

"Who are you calling?"

She raised a dark eyebrow at him. "Who do you think? Willy."

The same three faces sat around Pete's kitchen table.

"Joe Putnam took it," said Polly again. "He was in this kitchen. He saw it on the table."

Which was true, but despite what Pete had heard on the weirs that day, or maybe because of it, he couldn't see Joe Putnam sneaking into his house in the middle of the night and lurching off with the chest in his fist. "Dave Snow saw it, too," he reminded her. "And I'd like to know what he was thinking when he offered all that money for Cobie's boat. Joe Putnam said nobody in his right mind would give me a red cent."

"Right," said Polly. "Joe Putnam's had a lot of things to say about all this."

"And you said Esther Small was here," Willy tossed in.

Pete eyed him curiously. "Yes. But I don't see where that fits."

Willy grinned. "Me, either."

Pete gave up. He was tired of speculating. And besides, he was hungry. He got up and went to the refrigerator, but the refrigerator was unforthcoming. "Anyone for pizza?"

Willy pushed back his chair. "I guess I'll get going."

"You haven't eaten, have you?" asked Polly. "You must be hungry."

Pete turned, surprised. He saw Willy pause, half out of his chair, trying not to look surprised in the slightest. "Starving, as a matter of fact."

But the minute he sank back into his chair, the conversation seemed to dry up.

Pete dredged up the first thing he could think of. "Cobie's coin. You've seen it, Polly?"

"At Hugh Platt's. It's beautiful. Once you've seen it, you can't forget it. I keep picturing Cobie stumbling across that chest, smashing it open, seeing all that gold shining up at him."

"Gold digger," said Pete.

"You don't have to be a gold digger to get excited about that," said Willy. "It's not just money, it's history."

"That's it," said Polly eagerly. "You stare at King George's profile and remember how old that coin is."

"And where it's been," said Willy.

"And who touched it last," said Polly.

"Hugh Platt," said Pete.

They glared at him.

Pete moved to the phone. "Who wants what?"

"Mushroom and black olive," said Polly just as Willy said "Sausage and pepperoni."

Pete went to the phone and ordered one of each.

"So anyway," said Polly. "You should stop by sometime and ask Hugh Platt to show you the coin."

"I might do that," said Willy.

Silence again.

This time it was Willy who rescued them. "So how long have you two known Kay Dodd?"

"I've known her since I was sixteen," said Polly. "I met her at school. She moved here in our sophomore year. Joe Putnam was a senior. They've been going out off and on ever since."

Pete stood. "I guess I'll get the pizzas."

Polly whirled around, looking a little panicked. "Now? You've only just ordered."

"I know, but you got me curious. Hugh Platt is on the way. I thought I'd stop in and check out this famous King George."

Polly turned to Willy. "Don't you want to go with him?"

Willy yawned. Pete bet it was fake. "I'm beat. If you don't mind, I'd rather sit. So Kay and Joe met when they were in high school?"

"They met when Joe got kicked out for bashing somebody's head into a locker. And when they let him back in, the kid came up to Joe and said he guessed he'd never try that again, and you know what Joe did?"

"Bashed the kid into the locker again."

"Yes," said Polly.

"And Kay Dodd was impressed, is that it?"

Polly's eyes widened. "Yes, she was. The kid Joe beat up had been picking on her little brother. It was right after that Kay and Joe started going out."

"Interesting," said Willy.

"Yes," said Polly thoughtfully.

"Okay," said Pete. "I'm out of here."

They didn't seem to hear him.

Very interesting, thought Pete.

When Hugh Platt heard what Pete was there for, he blinked at him curiously. "You want to see the coin? The coin Cobie Small found?"

It sounded better than the real reason—that he was trying to get out of the house so his sister could start learning who to fear and who not to fear. But yes, he was curious about the coin. After all this, how could he not be? "If it's not too much trouble. Polly told me it was worth a look."

The great blue heron thrust out his neck, suddenly all smiles. "Oh, it is that, I assure you. Come with me, please."

He walked in that odd bent-legged strut to the library. "If you would care to wait here? I have not yet had the coin mounted and displayed with my other artifacts. It's in the safe."

He waved toward the divan in front of the window, but Pete didn't sit. Last time he'd been in this room he'd been dragged here by Polly and one of her supposedly pressing agendas. This time he could afford a closer look. Those funny, salt-pitted bottles, that heavy brass spike on the desk, the model ships . . . Pete moved to one of the ships. "Did you make these models?"

"Yes, yes, I did. But don't look too closely, I beg you. I'm afraid I've made the usual landlubber's mistakes. I'll be back momentarily. Please, make yourself comfortable."

Hugh left. Still, Pete didn't sit. Now it was the books that drew him. He moved to the shelves, cocked his head sideways, and began to scan titles.

It seemed as if every book ever written on New England history was in the room, from thin pamphlets published by local church groups to thick volumes in six-book sets published by the big conglomerates in New York. Where to start? Pete had been held spellbound in this room once already, listening to tales of rum in boots and roads of ice and frostbite. He decided to head for the shipwreck section. He sought out a thick volume and flipped to the index.

There it was, the *General Newcomb*.

The phone on the desk jangled. Pete jumped, already deep into the past, but the ring was quickly cut off. Pete hoped the call was for Hugh, that he had picked it up elsewhere. Pete was in no hurry to leave this book—he had just been reacquainted with an old friend, Captain Rum-in-the-Boots Harvey.

* * *

Polly got up and fished two Ballantines out of the refrigerator. She saw Willy wince almost imperceptibly. "I know. But it's all he ever buys these days. It's because of Connie. She's got him addicted to the rotten stuff." Polly took a sip of her own and grinned. "I guess I'm getting used to it myself."

Willy took a swig and gazed at the can thoughtfully. "People get used to lots of things. Sometimes that's a good thing. Sometimes it isn't. Take Kay Dodd, for example. From what you've said about her relationship with Joe Putnam, it wasn't so nice. But maybe she got used to it. Maybe it got to seem normal to her. Or maybe she didn't think so much of herself, felt she deserved no better, or decided he'd changed, decided she could go back and keep her dignity. Isn't that how it usually works? Then she and Joe cooked up this scheme about Cobie—"

Polly set down her can with a crack. "No. That's not Kay you're talking about. At least not the Kay I know now. If you'd heard what she said about him, or even seen her place before it got wrecked, if you'd heard her talk about the Pulitzer. You don't talk like that when you don't think much of yourself."

"Okay," said Willy, as if she'd actually said something that made sense. "So I guess the question then is, why is the new Kay back with the old Joe?"

"I don't know," said Polly. "Maybe . . ." she summoned all her nerve and looked straight into Willy's gray eyes. "Okay, maybe I've gone overboard about Joe. I must have if Kay . . . if they . . ." She looked down. "But even if I'm wrong about Joe, I'm not wrong about Kay. In the first place, I saw a picture she took of Cobie. I listened to her talk about him. And I was with her when she saw that apartment. You saw her soon after. Are you trying to tell me she acted like someone who did that to her own apartment? She was *upset*. There's no way Kay Dodd did that to herself."

"Or killed Cobie?"

"Or killed Cobie," said Polly.

"Okay," said Willy. "So who's next on the list?"

Apparently, Captain Harvey's feat aboard the *General Newcomb* during the blizzard was far from the only shining achievement of his career. He had commanded the privateer in numerous battles and had almost single-handedly managed to acquire a large number of cannon for the colonies, as well as enough gold and silver to amply supplement the colonial treasury. And there it was in black and white, the plundering of the *Royal Arms*, the entry ending with a regretful note about the never-recovered purser's box of gold. It was too bad Hugh Platt hadn't glanced through his own bookcase more thoroughly, thought Pete. He'd have found everything he needed to know about the treasure chest right here.

And where was Hugh? That phone call must have been for him, after all. Pete replaced the thick volume and pulled out a thinner but taller one, this one complete with pictures. Again he went straight to the index, and there, again, was the *General Newcomb*. Pete flipped pages. The story was much the same as the one Hugh had told, but this book also mentioned the plunder of the *Royal Arms*, the missing chest of British gold. So what was the big mystery? Here was the whole story, right here in Hugh Platt's bookcase. How could Hugh Platt have remained ignorant of the box of gold? Hadn't he ever opened these books? Pete looked at the book still resting in his hands. *Shipwrecks of New England.* He'd heard that particular title before, somewhere, somehow . . .

And then he remembered. He flipped to the inside back cover, and there it was. The cardboard pocket. The library card.

Pete heard footsteps. He turned. Hugh Platt stood in the library door, staring at the long-lost library book in Pete's hands.

It was all right there in front of Pete's eyes. The documentation on the *Royal Arms.* The missing library book. The ship models with the landlubber's mistakes, mistakes a man who "rowed like a drunk" might make.

And the panic in Hugh's face.

He lunged awkwardly toward Pete, reaching for the book.

Pete sidestepped, one hand holding up the book like a shield, the other hand pointing at Hugh like a sword. He had one second in which to feel ridiculous before the fury took hold. "A word of warning," said Pete. "I'm no sixty-year-old drunk. And you don't have an anchor this time."

Hugh Platt stepped back.

Phew, thought Pete.

And then he saw Hugh Platt's fingers reach behind him toward the desk and close around that long brass spike.

Chapter
31

His eyebrows were very black, and moved readily, and
this gave him a look of some temper, not bad, you
would say, but quick and high.

"Okay," said Polly, fully into it now, forgetting for the
minute who she was talking to, "who's next on the list? You
mean after Joe Putnam? Let's see. We can assume whoever
trashed the wreck trashed Esther's room and Kay's apartment."

"Never assume anything about anybody," said Willy, but
the second after he said it, he grinned sheepishly. "I'm
coming out with some great pronouncements today, aren't
I? But okay, let's assume that for now."

"And the person who did all that trashing is the one who
stole the chest from this kitchen?"

"I'd be willing to assume that, too."

"And that whoever did all those things also killed Cobie."
Willy nodded.

"So if the same person did it all, it should eliminate a few.
One person had to be at Cobie's wreck that Friday night, at
Esther's room a week later, at Kay's apartment two days
after that, and sneaking into Pete's kitchen the same night.
One person had to know that Cobie had money, that Esther
and Kay went out to the wreck, that we had the *Royal Arms*
chest. What do you think?"

As Willy looked at her, it dawned on Polly this wasn't the look she usually got—the one reserved for brainless girl-friends or dippy younger sisters.

"I don't know," he said. "What do *you* think?"

Hugh Platt stood blocking the one doorway, his eye on Pete. Pete stood back to the wall, his eye on that spike. It could make a nice, neat puncture wound in somebody's head. It could crush it if it was swung just right. Still, Hugh Platt had a good ten years on Pete, and he was face-to-face with him, not sneaking up behind him. And Pete was cold sober. *Boy,* was he sober. If push came to shove, there was no way Pete would end up like Cobie.

Was there?

"So this is why you came here," said Hugh. "To make sure I had the book. It wasn't to see the coin. You knew about me all along."

If Pete had known all along, he wouldn't have come here at all. He wasn't that much of an idiot. But he decided it couldn't hurt to let Hugh overestimate him a bit. "What else could it mean if you had the book? You must have taken it the night you killed him. But why did you want it? There are plenty of books on your shelf that told you all you needed to know about the *General Newcomb* and the *Royal Arms.* You lied to us when you told us you'd never heard anything about it."

"Of course I did. Did you really believe for one minute that a person in my position wouldn't know every last obscure detail of the events surrounding that shipwreck? Including every last tall tale of the missing chest of gold from the *Royal Arms?*"

"But they weren't tall tales."

Hugh's teeth gleamed. "No, they weren't. But even I wasn't sure Cobie had actually found it until I heard him spouting off that night at Lupo's. The drinks on the general. This money of his being a drop in the bucket compared to what was to come. I'd suspected the minute he came to me with the coin, of course. I attempted to talk to him adult to adult. But he wouldn't come clean. That night in the bar I knew for certain what he'd found. It troubled me. It ate away at me. I knew what would happen to that miraculous find if it were left in Cobie's hands. He would sell it off coin by coin, drink it away bottle by bottle. He would use the chest as a place to store his . . . his *teeth*."

"So you felt justified in killing him."

Hugh Platt winced. "I did *not* feel justified in killing him. I hadn't the foggiest notion he was there. I was driving home. I saw the wreck. I assumed if Cobie had found the gold, it would be out there somewhere. The dinghy was on the beach. I assumed Cobie was still on shore."

And now Pete winced. So Connie had been right. It had come down to them leaving the dinghy on shore after all.

"I rowed out to the wreck. I was sure the chest was there. I was sure a simple mind such as Cobie's couldn't have found a place to hide it that would escape me. All that was needed was a cursory search, and I would be home free. But as I said, I hadn't expected to find Cobie there."

"So he woke up and saw you. And you killed him."

Hugh Platt jerked his head from side to side. "No, no, no. Exactly what do you think I am? Yes, he woke up and saw me. I was perfectly honest with the man. I told him exactly why I was there. And again, I tried to reason with him. I spelled out the historical significance of what he'd found. I told him it belonged in a museum. And he laughed at me. He wouldn't even show it to me. He stood there in those ridiculous, foul-smelling long johns, gaping at me, sniggling away, and I'm sorry to say I was overcome with an emotion so intense it . . . it . . . I'm afraid I have to say it temporarily blocked any finer feeling I might ordinarily possess. The boat pitched suddenly, and I reached out for something to steady myself. My hand closed on the anchor. I don't know, I don't recall consciously thinking about it, consciously yanking it free, but the next thing I knew, it was loose in my hands. Cobie, too, had begun to lose his footing and he turned his back to me, clutching the edge of his bunk. There he was, an ignorant, useless human being, standing between me and my dreams. So I swung the anchor——" Hugh Platt stopped, gazing down at his hand, the hand that still clutched the brass spike. Pete considered taking a flying leap at him, but even as the thought crossed his mind, Hugh's grip shifted on the spike.

But Hugh Platt's mind had apparently never left Cobie's cabin. "I hit him in the back of the head. He pitched forward into the bunk. Dead. In that one instant he was dead."

"No, he wasn't," said Pete. "But you didn't know that, did you? He didn't die from the wound, he died from drowning. But you thought he was dead. Is that why you threw him overboard?"

"Of course I thought he was dead! Good *God,* you should have seen the blood! And he collapsed before my eyes, facedown onto the bunk, that hideous wound gaping up at me. I suppose I was fortunate in one way. He bled into a thick blanket, nothing else. I was able to wrap the blanket around him and deposit him over the side."

"With the anchor."

Again, Hugh Platt looked at his hands. "There was blood on the anchor. I had to dispose of the anchor. I don't know, I think for a minute I went mad."

"But not mad enough to forget to turn the cabin inside out looking for the treasure. And the book? Why did you keep the book?"

"I didn't know what to do with the book. I assumed sooner or later Cobie would wash up on the beach, someone would find him, and decide, as they apparently did for a brief period, that he'd tumbled overboard by accident. I was sure the anchor would sink to the bottom and stay there. I never imagined something heavy like that would travel all the way out to become caught in the weirs. But I couldn't run the risk of the *book* washing ashore. And I certainly couldn't leave it there."

But Pete still didn't get it. "Why not?"

"Because it was about shipwrecks! Because it was the first stop on the trail! The *General Newcomb* was in there! I couldn't run the risk of others stumbling onto the rest of it, of getting there ahead of me."

"So you stuck it in with all your other books, like *The Purloined Letter*. And that's where it was the day Polly came inquiring about it?"

Again, Hugh smiled. "No. As a matter of fact, it was your sister's visit that put me in mind of *The Purloined Letter* in the first place. Before she got here the book was hidden under those sofa cushions, but once I realized Polly knew and the librarian knew that Cobie had come here, I concluded it was at least conceivable that the police, too, would come here asking questions or, worse, poking around. And if they happened to find the book *hidden,* how would that look?"

"Incriminating," said Pete. "Right. But in your bookshelf it might just mean that Cobie left it here and you accidentally shoved it in the shelves. You have a lot of books to keep track of."

"I suppose my thinking might have run along lines similar to that," said Hugh, somewhat condescendingly, Pete thought.

"So the day Polly and I came here together, the book was right up there in the shelf. And you knew all about the gold that had been aboard the *Newcomb*. But you diverted us neatly, didn't you? You took our minds off it fast enough. It was some story, that story about the northeaster and the rum in the boots and the frozen bodies."

Hugh drew himself up. "That was no story. Every word I told you was true and fully documented. Any fool would have been diverted by it."

Pete decided to ignore that *fool* bit. Besides, he'd just realized something he should have picked up on sooner. Hugh didn't find the treasure in Cobie's cabin. If he had, he wouldn't have cared who found the book or stumbled on the trail.

And if he had, he wouldn't have had to do all the other things he had done later.

* * *

"Okay," said Polly, "let's start at the beginning. We start with someone killing Cobie and trashing his cabin looking for the treasure. Then he trashed Esther's room and Kay's apartment. Then he steals the chest."

"That's not the beginning," said Willy. "The beginning is Cobie showing up at Lupo's with the money."

Polly sat up. "No, it isn't either! The beginning is Cobie finding the gold coin."

Willy nodded. "Okay. So let's start with the gold coin. That's really the first inkling anyone had that Cobie might have found something. So who knew about the coin?"

"Cobie took it to Ben Hopkins at the coin shop over on Arapo."

"Ben Hopkins," said Willy. "Okay. Who else?"

"Let's see. Then he took it to Hugh Platt. Then back to Ben, where he sold it, and then it went back to Hugh, who bought it from Ben. And there it's remained ever since."

"Okay," said Willy. "Did anyone else know about the coin? Think."

"Cobie told Esther he would buy her a house and a car. But she says she didn't believe him, that she knew nothing about any gold, and she left. I can't think of anyone else who might have known about the coin."

"Someone who saw him find it, maybe."

"Someone on the water," said Polly. "Dave Snow. Pit Patterson. Jack Whiteaker."

"You've forgotten your friend Joe Putnam," said Willy.

Polly dipped her head, trying not to look too pleased that her horse was still in the running. "So these people could have known about the coin, might have suspected Cobie had money, might have killed him. Now which of them knew that Esther went out to the wreck?"

"Joe Putnam," said Willy again. "Or, again, anyone around the harbor—Dave Snow, Jack Whiteaker, Pit Patterson."

"Or anyone who heard she'd arrived, heard we'd found her out there."

"Or anyone you told. Did you tell anyone? Think."

Polly thought. She couldn't remember. She looked at the clock. "I'll tell you what I think. I think our pizza's getting cold." She got up and got two more Ballantines out of the refrigerator.

Chapter
32

I could see by the workings of his face that he was trying to think, and the process was so slow and laborious, that . . . I laughed out loud.

Think, Pete told himself. What was Hugh Platt talking about now? But it was hard to think with those knuckles still wrapped around that brass spike.

What had happened after the actual murder? Esther Small's room had been ransacked. Why? Because she'd been out to the wreck, might have uncovered the treasure. And Hugh Platt must have known that, too. And how had he known Esther Small had been out to the wreck? Because Pete and Polly had told him! Right in this room. Now all their own idiocy came crashing back to Pete item by item. They'd led Hugh to Esther, and they'd led him to Kay, too. Polly had told him about Kay Dodd's friendship with Cobie. She'd also told him they had the treasure chest.

But now what? How far was Hugh in? How deranged was he? Was he willing to kill Pete to keep him quiet about Cobie? He'd almost have to, wouldn't he?

And it seemed to Pete that the very minute the thought occurred to Pete, it occurred to Hugh also. The hand on the spike rotated, hefted.

* * *

"Okay, enough," said Polly suddenly. "We're not going anywhere. We're going in circles. Let's talk about something else. How'd you make out with that snapping turtle?"

"I don't know," said Willy. "I think we're missing something. Let's try Kay Dodd again."

Polly's eyes must have flickered.

"I'm talking about what happened to her apartment. Who knew she went out to the wreck?"

"Me. And I told Pete. But anyone who knew she was friendly with Cobie might consider her place a good place to check out."

"Okay. Now let's go back to the chest and the list of people who knew it was in this kitchen. That list should be shortest."

"I knew it was here. Pete knew. Joe Putnam, Dave Snow. Esther. Oh! And I told Ben Hopkins about it. And Hugh Platt."

They looked at each other.

Willy looked at the clock. "That's one cold pizza."

Pete said the first, no, the second thing that occurred to him. "Why did you steal Cobie's money?"

For a minute Hugh looked blank. Then his brow cleared. "Oh, *that* money. The money in the envelope under the mattress. I'm afraid after I killed Cobie and disposed of his body I acted illogically. I ran around the cabin tearing it to shreds, looking for the gold, looking for the chest. Once I'd exhausted the search, and myself, I collapsed onto the bench by the table. When I looked around and saw what I'd done, I was horrified. I knew I couldn't leave the place looking like that if it were to appear that his death was an accident. Still, I didn't dare stay much longer. I doubted Cobie had many friends, but it appeared he had one. Someone who had rowed him out and put him to bed and then gone home, leaving the dinghy on the beach. Would that friend come back to check on him?"

No, he wouldn't, thought Pete. But neither would anybody

else. The end result would probably have been the same, but God only knew how long Cobie would have lain on his bunk bleeding to death if Hugh hadn't tossed him overboard.

Hugh Platt rattled on, brow furrowed as he tried to retrace his actions. Was this the first time he'd thought about it in this much detail? It had to be the first time he'd spoken about it out loud, and there was something eerie about it, as if he were almost proud to be able to explain the clever way his mind had worked that last Friday evening.

"I decided the simplest thing was to pocket the cash and make the entire episode appear as nothing more than theft. Cobie had flashed his money around the bar. Everyone knew of its existence. So that's what I decided. That's why I took it."

"I see," said Pete. "Good thinking." Something in his tone must have sounded the way he felt.

"Oh, enough of all this," Hugh snapped. "Where is it?"

It wasn't what Pete had expected to hear next. The sound of his own skull splintering had seemed the best guess. "Where is what?"

"Please," said Hugh. "Let's not be more idiotic than necessary. You didn't come here to see my one measly King George III guinea. You have a chest of them. Or rather, I have the chest now, but you must have the gold. Where is it? Where did you find it? I'm warning you, I've come this far, I'll go the rest of the way without hesitating."

Pete thought fast. Or as fast as his exhausted brain would let him. "Don't *you* be more idiotic than necessary. First of all, you should be able to figure out by now that I don't have the gold, either. If I did, why would I come here at all? To gloat about it? Would I have stood around all this time waiting to take a brass spike between the eyes? I don't think so. If you ask me, Cobie hid the gold, and it looks like he hid it where none of us will ever find it. Polly found that empty chest in Garret Gold, right where Cobie had left it for safekeeping. But he didn't leave the gold there. At least, I don't think he did. I don't know where he left it."

Pete watched Hugh. He'd told him the truth. But did Hugh believe him? And if he didn't . . .

The two realizations hit Pete almost at once. First, that Hugh did believe him. Pete could see it in his face, the bleak despair as he saw the gold once again slip through his fingers. But the despair wasn't there long. It was replaced by something else, something that diminished Pete instantly in his eyes. But what had Pete suddenly lost?

The second realization came harder than the first. Pete had just lost his worth. He'd lost his bargaining chip for life. He had just admitted to Hugh he had no idea where the gold was. He was no longer of use to him.

And as Pete watched, Hugh's face changed again, filling with some sort of conviction, a resolve of some sort. But a resolve to do what? And then Pete saw what Hugh Platt had just resolved. He'd resolved to survive. He wasn't going to march calmly off to jail for Cobie's murder. And what was the only thing standing between him and freedom?

Pete.

Hugh Platt took a step foreward, spike clenched. *I've got two choices,* thought Pete. *I can jump the guy or I can reason with him.* Pete decided to try reason first. After all, even Hugh, before he'd resorted to murder, had tried to reason with Cobie.

"You might think of one minor point before you come any closer with that spike," said Pete. "You said something about since you've come this far, you might as well go further. Not true. So far you're only in up to your neck. You haven't gone under. You hit Cobie on the head. That's all you did. It resulted in his death, sure, but the worst we're talking about is second-degree, not first-degree, murder. There's a big difference." At least, Pete hoped there was. Actually he didn't have a clue what he was talking about, but as he looked at Hugh Platt, he decided Hugh didn't have a clue, either. "But if you kill me, that's murder one. That's big time. I suggest you think about that."

But the hand on the spike only worked its grip tighter.

Okay, so much for reason. Pete cast around for a weapon, and as his eye landed on the funny-shaped bottle, so did Hugh's.

"No!" cried Hugh. "Not that!"

Pete snatched up the bottle.

Hugh Platt lunged.

And Pete did what he'd seen a few thousand times in the old movies. He dropped horizontal to the ground and rolled. In the movies the maneuver knocked the assailant's feet from under him and sent him crashing to the ground. In life, Pete found, it worked differently. He rolled *under* Hugh's feet as Hugh leaped, and while Pete was under them, the feet came down square on top of him, smack in the middle of his solar plexus. The blow knocked the bottle out of Pete's hand and the air out of his lungs, along with a goodly portion of his enthusiasm. He lay on the floor struggling to breathe, looking at the brass spike and the mad eyes above him.

And then Pete saw something else, and it took everything he had in him to keep his eyes from flickering. He needed a minute. A second, even, might do it. It shouldn't be impossible. Obviously, Hugh was having difficulty dispatching Pete in cold blood or Pete would have been dead long ago. He sucked in what little air he could. "Murder . . . one," he croaked.

And yes, Hugh paused. "You have an interesting way of looking at things. But first-degree, second-degree, what does all that matter? A murderer is a murderer. If a murderer is caught, he goes to jail. What does it matter if he goes to jail for one murder or two murders?"

"Or if the murderer is alive or dead?" said the voice behind Hugh.

In one fluid motion Willy McOwat planted his gun muzzle above Hugh's ear and twisted the hand holding the brass spike behind him.

The explosion and Hugh's scream of agony came one on top of the other.

Chapter
33

What a supper I had of it that night, with all my
friends around me; . . .

"It was the spike," said Willy for the tenth time. "I twisted
his arm, the spike flew out, landed on his foot and smashed
the bottle on the rebound. He screamed bloody murder."

"I thought you shot him," said Polly.

"And I thought you were going to wait in the car," said
Willy.

"I wouldn't be sitting here talking to you if you'd shot
him," said Polly.

"And I might not be sitting here talking to you if he
hadn't at least considered it," said Pete hotly.

It was late. Very late. And they'd finally met up in Pete's
kitchen to consume a couple of revamped pizzas.

"Hugh Platt," said Willy after a few silent bites. "Funny
how we all sort of figured it together."

"It was crazy," said Polly. "It was the pizza that did it,
finally. Thinking about you over there while we were
starving to death, listening to some jolly old tale about
shipwrecks."

"Yeah," said Pete. "Real jolly."

"We'd been talking about Hugh and about how I'd told

him we had the chest. And then I remembered that wasn't all we'd told him."

"Yeah," said Pete again. "We told him everything. About Esther going out to the wreck, about Kay being buddy-buddy with Cobie."

"And the only reason he didn't fall for our trap in the woods was because he wasn't here to get the rumor. He was giving a lecture in Bradford. He told me."

"So finally we looked at the clock," said Willy. "And it occurred to us that even you wouldn't leave a pizza sitting around cooling its heels forever."

"And that's how we figured out Hugh might have done it and that you might be in trouble," said Polly.

"Well, you took your sweet time about it," said Pete.

"And so did you!" cried Polly.

Pete was about to snap at Polly in protest, but when he raised his eyes from his pizza, he saw she wasn't looking at him. She was looking over his head, grinning from ear to ear.

Pete turned.

Connie.

"But we said *Wednesday,*" said Pete for the third time.

It was the third time that did it. Connie unwound herself from his arms and pushed back the covers. "Okay, I'll go back. At least my mother will be glad to see me. She said good-bye as if she never expected to see me again."

Pete pulled her against him. "At last your mother and I have something in common. That's just how I felt when you left. I convinced myself something would happen, an old boyfriend, a life change—"

"Oh ye of little faith," said Connie, but she held on to him tighter. "I wanted to come home, really. It was just that they were so glad to see me."

"I know. I'm sorry. You felt you had to stay. I should have respected your judgment."

"Oh, I don't know, sometimes my judgment's lousy."

She could feel Pete's grin against her forehead in the dark. "We all lapse occasionally."

For a while neither of them said anything, did anything, except to lie wrapped up in each other. But finally Connie found her thoughts drifting back to other things, things that still needed explaining.

"So Hugh Platt killed Cobie. Over an empty box."

"Mmm," said Pete.

"And you still haven't found the treasure."

"Mmm," said Pete.

"So where did Polly and Willy take off to like that?"

"Burgers."

"On Nashtoba? At this time of night? And didn't they just eat a pizza?"

"Mmm," said Pete.

And *hmmm,* thought Connie. It was something else she'd have to thank them for. She clutched Pete even harder. "I tell you, I'd like to think that I could go away for a couple of days and not come home just in time to miss seeing you murdered."

Pete didn't answer.

Connie drew away just far enough to look at him. They didn't have any curtains yet, and there was just enough moonlight for her to be able to see him. His eyes were closed. His face seemed thinner, with circles under his eyes, the shadow of tomorrow's beard dusting his jaw, a drawn look around the mouth. But despite the fact that his face looked thinner, the rest of him felt bulkier, as if he'd been lifting weights. Pete? Weights? Still, it didn't appear that his vacation was doing much for him.

Well, Connie would have to see to that. She brushed his eyebrow with her lips, the bridge of his nose, the corner of his mouth, his neck . . .

Nothing moved.

He was asleep.

Okay, so she'd see to it in the morning.

* * *

Polly woke again to the sound of Pete dragging his feet down the stairs. He was late. She could hear him charging around the kitchen, shuffling through cupboards, dragging his boots in from the porch. Polly stayed put till she heard the door close behind him, then she got up, took her shower, packed up her bags, and crept quietly down the stairs.

Polly took a look in the refrigerator. It was bare. So she'd have to hit Mable's Donut Shop on the way out of town. She reached into the side pouch of her suitcase and pulled out a lumpy parcel. She peeled away the tissue paper and lined up the marble chessmen on the kitchen table, slipping her note under the king. She stepped back and studied her arrangement. No. She removed the note from under the king, placed it under the queen, and grinned. She hefted her bags, took a last look around Pete's kitchen, and went out the door.

She was surprised to see the signs of a nice day pending. The sky was just flushing with sun, the fog was wheeling off the marsh, the faint breeze carried, not a hint of summer, maybe, but at least a hint of better things to come. And as Polly's gaze floated toward the water, a curious urge struck her. She dropped her bags where she stood and ran.

She ran till she hit the sand and stopped. The sound was pearly blue and calm. She looked to the right, where the sand curved like a sickle and disappeared around the bend. Then she looked to the left.

His house wasn't far down the beach.

It was only polite, wasn't it, to tell him she was leaving?

She set off across the sand, and whether she would have persevered all the way to his door she'd never know, because the minute she rounded the bend that brought his path into view, she saw him sitting in the sand, khakis rolled up, feet bare.

He started to get up. Polly started to sit down. They did an awkward up-down thing and grinned. Willy pointed to the sand and half bowed. Polly sat and he joined her.

"You do this every morning, come out here and sit in the sand?"

"When I can."

The tide was on its way out. Polly watched a gull scoop a quahog off the newly exposed sand, soar high, open its beak, and let the clam fly. It hit the rock dead on. They heard it crack open.

"Good aim," said Willy.

After a minute Polly said, "So tell me. Do you think Cobie found a full chest? Do you think there's still some treasure out there somewhere?"

"Probably."

Polly whipped around. "So why am I the only one who cares? You and Esther Small! And *Pete*. I tell you . . . Listen," she started again, "I just came to say good-bye. I'm heading out. I forgot to tell you last night. Thanks for that, by the way. I was trying to figure out how to get out of there and give them some room when you hit on that idea about the burgers."

"Some great idea. Burgers. At eleven o'clock. Here."

"So what? They don't have to know we drove to the dock and sat in the car. But I wanted to say one more thing. I shouldn't have said what I said last night about you shooting Hugh Platt. You'd only do what you had to, I should know that. And if you hadn't been there—"

"He might have dropped the spike on *Pete's* toe."

Polly laughed.

Willy stood. "I'd better get moving."

"Another big case?"

"Pete's case, actually. That kid staying in Hillerman's boathouse. Pete smelled something fishy, I ran a check on the kid, and sure enough, he's a fifteen-year-old runaway from Westwood. His parents arrive this morning to collect him. I told him I'd take him out for pancakes first, get his strength up." Willy grinned. "And you think life here is dull."

Polly thought of the night before, Willy's gun to Hugh Platt's head, her brother's face. "No," she said. "Not anymore."

213

Willy held out a hand. Polly took it, and he pulled her to her feet.

"Good-bye," he said.

"Good-bye," said Polly.

She turned, paused, turned back. *He's not stupid. He's not sixteen, either.* "I guess there's one more thing I want to say. To . . . to explain, I mean. When Pete said . . . I didn't want you to think . . . It wasn't because I—" she stopped. "I guess I just wanted to say that I enjoyed our dinner."

"Good. Me, too."

Encouraged, Polly pushed on. "And I know I've acted a little strangely. It's just that this isn't the best time for me right now. I guess I just need a sort of a . . . a sabbatical."

For some reason Willy nodded as if she'd made perfect sense. "Okay. Keep in touch. Call me if you find any stray turtles."

Polly grinned, turned again, actually got ten yards down the beach this time, paused again. "And you call me if you find that treasure!"

Chapter
34

That was, at least, the end of that; and before noon, to
my inexpressible joy, the highest rock of Treasure
Island had sunk into the blue round of the sea.

"It's drying up," said Joe Putnam. "Couple more days and
we'll be out of here."

Pete peered over the side of the skiff into the crystal clear
water. He saw the shadowy backs circling underneath them.
Still a lot of fish, but even Pete could see that there were
fewer of them. A couple more days? That would put it at
Wednesday. Suddenly those four remaining vacation days
began to glisten brightly. He and Connie should get out of
here, he thought. Go to Boston, check into a nice hotel.
Okay, it was no world tour, but still, it would leave the
phone, the responsibilities behind them.

Pete reached for his net and was surprised to see Joe
Putnam standing still, staring off toward the horizon, as if
he were trying to find the exact spot where soft sky reached
down and touched hard water. "I don't know," said Joe.
"Damn tricky business. Don't know as I'll ever figure it
out."

"Figure what out?"

"Oh, Kay. I told her it finally made sense her hanging out
with Cobie once I found out about that treasure. I figured

that's what she was kissing up to him for. What else could she see in the old coot? And know what she said? She said I was deaf, dumb, and blind, that I couldn't tell a soft-shell clam from a quahog, and she didn't care how many chests of gold there were out there, because nobody could buy the Pulitzer. Now I ask you, what the hell is that supposed to mean?"

It seemed plain enough to Pete, but he knew that wasn't the point.

"I don't know," he said. "Why don't you ask her?"

Joe turned. "Yeah. Ask her." He picked up his net and lit into the fish, but he didn't get far before he stopped again. "Tell me something. You think there's really a treasure out there somewhere?"

Pete paused with his netful of dripping mackerel in midair. "Yeah, somewhere."

It was a toss-up which one of them was more surprised at his answer.

It was like seeing a mirror image, one of some years hence. Esther Small sat in Mable's Donut Shop with her suitcase nestled in tight by her ankle, a cup of coffee in front of her.

Polly, her bags in her car, her own coffee to go in her hand, found herself unable to walk past. "You're leaving?" she asked.

Esther looked up, saw Polly, nodded. "I'm through here."

But she wasn't. And Polly felt compelled to tell her so. She slid into the seat across from her, uninvited, more than likely unwelcome, and she didn't care. "I don't think you understand. Cobie found a chest full of gold, the purser's box from the *Royal Arms*. We have the empty box. We have evidence that he'd come into a whole lot of money. But we can't find the gold. It's still out there somewhere."

Across the booth, Esther Small's face never changed. She set down her coffee cup. "I told you once before, it's *you* who don't understand. You talk of this treasure. To you it's a beautiful dream. Can't you see how tired I am of dreams?

Don't you know how long I lived under the curse of yet another and another and another of these fantastic dreams? That's how we lived. From dream to dream. And none of them ever came any closer. Once they faded into the horizon, they got replaced with another dream. And another bottle. And in some strange way it seemed one was always dependent on the other. There he sat, drinking and dreaming, day after day. He never ever understood that his dreams didn't interest me. I didn't want to be rich or to have an important husband. The Cobie I used to know was fine by me, as long as he did his best, as long as he was there with me. But when I say there I mean *really* there, in this world, facing up to its bills and its sorrows, not off on some Treasure Island a million miles away. You say you think he found a box of gold—"

"I *know* he found a box of gold," said Polly. "Don't you see? This time his dream came true."

"It did?" said Esther bitterly. "And when was that?"

Polly fell silent.

After a minute Esther Small reached across the booth and touched her hand. "I'm sorry. Go ahead and dream. But don't waste your time dreaming of stumbling over boxes of gold. Dream of something you can make come true with your own two hands."

"Right," said Polly. "But what if your dream is the kind you *can't* make come true?"

"And what is your dream? Love, I suppose?" Esther smiled. "Ah, yes, I see your point. That's the kind of dream that has to pop up in its own good time. And it usually waits until you've given up on it and gotten involved in something else."

"But involved in what?" said Polly. It was a rhetorical question, aimed at herself. She was surprised when Esther answered it.

"Involved in whatever you have to, to survive. Working. Eating. Sleeping. Nobody said it was fun."

They didn't? Polly could have sworn somebody told her it was. Once.

The sound of air brakes reached their ears. Esther drained her coffee and stood. "My bus."

"Good-bye," said Polly. "I'm sorry for how things turned out. Good luck."

She should have known how Esther Small would answer her.

"I'll make my own luck, thank you."

Chapter
35

By this time the whole anchorage had fallen into shadow—the last rays, I remember, falling through a glade of the wood, and shining bright as jewels on the flowery mantle of the wreck.

Pete was standing at the kitchen table, boots still on, eyes glued to the marble chessmen, Polly's note in his hand, when Connie walked in. He looked up. "She's gone."

"She was gone when I got up," said Connie. "But at least the note explains."

Pete looked down. *Thanks for everything. I'll be back for another visit soon. But right now I think it's time at least one of us got to revel in his dream.*

"An hour of peace and contentment alone in your own home with me. That's what you said, wasn't it? So when do we start counting?"

"I think she gave me that hour last night."

Connie pulled out a kitchen chair and pointed Pete to it. "You know, I don't think you'd be out of line if you asked for an hour today, too."

But Pete was still studying the chessmen. "I don't get it. How did she know I wanted these? My grandfather had some. I used to play with them all the time."

"So she noticed. And remembered. She's not stupid."

"I know that. The question is, does she?" Suddenly Pete sniffed. "What's that smell?"

"Meat loaf. It's almost ready. Will you sit down? You can explain everything to me while we eat."

"Explain what?" asked Pete, trying not to look surprised about the meat loaf. Cooking wasn't Connie's strongest suit.

"Well, Hugh Platt, to start. I just can't buy it, somehow. He doesn't seem the greedy type."

"I know. But he insisted the money had nothing to do with it. It was the history he wanted. He wanted to preserve the history. And in Hugh's mind, compared to a once-in-a-lifetime find like that, a guy like Cobie didn't count."

A timer went off. Connie hopped up, pulled out the meat loaf, and busied herself putting dinner on the table. There were baked potatoes with chives. And a salad with croutons in it. And a bottle of cabernet sauvignon. She set a wineglass down in front of Pete and pulled out a Ballantine for herself.

"It's funny about Joe Putnam, though," said Pete. "I don't think he's the ogre Polly had him pegged for, but other than that, her ideas weren't far off. Joe made it clear the other day. He felt like a fool, getting teased about Kay and Cobie. He acted like a jerk, drove Kay away, then tried to pretend everything was all right when it wasn't. True, he didn't want anyone looking to him when they came after whoever killed Cobie, but if he could have discouraged any looking into it in the first place, so much the better. He didn't want Kay dragged into it."

Pete shoveled more meat loaf into his face. "You know, this is really good. All week Polly just sat there and let me cook and clean and wait on her hand and foot. Then all of a sudden she started making French toast. And omelettes. And doing the dishes. I can't figure it out."

"Not so tough. Everybody likes to be taken care of once in a while. What do you think I was doing the whole time in New Jersey? Cooking, cleaning, waiting on them hand and foot. This is Mom's meat loaf recipe, as a matter of fact."

"But what made Polly decide to pitch in all of a sudden like that?"

"You got tossed in the drink. She started to worry about

you for a change. She must have realized you could use a little help. Have you looked in the mirror? You look like hell."

"I told you, those weirs are hard work. And thanks to you, I'm working off three hours of sleep."

They grinned at each other idiotically.

Finally Connie said, "Pete?"

He looked up, smiling.

"There's something I'd like to do."

Pete held up a hand. "Let me tell you my idea first. I'll be through with the weirs in a couple of days. How about if we go to Boston, find a hotel—"

Now it was her turn to look surprised. "All right," she said. "But I was talking about right now, tonight. It's coming home and thinking about Cobie all over again. I want to go out to the wreck."

The sun had set, but there was still enough light to have turned the harbor into liquid silver. A lone gull wheeled and cried over the boat, a school of minnows peppered the glassy surface of the water, the salt scoured Connie's nostrils clean. She stood on the beach and drank in the sights, the sounds, the smells. She felt as if she couldn't get enough of it. True, there had been a minute out on the highway when it had felt good to get away, maybe another minute, right after Pete hung up on her, when she felt like *staying* away, but not now. The Boston idea was nice, but for another time. Right now, it felt good to be home.

Boy, did it feel good.

Beside her, she saw Pete lift an arm. She turned in the direction of his wave and saw Dave Snow coming down the beach.

"Connie. Welcome back. Okay, Pete, what's it gonna be? Are you gonna sell me that boat or not?"

"You still want it now the murder's solved?"

Dave peered at him curiously. "What's that supposed to mean?"

"Just something I figured out along the way. You had no

use for Cobie until we came around asking questions. Then suddenly you thought he was God's gift to advertising. You wanted to buy his boat to attract your customers. Pit Patterson did a pretty smart about-face, too. All of a sudden he and Cobie were best friends. Did the two of you think you were going to get accused of his murder?"

Dave shot them both a half-guilty grin. "Maybe. Maybe. It was one thing when everybody thought he rolled overboard and drowned. It was another when it turns out he got coshed. Pit and I figured we'd better make out we were all right with Cobie."

"But why do you want that old boat?" asked Connie.

Dave shrugged and looked away. "It's been there a long time. Cobie'd been there a long time."

A mournful whistle traveled across the sand on the breeze. *Danny Boy.* Dave Snow looked up. "He's early tonight."

"Early?"

"Jack. He walks the beach every night, whistling that God-awful depressing song. Look, I've got to get back to work. Are you selling or aren't you?"

Dave waited, but still Pete hesitated.

"Let me think about it overnight. I'll call you tomorrow."

Dave Snow rolled his eyes at Connie and wandered down the beach.

Connie started toward the dinghy, but Pete put out a hand, holding her back.

In a second Jack Whiteaker had reached them. He greeted them with the trademark flash of teeth, the toss of his hair. "Fancy seeing you two out here. Nice night."

"Yup," said Pete. "Nice night."

Jack looked out at Cobie's wreck. "I find myself walking by here every night. I can't get used to it, somehow, Cobie gone."

"Still," said Pete, "it must be a relief in some ways. He couldn't have been good for business, stealing from your guests."

222

Jack Whiteaker chuckled softly. "No, it wasn't. Mind you, I still don't know for sure if he was a thief."

"Eunice Dipple was convinced. What did you do, buy her off to shut her up?"

"Eunice, the Donaldsons. And there were other complaints."

"But why did you do it? What did you care if Cobie took his lumps?"

"I didn't when he was alive, but then he died. And somehow, it just didn't seem right to leave that for his poor wife to think about. And he was a scavenger by trade, we have to remember that. I think he truly believed that whatever was left unattended, whatever he could pick up off this beach, belonged to him by right."

"Including lobsters out of Pit's traps?"

Jack chuckled again. "Oh, I could see Cobie devising a way to stretch that moral point. Maybe the lobsters weren't actually in the traps. Maybe he figured Pit owed him something for keeping an eye on his pots. Who knows what Cobie thought?"

"But you told your customers you reported Cobie to the police. You didn't."

"I said I was *going* to report him. Could I help it if he died before I got around to it? And once he was dead, I couldn't see the point. So I replaced the lost items and added a small bonus if they agreed to keep quiet if the subject ever came up. And it did. You saw to that."

"So tell me something," said Connie. "This rumor about Cobie finding treasure. You're out here a lot. Did you ever see anything? Did Cobie ever say anything?"

"I never saw Cobie with anything more than a basket of clams, an old buoy, a bunch of line, those plastic fish totes that keep washing up. And he never said anything to me that he didn't say to everyone else. Now if you'll excuse me, I'd better finish my walk."

Jack Whiteaker walked off, whistling.

Danny Boy, of course.

* * *

The row out to the wreck was a kinder, gentler version of the last trip they'd made this way together. It seemed to Pete a lot had gone on in the interim. They talked about some of it but fell silent as they climbed aboard, mutually according Cobie a moment of silence. Pete led the way into the cabin and sat on the bunk. Connie sat on the bench along the table.

"Why don't you want to sell the boat?" asked Connie finally.

Pete gave her a sheepish grin. "I'm not sure. I think it's Polly and that damned treasure. And I haven't trusted Dave Snow since he gave me a free beer."

"You think the treasure's on this boat?"

Pete stood, giving himself a mental shake. "No, I don't. I'm getting as kooky as Polly. I'll sell it and send the money to Esther. But I'd like to clear out Cobie's stuff, just in case she changes her mind."

Pete started with the drawers under the bunks. One denim shirt so thin it was translucent in spots. One pair of torn overalls.

Connie wandered the three steps to the galley and opened the refrigerator. "We should toss these clams. They've been sitting in here for weeks. I suppose the beer's still good. Want one?"

Pete shook his head. Connie shut the refrigerator and moved to the cupboard. "It seems so long ago, Cobie spouting off in the bar. What do you suppose got him drinking again?"

"What got him to stop?" asked Pete. "Short-lived though it was."

"That's easier, I think. He wanted to get Esther back. He must have known the money alone wouldn't do it. But he never really meant it. The minute she walked out again, he started drinking again."

"I guess." Pete opened the second drawer. Two pairs of socks that had once been thick wool, now down to threads at the toes and heels. A grimy pair of boxer shorts.

"And all that drunken gibberish. Who'd have thought he

meant anything by any of it, the business about the drinks being on the general, and pearls, and . . . Hey, that reminds me. What about *your* gibberish, Pete? All that over the phone about pearl rings, and lottery tickets?"

"There weren't any. At least I don't think there were. I got to thinking about it when Polly started all that talk about dreams. I think it came down to a few people projecting their own fantasies onto Cobie. They knew he'd suddenly come up with some money, so the guy who was into the lottery decided Cobie'd picked a winning number. The woman who dreamed of a hot romance imagined a pearl engagement ring. At least she had something to base it on. Cobie did say something about pearls."

"Pearls in oysters. Whatever the hell that meant."

Suddenly Pete heard a gasp. He turned around to see Connie yanking open the refrigerator door. She grabbed a quahog, hefted it, peered at it. "Glue," she whispered. Then, "Pete! Give me your knife."

Pete fished his Swiss army knife out of his pocket and rose. Before he'd moved farther, Connie rushed at him and grabbed the knife, applying the point to the clam. She pushed, grunting. Pete tried to take it from her, but she twisted away and, in a fit of impatience, banged it against the shelf.

The quahog sprang open.

And a shower of gold coins rained onto the floor around their feet.

Chapter
36

All of us had an ample share of the treasure, and used it wisely or foolishly, according to our natures.

Bert Barker sat on the steps of Beston's Store, his face the color of an eggplant. "Hit me with that again."

Evan Spender winked at Ed Healey. "They kept one coin. One King George III gold guinea. And they sent it to Polly."

Bert got up, crossed the porch, put a quarter into the rusted old Coke machine, and extracted the long, cool bottle. He snapped off the cap under the bottle opener and took a long drink. It seemed to restore him.

Partly, anyway.

"You mean to tell me, here's Pete, handed the contents of that old wreck fair and square by Cobie's widow, and they find upwards of half a million dollars glued into a bunch of quahogs *and they give it all back?*"

"Mostly. 'Cept for the one coin I already told you about. Esther tried to split the whole thing with them, but they said no, all they wanted was a remembrance."

"A remembrance of *Cobie?*"

"A remembrance of something, anyway. Pete called Polly, told her she could have half if she wanted it, but Polly said the same thing as Pete and Connie. Cobie wanted it for Esther, so that's where it should go—to Esther."

"Bet I know what she's going to do with it," said Ed. "Bet she's going to buy back that house on Paine Road."

"No," said Evan. "Turns out she's moving to Florida."

"That's funny," said Ed.

"No, not really. Turns out she was pretty cold and clammy the whole time she was here."

"Dreams change," said Ed.

"I'll tell you what'll change," said Bert. "Pete and Connie. *And* Polly. They'll get to thinking about it, thinking about what a quarter of a million coulda got 'em. They'll change their minds in a hurry. Me, if I stumbled onto a couple dozen quahogs stuffed with gold, you know what I'd do with it?"

"What?" said Evan.

"I'd . . . I'd . . ." Bert's voice trailed off. It was too much. He stared around him helplessly.

Ed Healey eased his jellied form off the bench and patted Bert on the shoulder. "You keep dreaming, Bert. Don't cost you anything to dream."

"Oh no?" said Evan. "I'd say it cost Cobie plenty."

"True," said Ed. "But at least his dream came true. He gave Esther some security. Finally."

"Thanks to Pete and Connie," said Evan.

"And Polly," said Ed.

"And the *General,*" said Bert. "Jesus, God Almighty. To think that for two hundred years a half a million dollars in gold has been sitting right here under our feet someplace. And look who finds it. *Cobie.*" And Bert's face, which had finally paled to a nice sea lavender, quickly returned to a rich royal purple.

"Cheer up, Bert," said Ed. "Another couple hundred years, another half a mill'll turn up someplace else."

Somehow, the idea didn't seem to cheer Bert up any.

ENJOY SOME OF THE MYSTERY POCKET BOOKS HAS TO OFFER!

SAMUEL LLEWELLYN
MAELSTROM 78997-X/$5.99

ANN C. FALLON
HOUR OF OUR DEATH 88515-4/$5.50

AUDREY PETERSON
DARTHMOOR BURIAL 72970-5/$5.50

TAYLOR McCAFFERTY
BED BUGS 75468-8/$5.50

WILLIAM S. SLUSHER
BUTCHER OF THE NOBLE 89545-1/$5.99

ELIZABETH QUINN
LAMB TO THE SLAUGHTER 52765-7/$5.99

SUSANNAH STACEY
BONE IDLE 51062-2/$5.99

JOHN DUNNING
THE BOOKMAN'S WAKE 56782-9/$5.99